D1744152

SPUNKY SAILOR

ALSO BY KEN SMITH

Riding the Big One
Going Down
Skin
Run Naked, Run Free
Virgin Sailors
Brad

SPUNKY SAILOR

Ken Smith

Lethe Press
Maple Shade, NJ

Copyright © 2007 Ken Smith. All rights reserved. No part of this book may be reproduced, stored in retrieval system, or transmitted in any form, by any means, including mechanical, electronic, photocopying, recording or otherwise, without prior written permission of the author.

This paperback edition released 2009 by Lethe Press, 118 Heritage Ave. Maple Shade, NJ 08052

ISBN 1-59021-029-8 / 978-1-59021-029-1

Contents

TOMMY

"That Heathrow airport?" asked Tommy.

"Yes, sir," came the polite, female voice.

Tommy giggled drunkenly. "Any planes crash to-day?"

"Certainly not, sir!"

"'Spect they will once them pilots have seen the size of those tits of yours." Tommy slammed the phone down, collapsing into a fit of giggles. He just couldn't help doing it, playing that schoolboy prank he should have grown out of a long time ago being an eighteen-year-old sailor. He'd already phoned a 'Smelly' and a vicar called 'Boyes', Tommy telling the vicar he was looking for boys himself, and that a vicar would probably have a couple of nice lit-tle lads tucked under his cassock. A threat to inform the police by the vicar was repelled with, "Bend down and kiss my altar-boy bum."

My lovely mate sank his palm back inside his bell-bottom's pocket and rattled some coins. I grabbed his arm, pushed open the door and gave him a tug toward the street. "Enough, Tommy. Come on, let's find another boozer."

Withdrawing a coin, he hastily slotted it into the pay phone. "Just one more, Sandy."

"Cops are already on their way," I warned, dragging my spunky sailor from the telephone kiosk. "I don't fancy getting banged up tonight, even if you do."

"I bet you do." Tommy bent over and offered his delectable little bum. He giggled; giving the firm mounds a gentle pat. "Banging your lovely big cock right up here."

His offer meant nothing. It was gay play, common among us sailors. I suppose there was the possibility he was gay himself, the chance it might have been a genuine offer in the guise of play. He certainly had an air of availability about him. If so, he may well have seen that porno video I'd made before I'd joined the ship, the earnings of which were still providing me with regular runs ashore. I certainly hadn't forgotten it, the memory still fresh in my mind and my hole still sore from riding that big one. I guess time would tell. Anyway, I was in no hurry to find out. Being in his lovely company was enough to be getting along with. And living in the same mess deck there was plenty of opportunity to scan his smooth skin and savour every centimetre of his soft or hard sex depending on his thoughts at the time.

"Where now?" I asked, pleased and relieved that I'd dragged him away from the phone box and moving along the pavement, albeit in a snakelike fashion.

"The Beachcomber. It'll be filled with fillies." Tommy gripped his dick through his bell-bottoms and made the head bulge with a squeeze of his fingers. "Wanna find me a nice lass and slip her a length."

My own cock jarred in my bell-bottoms at the sight of that. I knew how happy the lass would be once she'd caught sight of the nine inches he had to offer and had it sinking down her throat or sailing up her pussy. Already I was jealous knowing he'd pull his filly effortlessly, suspecting I'd be waiting close by, no doubt tossing myself in frustration until he'd ridden her to the finishing line.

"Beachcomber it is." I tried not to sound too disappointed aware that before we reached the straight club we'd have to pass a gay one. It really didn't matter we were heading for the straight club. I knew there would still be scores of half-naked youths to admire; topless boys, chests glistening with sweat; slender waists and muscled abdomens aplenty; fuckable bums and gyrating packets thrusting at me from all angles. And I could always live in hope that there might be at least one randy lad available in that pool of promiscuity, one youth that batted for both sides. Even a chance of a blowjob in the heads, or quick excursion outside the club and down some darkened alley for a fuck. With this possibility fixed firmly in my mind, I began to cheer at the prospect of going to a straight club.

The next street saw us stroll by the gay club, aptly named The Meating House. I watched with envy as all that available boy-flesh floated around outside and flaunted itself. I almost suggested to Tommy, somewhat hypocritically, that we step inside for a 'laugh'. After a barrage of wolf-whistles and other fruity comments from the clubbing boys, and Tommy's hands on hip camp response, that I wished I had. It was clear he had no problem with gay boys. Whether he'd have a problem with his best mate being gay had yet to be determined.

The next turning brought us face to face with a couple of lager-slaughtered louts. Unfortunately, a uniform could often bring unwanted grief upon its owner. The comments we received from both were not at all pleasant. Although Tommy was a slightly built youth, his body was as strong as any lightweight boxer; a little stick of dynamite if ever there was. If riled, he could really let loose with his fists, and legs. Not surprisingly, I needed to grab his arm to stop him from wading into them.

Verbal abuse stabbing into our backs, we continued on our journey.

Halfway down the street leading to the Beachcomber, Tommy gave me a nudge as we approached one of the few lamps lighting a shop doorway. A couple of kissing boys were standing inside the secluded cavern—brave boys at that, so close to the straight club. Both in their teens, they were well and truly into each other's faces. The black teenager, dressed in leather harness and matching leather trousers, was being fondled with enthusiasm.

My heart pumped enviously at the pleasing sight when the shorter, jeans-clad white youth teased and tormented the black boy's cock. Already I could imagine the soft tongue of the white lad slipping down my own throat while the thick cock of the black youth pressed between my buttock cheeks and fucked me. I'm not sure if Tommy noticed my obvious joy but he gave me a crafty wink that suggested I fetch a bucket of ice cold water.

"Hell, Tommy. If those two bastards we've just passed had spotted them..." My body shivered. "Jesus... they might have been..."

"Don't you believe it, Sandy," Tommy butted in, pre-empting the scenario. "I've seen faggots fight before. Forget all that handbag and powder puff crap. Some of those little fruits can throw a fair old fist when they're cornered." Tommy's choice of 'fruits' and 'faggots' might not have been to my liking, but they were common terminology used by us sailors. I knew he didn't mean them offensively.

I gave him a nod of agreement, suspecting he had much respect for the lads. "Don't I know it," I said, giving him a snippet of information about my own sexuality, then wondering if he may have just given me a snippet of his.

As we came closer to the lovemaking pair, the black lad caught sight of us over his friend's shoulder. Giving his seducer a gentle nudge, the pair stepped from the doorway and onto the pavement. I couldn't be sure if it was for safety reasons on their part but it seemed a sensible tactic, allowing a quick escape. Or, as Tommy had pointed out, space to fight if absolutely necessary.

"Seafood!" delighted the black youth, with an appreciative whisper when we drew level.

"Having fun, boys?" chirped Tommy, removing any doubts of danger the youths might have had, his tone soft and free of threat.

"Sure are," the younger white lad replied, his expression radiant and ruthlessly seductive, his solid cock rampant and ready. "You?"

"Soon will be," I said, giving him a disrobing scan that only another gay lad could read.

"You will if you *come* with us," the youth flirted, the emphasis on 'come' more than obvious.

Tommy squeezed his soft cock down the leg of his bell-bottoms and got the big bud bulging against his thigh. "Fancy a nice big.... Golden Rivet?"

"I fancy some salty spray splashing all over my face," parried the bold youth.

"Sorry, but my tank's empty at the moment." Tommy continued to play, surprising me that he knew of such things as golden showers.

"Why don't you come and fill it up?" suggested the black lad, the contents of his leather trousers again beginning to take on the proportions of a pound-and-a-half of juicy salami.

I played it straight. "Sorry, but we're doing girls tonight, boys."

"We can do girls as well," said the white lad. "Got some nice sexy numbers at home." He gave his companion's leather-clad bottom a slap. "Haven't we, Tyro?"

Tyro wriggled his hands over his hips, as if slipping into one of those skimpy leather skirts. "Sure do, Shaun."

I didn't fancy girls in the least but would loved to have seen the pair in skin-tight tops, smooth midriffs and lickable navels revealed, their fine young cocks bulging against the tight, leather mini-skirts. Excitedly I waited for an '*I'm game*' response from Tommy.

Tommy winked and began moving on. "Another time, perhaps?"

"Night, Shaun. Night, Tyro." I reluctantly bade them goodbye, setting off after Tommy.

Tommy turned and gave them a wave when I reached his side. "Goodnight, boys. Take care," he called back.

"Luv you… you lovely sailor boys," sang Shaun, his blown kisses drifting on the breeze.

"Me too," sighed an also disappointed Tyro as he reached for Shaun's hand.

"Nice pair of lads." I slapped Tommy's collar. "Reckon you were in there."

Tommy laughed loud and deep. His hand flicked upward behind the back of my head and sent my cap spinning skyward. "'Course I was. But I didn't fancy yours." He began legging it down the lane and toward the club.

I dived into the road, scooping up my cap just before it went under the wheels of an empty cab that had just dropped a gaggle of giggly girls at the club. A quick sprint and I was soon alongside Tommy. An intuitive duck by him saw my hand skate through the air and me spin in a circle from the effort of trying to knock the cap from his head.

"I suppose yours was the black guy with the big cock?" I said, suddenly realising that perhaps I shouldn't have admitted noticing that part of the lad's anatomy, at least not revealed to Tommy that I had.

Tommy's eyebrows rose. He gave me a knowing look. "You queer, or something?" I quickly checked his expression for any seriousness but could see none. Seconds later, he gave me a poke in the ribs and laughed that incredibly butch laugh of his. "Mine was the white lad with the tight little tush."

Again, my cap left my head.

"Come on, let's get a shag. I'm as horny as a hound dog in a harem of bitches," Tommy shouted over his shoulder as his legs raced him toward the group of excited girls waiting to enter the club.

"I guess the sight of that lad's tight little bum has got you nice and horny, then?" I called after him. His head swivelled around. Although I couldn't see from the distance that I was, I'm sure those sexy little eyebrows wrinkled his brow again. I was more than sure his cock had begun to rise the moment he vanished into the group of flirtatious fillies and instantly rewarded with snogs from several lipstick-laden mouths.

Bless him for it, Tommy actually waited for me to catch up, and left the lasses to enter the club alone. Reaching his side, I had another go at his cap but failed miserably.

"Careful, Tommy, your personality's showing." I winked and nodded toward his cock, which had reached six of its nine-inch capability.

"Reckon I scared them off with it." He grinned wickedly. "They were too keen, anyway. Sailor-hunting-slappers. Give them a good poking and they'll say you got them pregnant next run ashore."

"Lucky you've got me, then. Never got pregnant yet."

"Think I'd rather shag the bouncer."

I gave the mountain of brainless bouncer meat a quick once over. "Reckon it'll do him the world of good. Probably rolls over in bed anyway."

Tommy slapped my wrist and slung his arm around my waist. "Can't take you anywhere, can I, darling?"

I gave his bum a deserving slap. "You can take me anytime you want, dear."

Brainless bouncer and mate pushed their bodies together when we stepped forward. "Gay club's down the road, girls," said Brainless. Again, the problem was our uniforms. Sometimes they just invited sarcasm or thoughts of impending trouble.

"So why ain't you working there?" Tommy opened his big mouth in a drunken blurt.

"That's right, Tommy. Those queer boys could do with a nice big bloke like him to protect them." I did my damage limitation.

"That's exactly what I was saying, Sandy." Tommy suddenly realising he may have blown the chance of a finding a filly to shag. "Anyway, we're not queer." He blew me a kiss. "Well, I'm not."

I smiled my best smile at Brainless. "Take no notice of my mate. Viagra. It's the only way he can keep his little pecker up."

"I can believe that," said Brainless, proudly beefing up his body.

Bouncer number two gave us another once over and then nodded to Brainless. The two tons of beefcake parted. "No trouble!" they barked in unison.

My shove on Tommy's back sent him swiftly between the pair when I saw his kissable lips begin to open for a second verbal attack. "You want to get into this club and find a shag, or what?" I whispered when we were out of earshot. "Jesus, Tommy."

Tommy shrugged his shoulders. "Not bothered, really." He patted my bottom affectionately and giggled. "'Cos, as you said, I've always got your slack old arse if I'm desperate."

At reception, our caps and my cash went over the cloakroom counter. Caps had a habit of going walkies. As they were expensive little buggers to buy, about the same as the entrance fee to the club, it was always best to check them in.

A cloakroom ticket apiece and a logo stamped on the back of our hands was our reward; the logo being our pass back into the club should we decide to pop out for air. Tommy insisted his was stamped on his forehead. Succumbing to his drunken charm the filly obliged but stamping it onto his cherub cheek. However, his request for a snog got rebuffed by the lass but was spotted by Brainless, who was still keeping a wary eye on him.

"She can't wait to jump on me bones and bounce on me cock," Tommy boasted as we walked onto the dance floor and were almost bowled over by a deafening noise that was supposed to be music.

"Dumping me already?" I shouted against the din. "Call yourself a date?" Tommy didn't hear, or if he did wasn't interested. Keenly, he'd vanished beneath an array of flashing and rotating lights, into a fog of dry ice and deliciously tasty, half-naked youths or, from his perspective, scantily dressed lasses.

"Bud!" Tommy hollered his order, already gyrating his hips and thrusting his big cock toward every lass within fucking distance, carnivorously homing in on a buxom lass who had more than enough cleavage to cram his pretty face between and begin his night of gorging.

"Sir!" I accepted my fate as slave.

A frantic bout of jostling saw me returning with two Big Buds that had had their caps decapitated by the stressed-out, overworked barman. I took a swig from each of the quarter-of-a-gallon containers as I fought my way through delicious boys, making sure I brushed against their smooth and sweaty torsos whenever the opportunity arose.

Deep in the heaving mass of fermenting flesh, I eventually found Tommy. Had he not been dressed in his sailor uniform I doubt I'd have done so. I handed him his ice-cool Bud. "Your drink, sir."

"'Bout bloody time," Tommy complained. Gripping his filly's tiny waist, he pulled her pelvis into his. Taking the wide-necked bottle in his free hand, he downed a hearty gulp before offering it to the lass. With a cock-sucking action, she sent her mouth halfway down the long shaft. That sure put a smile on his face. Straight away, I knew she'd have no problem swallowing all of his delicious cock. And the way she pulled him into to her perspiring body and planted her mouth on his, and began to tongue him within an inch of his life, neither did he.

As was the norm, there was a 'gooseberry' dancing with Tommy and his bit of skirt; a not-so-pretty lass to be brutally honest. I read Tommy's thoughts and knew I was destined to be Gooseberry's dance partner.

The wonderful thing about clubbing, you could pretend to dance with a person while your actions and thoughts were directed elsewhere. In my case, the youth to my right dressed in the tightest pair of satin hot pants imaginable, his naked chest covered in glittery dust. A lad who had a dick to die for that was in serious danger of bursting those skimpy pants apart.

Thus targeted, at frequent intervals I placed my randy body as close to his sexy one as legitimately possible, painfully tormenting myself with the prospect of probing every delightful orifice of his twitching torso.

"Great place!" hollered Tommy after he'd withdrawn his tongue from the depths of his filly's stomach. "Should have come here earlier."

"Great!" I hollered back, sweat already dripping from my brow, and still wishing I were in the gay club or with the lads we'd met earlier. Better yet, in bed with my hot pant silent partner who appeared to be pushing his bottom closer and closer on each of his provocative pirouettes.

"I'm Sharon," Tommy's girl flirted, giving me a kiss on the mouth. I got the impression she was willing to ride two stallions at the same time if needs be. Not surprisingly, Gooseberry remained silent and shy.

"Sandy!" I yelled my name, only for the whole club to hear my introduction when the music suddenly hit a silent void big enough for the entire population to disappear.

Tommy had laughed when my name sailed out over the dance floor. "Sandy's gay!" he shouted, completely surprising me. Thankfully, his untimely revelation became swamped by more brain busting beats blasting from the barrage of speakers, and only reached the ears of those closest.

I shot him an '*I'll slap your face*' glare, but suspected he was just staking out his claim, trying to ward Sharon off.

"Bisexual," Tommy corrected with a grin.

"Fantastic!" sang Sharon, whose reactions were surprisingly sharp for someone so pissed. It appeared she didn't seem to mind in the least of what my sexual preferences were, might have even been turned-on by the three of us in a bed. Childlike, I poked my tongue out at Tommy.

"I'm Simon," my hot pant lad surprised me. His smile was sexual; his kissable whispering lips close to mine, his soft voice slipping over me like Liquid Silk lubrication sliding down a thick cock.

I decided to do my own bit of flirting and wind Tommy up. I stroked my finger intimately from Simon's tiny navel and up to his small pecs, collecting glitter on the tip as I did so. "Hi, Simon." I seduced him with a suggestive wink.

Tommy shook his head. I think he mouthed "Slut."

"Hi, Simon," greeted Sharon, again puckering up. The lad tactfully avoided her voluptuous lips and brought his attention back on me.

Why a foursome suddenly flashed into my mind, I really didn't know. I say *foursome* because Gooseberry, bless her, had already returned to one of the many vacant seats and looked about as happy as any gooseberry should.

But a foursome did enter my mind. Soon, my dirty little brain had visions of Simon's tight little hot pants dropped to his ankles; his cute buttocks getting a right old rogering from me—which they most certainly warranted—while Tommy's big dick was being sucked and savoured to the point of being totally devoured. I'm sure Sharon was in there somewhere. I'm not sure where.

"We will, we will, rock you! We will, we will...." The group sang.

The words blasted into the heaving mass from every direction imaginable, arms rising high above the heads of jubilant and joyful clubbers as feet stomped and voices sang in one ear-splitting crescendo the all important, "Rock you!"

"We will, we will..."

"Cock you," hollered Tommy, well out of key and slightly adrift of the crowd when the chorus came around again. On his next "Cock you!" he moved closer to Sharon and thrust his rampant dick hard into her fanny. My mouth dribbled enviously.

"Yes please," seduced the horny Sharon, shoving her big juicy tits into Tommy's face and her pelvis hard into his solid cock. She smacked her lips onto his and sent her tongue deep again.

"Suck you," was what I thought whispered from Simon's succulent mouth when the chorus next came around, followed by his finger stroking my cheek. Our newfound friends were simply disgusting. Just the way I liked them.

I was somewhat puzzled why Simon had come to a straight club rather than the gay one just along the road. I suppose he could have been yet another bi guy in the making, a phenomenon that appeared to be increasing daily. If not, there was something quite rewarding about pulling a straight guy, if gay, especially if you got him to blow you or, better yet, you managed to fuck him.

What did it matter? I was more than happy to be in his company and relish his boyish beauty. It also gave me a chance to keep my mind away from what was developing inside Tommy's bell-bottoms. Something only Sharon was aware of; her massaging hand stuffed deep inside his pocket.

I was sweating profusely and needed a rest. A sailor's uniform is not the most suitable attire while clubbing; not even the lightweight outfit made by a Chinese tailor in Singapore that I was currently wearing.

I made a zigzag move toward the chairs and tables. Simon grabbed my arm. "Going for a pee?" he asked. His seductive gaze was fiery; the rays kindling an instant flame deep in my groin. "Me too."

His offer for me to accompany him was unmistakable and irresistible. I could hardly control my excitement as the pair of us cut a swathe through hot and horny half-naked youths and headed toward the toilet. The head of my cock was already rising to greet the waistband of my black boxers, a familiar stickiness apparent in eager anticipation of what might happen once inside.

At the end of a dark passage, we casually entered the urinal area of the toilet, me following Simon and worshipping that irresistible bottom as he flexed the cheeks flauntingly. He checked each of the cubicles for occupation. The scrumptious bulge inside his hot pants had already developed into a thick sausage of succulent flesh as it fought its way between tender young thigh and silky material. I was in no doubt of his intentions.

Finding each cubicle locked and occupied, he looked more than disappointed that he was unable to drag me into one. Even as horny as I was, I did doubt the wisdom of the pair of us popping into a cubicle, even if it had been vacant. It was common knowledge bouncers regularly checked the toilets for 'drugs users' according to the warning notices on every wall.

Putting my sensible head back on, I faced a urinal, pulled out my painfully stiff cock and tried to pee. An excited Simon was beside me in an instant.

I hadn't noticed when we were on the dance floor but Simon's hot pants hadn't any fly. Like the bold youth that he obviously was, with a quick wrench he had them well below his low-hanging balls and was soon firing jets of piping-hot pee against the urinal. Firing it from what I can only describe as an incredibly thick, eight-inch cannon, a beauty sporting the cutest tuft of black curly hair above the solid shaft.

As Simon peed, his petite buttocks squeezed tightly together, and then relaxed as they propelled each squirt of golden liquid against the porcelain bowl. Frequently his beautiful mouth sent smile after erotic smile showering over me, his excited eyes flitting from my cock to my face and back with the speed of a thrashing foreskin. Like an embarrassed kid my own pee remained under pressure and unable fly, my cock having grown, so fully, the foreskin had tightened over the bulbous head, making the task impossible.

It was a set of brave and desperate digits—fingers slender, long, and feminine—which caused me to jump when they darted to my dick and wrapped around the shaft. Before I had time to warn of dangers Simon had sunk to his knees and his hot mouth had engulfed the head of my cock and was now frantically sucking. On Simon's third deep swallow—soft throat muscles massaging—I felt my spunk rise through the shaft surprisingly early, the sight of his boyish face and consuming mouth causing my balls to tighten and spin.

The fourth and fifth sensational swallows saw the first bubble of spunk jettison from the eye of my cock and onto his lapping tongue. On tasting my spunk, he rewarded me with deep swallow number six.

On sensational swallow seven, a torrent of spunk let fly and began to spurt and splatter deep into his magnificent massaging throat.

"We will, we will, rock you!" bellowed a bunch of drunken lads as they came along the passage and approached the entrance to the toilet.

Sensational swallow number eight didn't materialise. Simon's fantastic working mouth had vanished, my lad rushing into a cubicle when vacated, his hastily hoisted hot pants covering his balls, his stiff cock still pointing high.

My face flushed brighter than the section of red-tiled floor on which I was standing. My heart began to pump fast, furious and fearful. Spunk still siphoning from the eye of my cock, I nearly broke it in two as I hastily stowed it back into the secrecy of my bell-bottoms.

"We will, we will..." sang the gang of unwelcome visitors who had disturbed my magnificent blowjob.

"Shaft you! Shag you! Smack you!" came their assortment of punch lines as the three lads tried to outdo each other's crudity, all the while bouncing off each other's bodies and the walls as they drunkenly jostled through the doorway.

Decent, but decidedly sticky in the boxer department, I waited for a gap to appear between the butch-acting bunch before making my way toward the door.

"Watch your backs, lads," spouted the ugliest of the three on catching sight of me, "The Navy's in town."

"Don't stick your head through any portholes, boys," spluttered the second beefy number who had a rather sissy rose tattoo with *LUV MUM* beneath it.

"I'm gonna throw up," gurgled the youngest of the gang, and then promptly obliged.

"You pissed pig!" cursed complaining voices when chunks of spew splattered everywhere, painting a pretty mosaic pattern on the speckled floor, the carroty bits blending with the background.

"That fucking vegetable curry," cursed the vomiting lad, retching again and adding more colour to his creation.

It was the ideal opportunity to get my arse away from possible trouble. Glancing back at the cubicle in which Simon had vanished I waited briefly to see if he too was about to exit. With no sign of his imminent appearance I bustled my way through another bunch of beer bloated bellies and headed back along the passage. At least Simon was locked safely away, doing what I could only imagine. Whatever it was, he should have been doing it with me.

I stood in a darkened area beside the dance floor, vacant chairs scattered around bottle and glass-laden tables, while I scanned the club for Tommy and Sharon. Just beyond a low dividing wall—also covered with bottles, glasses and overflowing ashtrays—the sea of bodies continued to gyrate, remain motionless or sway from side to side. All the while, the brainless beats relentlessly banged into their drug-addled brains, sending them into their own catatonic or superficially blissful worlds.

Tommy's uniform was not among them so I decided to stay put and wait for the return of Simon. After all, my sailor buddy had already found his fuck for the night and I knew he wouldn't think twice about making a bolt back to her flat without me. Maybe drag her off to some other tasty lovemaking retreat, like a church graveyard or shop doorway. With his *correct* assumption that I might be gay, he too may have thought I had already left the club and was now doing a similar wonderful thing with Simon; also in some darkened alley.

When I plonked my bottom on the plastic chair and lit a cigarette, I glimpsed my lost shipmate. Looking absolutely slaughtered, and a good deal drunker than an hour ago, he'd propped himself against an eight-foot bank of speakers. He had obviously not spotted me. Giving him a wave, I stood and headed toward him.

"Where's your bit of *skin?*" asked Tommy—referring to Simon—when I reached his side. He handed me a fresh bottle of Bud. "Thought you'd fucked off without me."

"In the heads having a wank." I suspected that was the truth, still wishing I were in there with him. "Where's yours?"

"Powdering her nose. Shit, I could do with a fucking wank myself."

"Be patient, darling. I expect she's blowing up her tits and getting them even bigger for that fantastic fuck you've been on about all night."

Tommy grinned. He took a good gulp of Bud and pinched my tit painfully hard. "She has got a big pair, ain't she?"

"Whatever turns you on." I was still feeding him more information of my disinterest in the female sex.

Tommy grabbed my cigarette and began puffing on it. "You're not really queer, are you, Sandy?" Embarrassed laughter accompanied his question.

I took another ciggie from my pack and lit it. I decided I'd be up front with him. "Fraid so. Problem?"

Tommy slapped my shoulder. "Hell, no." He roared his lovely butch laugh. "Means you won't be after my shags when we're ashore."

I winked. "Might be after you though."

Tommy grabbed his cock and gave it a good squeeze, ignoring my statement. "Fucking hell, what's she doing in there? I'm rampant."

"Told you. She's blowing up her tits. You wait until she comes back out. Hot air balloons or what? Shit, you'll be floating up to heaven together."

Tommy squeezed his cock again. "For fuck sake, Sandy. Fucking hell, I'm getting a boner just thinking about stuffing my cock between them."

I glanced down at his stiffening cock, gave his head a rub, and then pulled my uniform jacket open. "You poor old dear. Here, have a good feel of my knockers to keep you going."

Two palms went inside my jacket and twisted my nipples. I couldn't resist and sent my hand onto Tommy's cock and gave it a firm squeeze. For sure, he had a juicy big boner packed away beneath his bell-bottoms. When Sharon left the club with him, she was going to get the shafting of her life, the lucky bitch.

"Who's a big boy, then?"

"Bandit!" Tommy reached for my cock and gave it a good tug. "Not a lot to write home about there, though."

"You wait till you see it when it's happy."

"I think that's your young skin's department," he said, rejecting the offer.

"Hope so. Where is the little runt?"

"And where's my juicy pussy?" Tommy impatiently sulked again.

"They're probably shagging each other." I suggested the unthinkable.

Tommy's eyebrows did their usual trick and jiggled on his forehead. "Better not be."

Whilst we chatted, smoked, laughed and joked, and continued to sup our Buds, the two of us frequently scanned the entrance to the passage that led to both toilets, for our respective dates.

A baseball-capped youth joined us and leant against the speakers, his body close to Tommy's. There was something about the way in which the youth was eyeballing Tommy that I didn't like. I knew if he became aware of the fact, there might be a scene. Deciding we needed a swift change of loitering position, I suggested we sit at one of the tables. Never the one to do anything that didn't come from his own mind, he told me I could sit if I wanted but he was happy where he was.

Just as I was about to go and sit down, hoping Tommy would join me if I did, I spotted my hot pant Simon heading toward the exit. By the way he was scanning his surroundings, and the look of disappointment on his face, I guessed he was thinking I'd left.

"There's my skin, Tommy." I nodded toward my lad. "Back in a tick."

"Lucky you," Tommy sulked. Just as I set off, he swivelled his head back toward the toilets, catching sight of his present company. Reluctant to leave him with the dubious character, and keen to get back as quickly as possible, I did a quick charge through tables and chairs and was soon right behind Simon.

Shattering glass caused me to hesitate just before my hand went upon Simon's shoulder. Although it wasn't an unusual sound to hear in pubs or clubs, my instinct told me something was up, something that was about to involve me. Tommy yelling my name at the top of his voice confirmed my worst fears.

I swung about. Deep into the first row of tables and chairs I spotted Tommy, arms and legs lashing out in all directions, furniture bowling over, glass shattering all around him, girls screaming and backing away while excited guys looked on.

I managed to leap the first chair that blocked my path and circumnavigate a table laying on its side, my boots crunching broken glass into the carpet as I raced toward my buddy. Within feet of coming to Tommy's aid strong hands grabbed both my arms with vicelike grips and began pulling me roughly backward.

"Get off me, you fucking bastards!" I yelled. "That's my mate in trouble."

"You're leaving, Jack," growled a gruff voice that I instantly recognised as the one belong to Brainless. His bonehead buddy was the person holding my other arm.

Travelling backward there was little I could do, apart from let my heels drag over the carpeted floor. There was little I could have done anyway, these bastards being bigger than Mount Everest and Mount Everest's sister.

"I warned you and your mate about trouble," Brainless barked into my ear. So close was his mouth, I thought he was about to bite it off.

"And I'm warning you… If you hurt my mate I'll have the whole fucking fleet down here." It was a pointless threat really. Sailors seldom did that sort of thing anymore.

"Don't worry, Jack. We're not bullies," Brainless lied. "This is a decent club. We just don't like troublemakers."

"That right!" I turned my head and glared into the bouncer's eyes. At the same time, I caught sight of Tommy on a similar humiliating backward run.

Tommy landed heavily on the pavement seconds after my body had hit the deck. I struggled to my feet and offered my hand. Remarkably, he didn't have a mark on his face but his knuckles were in a bad way.

"You okay?" I asked as calmly and as casually as I could, although my whole being was all a tremble with adrenaline and fear.

I could feel Tommy's hand shaking in my own when I helped him to his feet. "'Course I'm bloody all right," he growled, sweat trickling over those sexy eyebrows. "Fucking arseholes!"

"So what the fuck was that all about!" I barked, switching my anger to him, mainly because I'd lost my Simon shag for the night.

Tommy didn't reply. He stomped straight up to Brainless and Bonehead. Screwing up the cloakroom ticket, he tossed it toward them. "Where's my fucking headgear? You fucking bastards!"

Two white Frisbees sailed through the air and spun on the pavement when they landed. "Here's your hats, girls," snarled Brainless. "Now piss off and don't come back!"

"They're *caps*, you thick fucking bastard!" barked Tommy.

Sensing yet worse things to come I rushed forward and grabbed Tommy's arm and began pulling him away. "Leave it. We'll find somewhere more friendly."

"So what about throwing that other bastard out?" Tommy continued with his attack, not willing to let matters alone.

"Just fuck off," grunted Brainless.

"One of you, is he? Another lump of shit!" fumed Tommy, pulling away from my grip and bravely taking yet more steps toward the beefy bouncers. I grabbed his arm a second time and gave it a firm tug. He tumbled backwards into my arms, almost falling over.

"That's it, Jack. Take your girlfriend away before we take him out," Brainless fanned the flames.

Tommy's face exploded, turning crimson with rage. He rushed toward the big men. Strong as he was, I somehow managed to wrestle him out of harms way, spinning him around and directing him down the road and away from the ugly scene.

"There's another dozen of them in there, Tommy. You're not going to win." I argued as calmly as I could. "You'll just get the crap kicked out of us." I rubbed my hand over his locks. "I think you'd rather stay a pretty boy, wouldn't you?" I thought attempted humour might calm him.

Tommy punched his fist into his palm. For one dreadful moment, I thought it was going into my face. "You tell that fucking cunt in there I'm coming back to get him," he screamed down the road, shaking his fist and spitting at both bouncers.

I was more than relieved when Tommy began walking away. I turned us around the first corner we came across and got us out of earshot and sight of the bouncers. "Well?"

Tommy ignored my question, anger still rushing throughout his small frame. "I need a bloody drink."

"I thought it was a shag you needed?" I continued to lighten things as I put yet more distance between us and trouble. Tommy merely grunted and remained silent for the next ten minutes.

Two bottles sitting on a wall beside a bus stop suddenly cheered him. Both were almost full. "Booze," he delighted, breaking his silence and grabbing the pair. Without thought of their contents, he took a swig from one and offered me the other.

"Gross!" I said, somewhat disgusted at his actions.

Tommy glanced at the label on his bottle and laughed. "Close. Grolsch."

I shook my head in disgust. "What are you like?"

"Booze is booze." He defended his actions. "Don't be such a bloody pussy. Look. They're fresh." He took another gulp. "Hardly touched."

I had to admit they did look recently opened. Being so close to the bus stop, they'd more than likely been discarded by their owners on the bus driver's orders before he allowed them to board. Just to be sure, I gave mine a healthy sniff in case some wicked bugger had pissed in the bottle, knowing that some desperately drunken sod, like Tommy, would pick it up and drink it.

I held up the free booze in a kind of relieved toast. "You're right, Tommy. Tastes fine." I was a little surprised that it actually did.

"Ain't I always?"

I spotted a red band around the top of Tommy's bottle as he tipped it toward his mouth. "Lipstick!" I laughed, pointing out the scarlet ring. "Your favourite colour, as well."

"Told you it was okay." Tommy grinned, already halfway through his. He pushed the neck of the bottle deep into his throat; blowjob like. "Just think, Sandy, some bird's had her lovely soft lips going right down on this."

I shook my head. "You're a sad case, gal. There's just no hope for you." Tommy tormented me further with more deep-throat bottle sucking.

We continued to walk to nowhere in particular. I desperately wanted to resolve the club incident, but decided I'd let him spill the beans in his own time. He appeared to have calmed a good deal since the fight, although his fingers still had a tremble in them when he lit fags and passed one to me. I also noticed the back of his hands had a fair amount of bruising and blood on them.

Whilst we continued on our calming journey, I heard a clock somewhere in the distance strike one. It mattered little, we had until zero eight hundred to get back to our ship and join our respective watches—mine on the flag deck, Tommy's the forecastle or some other seamanship duty allocated him.

Tommy's empty bottle went into a Council bin when we passed it and didn't find itself disintegrating against some brick wall, which it would have a half-hour back. He had definitely calmed himself.

A couple of young lads, about fifteen-years-old, were the first humans we came across after leaving the club. Huddled together in a graffiti-ridden shelter close by the park, they were smoking what appeared to be joints. Beside both sat four cans of super-strong lager. Both appeared too young to be drinking. After a closer look at their delightful young faces and slim bodies, tucked up in bed some hours ago is where they should have been—my bed.

"Give us a can, lads?" Tommy's tone was very butch but quite friendly. The boys shook their heads; the prettiest pulling his wares close to his side, no doubt suspecting Tommy might steal them.

"S'okay, I'm not going to nick them," reassured Tommy. He pulled out his wallet and withdrew a fiver, holding out his bloodied fingers. "There you go; two cans for a fiver."

I could see the horror on the cute, but hardly innocent, young faces when they saw the state of the trembling hand moving toward them. "S'alright, guys. Some hit-and-run drunk driver just knocked Tommy down. He's a bit shook up. A few cans would really help calm him." I gave the lads another reassuring smile. "Tell you what…" I stuck my hand into my pocket and pulled out three fivers from my wallet and added it to Tommy's five, "twenty quid for the lot."

Neither lad spoke but simply shot delighted glances across to each other. A hand quickly darted out and twenty quid, a tenner for each, speedily vanished into their respective pockets. Without a word, eight cans were duly handed over.

"You've saved my life, boys," thanked Tommy. "See you around."

"Thanks, lads," I said, handing a pack of four to Tommy.

When we walked away, my eyes gratefully etched a pair of bulging packets and two pretty faces into my memory for later retrieval.

Whispering young voices and giggles came from behind as we continued on our journey beside the park, each of us holding our cache of fermented fuel. With a click and a frothy fizz Tommy's first can pressed against his thirsty mouth, its contents refuelling his empty tank.

Tommy released a satisfied burp. "Nice one, Sandy. Where did you learn to lie so damn good?"

"Navy training. Habit now."

"Still, twenty quid for eight fucking cans... Thieving little buggers."

I slapped his bum. "Glad you reminded me. That's a fiver you owe me."

"You sure? Didn't I pay for us to get in the club?"

"No, I did! Thanks again. That's twenty quid you owe me."

Tommy took off his cap and held it over his face. "Me and my bloody big mouth."

I cracked open a can. "Please don't remind me."

TOMMY'S TORMENT

A half-moon roamed in and out of clouds as we made our way beside the large park. It was a warmish night so neither of us was in danger of freezing to death. We might have been in danger of getting so pissed we'd fall asleep somewhere and be late back on board though, an unthinkable and punishable offence, especially if the ship happened to sail without you.

"Into the park," sang Tommy, dashing toward a pair of iron gates a few yards further on. Having had enough of chasing him for one night, I didn't chase after him and casually strode toward the entrance, taking regular sups of my lager which I really didn't need.

"Damn! It's locked," cursed Tommy, rattling the padlock and chain when I pulled alongside. "Looks like we'll have to climb over."

I glanced up at the six-foot metal structure with spiked top and barbed wire headdress woven in and out of the framework. I'd scrambled over many an assault course during my training and found it hard sober. No way was I going to attempt one when pissed. "You're joking?"

"Hold my cans." Tommy shoved them into my body. "I'm going for it."

"Please don't. There has to be some other way."

"Wuss," called Tommy, already hoisting himself upward.

No way could I watch him do it. Watch him fall six feet or become impaled on those nasty spikes. I told him I was going and moved off hoping he'd follow.

It was another five minutes before Tommy's body landed next to mine, with a not so graceful thud and a curse. "How the fuck did you get in here?" He was clearly puzzled to see me on the other side before him.

"Gap in the railings." I was grinning boastfully. "Told you to come with me."

"Where's me beer?" he grunted, standing up and brushing the afternoon's freshly mown grass from his uniform.

"Shit! I've left yours on the other side."

Tommy peered through the railings, a desperate look, if ever there was. "Where's me bloody cans?"

"What's your problem? I paid for them, didn't I?"

Tommy made a grab for one of my cans. "Fiver was mine. That's two cans."

I gave my head a scratch when I stepped backward and out of his reach. "Now let me see… eight into twenty…"

"Two-fifty a can. Gimme. And the one I didn't finish."

I moved behind a tree and gathered up Tommy's booze. "Here, Einstein." I took a quick sup from his half-empty can before handing him the rest. Tommy guzzled down the remainder of the opened can, then sent it flying with a kick, disturbing the tranquillity of the night as it clattered into the branches of a silhouetted tree.

"Where now?" I asked, scanning the moonlit surroundings of open space and thick woodland way off in the distance. Tommy shrugged his shoulders, unconcerned, and continued to stagger up the grassy slope. The image of an intrepid explorer didn't spring readily to mind.

A large lake—void of wildlife and water foul—was what we came across on the other side of the steep hill, the reflection of the moon shimmering on the calm surface. Haphazardly placed were several small islands each with nesting boxes set upon them. Most of the lake's perimeter had been planted with reeds, bulrushes and other water-loving greenery. A rocky waterfall feature completed the serene setting, the trickle of flowing water soothing and sedating.

"Need to dunk me head and wash this blood off me hands." Bending over, Tommy scooped water into cupped hands. "Shit! My knuckles hurt like fuck."

Yes, Tommy did have a bit of a temper and was a fiery little bugger when riled, but he wasn't a scrap for a scrap's sake kind of guy, a "let's beat the crap out of this bloke cos I don't like the look of him" kind of person. I was sure he wouldn't have let fly without good reason. Although now seemed the perfect opportunity to get into why he'd lost it in the club, I decided not.

"What a beautiful place. Reminds me of home."

Tommy shrugged, sent some water splashing over his face, and began washing his hands. "Broke the bastard's nose with the first punch," he revealed, recalling his brawl. "Ouch! I think I might have broke me bloody finger as well."

I thought he'd given me the green light. "Wanna tell me about it?"

Tommy didn't take the bait. Jumping up from his crouching position, the ring clicked on his second can and a quarter of the contents went down his throat in a single guzzle. "Let's find somewhere to chill."

I sensed sadness in his tone but still didn't pursue the matter. I was sure there were some not so cheerful thoughts churning around his brain, something important to him. I decided to move us onto our favourite subject—sex. "D'ya think Sharon would have?"

Tommy began laughing. "Would've? She was tossing me off inside my pocket. Shit, I nearly came on the dance floor."

I could have kissed that luscious laughing mouth right there and then. Stuffed my own palm deep inside that bell-bottom's pocket and played with his throbbing cock all day long. "Don't tell me you've cut away the bottom of your pocket for easy access?"

"You bet. Getting your lass to reach into your pocket and pull out your fags can produce some real fun when she suddenly finds she's got hold of twelve inch packet instead of a packet of twenty."

"Don't you mean nine?"

Tommy poured more booze down his throat. "Fuck off. Twelve."

"Twelve, eh?"

He took another large swig and emptied the can. "'Course."

I made a grab for his cock. "Come on, then. Get the bugger out and prove it."

Tommy shook his head.

"I'll show you mine if you show me yours," I offered, doing a schoolboy retake and hoping for a result.

"Don't wanna frighten you."

"Try."

Tommy jumped to his feet. His hand went to his fly. My heart began to pump and my dick started to stir inside my boxers. Throwing out his big cock he turned and faced the lake and began peeing, a yellow circle of ripples appearing in the clear water.

My face was close to his bum in a flash, my arms embracing his thighs as I peered around his waist. "Wow!" I praised on glimpsing the suckable snake. "You've got a python in your pants."

"Told you," he said, drunkenly falling backward when he'd finished peeing and almost rolling into the lake, his soft cock hanging loose and dangling from his fly.

"I'm really scared of snakes but…" My hand accidentally brushed against his cock as I attempted to roll him over and pretend to fuck him. It was as if I'd thrown a switch, pressed some lethal button. Several spiteful comments spat from his mouth. I rolled from his body, a little taken aback and not sure what I'd done wrong, such play quite the norm. "Joking!"

Tommy tucked his cock speedily away, his face red. Fearing the worse, I backed off. He stepped forward and slung an arm over my shoulder when he sensed my bewilderment. "Sorry, Sandy. Come on let's walk for a while." He patted my back. "Christ, I'm pissed. I didn't mean nowt. Honest."

I threw my arm tentatively around his waist and pulled him close. "No big deal." Brushing the incident aside with a smile, our stroll saw us circumnavigate the lake. I could see Tommy was still toying with whatever was tormenting him. His third can clicked open. I was still on my first.

"Sorry, Sandy." He lit cigarettes. "Hell, I ain't got anything against queers. I feel real good that you told me you're gay. It's just…"

I got the gist of where he was going and thought I'd help. "It's just that you don't like guys coming onto you."

"No, it's not that. Hell, I know you were only playing… but there are some guys out there who do touch you up. You know… come on real heavy. Interfere with younger lads and shit like that."

I knew exactly what he meant and gave him another hug. "I know what you're saying, Tommy. But you know I wouldn't try it on with you, or anyone else for that matter. I think most gay guys stick to gay guys, especially gay sailors. It's far safer." I took a good gulp from my own can. "Hell, I was only playing, like loads of guys on board do." I poked his tummy. "Even you."

"That's true." He laughed when some of his own antics sprang to mind.

"It don't mean they're looking for a shag. It's just sailor play. You must know that?"

Tommy removed his cap and ruffled his hair, his thoughts deep and still disturbing him. "Yeah, I know. But some aren't playing. Some do abuse the power they have. Make guys…" He cut his sentence short and left it hanging in the air like some guillotine blade waiting to fall.

I slung my arm over his shoulder, still tentatively. "You got problems on board with someone, Tommy?"

Tommy laughed, unconvincingly, gulping more beer into his saturated belly, still leaving my question to simmer and stew—boil! "Where now?"

I pointed to the trees way in the distance and giggled drunkenly. "To the woods, you tart."

"I'll scream!" He surprised me with the follow-up line; his voice all feminine and vulnerable as he began to cheer and become all playful and camp.

"How loud can you scream?"

"Aaaah," was his whispered response.

"To the woods!" I did the punch line, the pair of us laughing uncontrollably at our own silliness as we rushed away hand in hand.

We passed a bench sheltered beneath a gathering of chestnut trees as we walked along the path leading to the wooded area of the park. Upon it lay a guy about the same age as both of us. Fast asleep, his only bedding was a cardboard box that lay both above and below his vulnerable body.

"Poor sod," whispered Tommy, desperate not to wake him. "What kind of life is that?"

I nodded agreement as we walked by. "Can happen to any one of us. You never know what's around the corner."

"Shouldn't be allowed. Everyone should have somewhere to live; someone who cares about them." Tommy sighed.

"Tell the Prime Minister and his Government that."

"Hang on!" Tommy moved over to the youth and placed his last remaining can of beer beside the lad's hand. "That should cheer him when he wakes."

Silently we moved away from the lonely soul.

"I reckon I've seen it all now, Tommy," I said when we approached the perimeter of the woods. "You giving away your last can of booze. Mother Teresa would be proud of you."

"She'll be even prouder of you when you let me have one of yours after I've finished this one."

A pair of fox cubs scampered silently by as we entered the wood. I suspected they were off on a bin crawl around the local houses. Sensible move really. Why go hunting in a wood when you've got your very own takeaway right on your doorstep?

"What the fuck was that?" Tommy grabbed my arm like some frightened kid.

"What?"

"Those things that just run down the hill."

"Think you've had one to many, gal. Were there any pink elephants with them?"

"Piss off! I'm not that pissed."

"I didn't see anything."

"You must have done. I think they were rats."

I laughed. "If they were, God help the cats."

"So you did see them?" Tommy was clearly relieved he wasn't imagining things.

"They were fox cubs, Tommy. Never been in a wood before and seen all the wonderful wildlife?"

"I forgot… you grew up in 'turnip' country, so you'd know about such things." His attempted Dorset accent was appalling.

"True. But if those fluffy little fox cubs scared the shit out of you, you wait till we bump into Daddy fox that hasn't had any grub all day. You'll probably give birth." Tommy shook his head but I did notice a look of doubt on his face when we walked between the first clump of trees and further into the darkness of the undergrowth.

"What we going in here for?" Tommy asked.

"Come on. Nothing to be afraid of." I held out my hand and slotted my palm into his. "Just you hold onto me and you'll be all right. I promise I won't let the big bad wolf eat you."

Tommy yanked his palm away and confidently rushed into the thick of the woods. "You think some little dog is going to scare me?" Deciding a prank was called for I silently shot away to my right and secreted myself behind a large birch tree as he marched away.

Tommy spun around and began scanning the undergrowth. Cautiously, he began creeping back to the safety of the open park. "Sandy! You there, Sandy?"

He stopped right beside my hiding place. "Little Red Riding Hood!" I barked when I jumped from behind the trunk and made a grab for his arm. "I'm going to gobble you all up." Which I'd have gladly done.

A pair of hands shot into the air. Beer came flying from his can. I'm sure I saw his skeleton jump clean from his body and then fly back in again. "Jesus, fuck!" yelped Tommy, pressing his palms against his racing heart and then into his frightened face. "You scared the fuck out of me."

"It's only Granny, not the Big Bad Wolf, you frightened tart."

Tommy panted, dropping onto the leafy soil like a soldier shot, his hands still clasping his thumping heart. "I think I've shit me pants!"

I fell about in hysterics. "Granny told you not to go into the woods alone, now didn't she?" I scolded, wagging a finger at him.

"I'm gonna fuck you for that. You see if I don't."

I began moving back into the woods. "Promises, promises, promises."

As we moved further into the woods in search of a road leading to the dockyard, it became clear Tommy hadn't spent much time in such places, if at all. Constantly he was glancing nervously from side to side, every rustle or cracking twig spooking him. The moon creating eerie shadows when branches bobbed in the breeze also caused the occasional jump and jitter. Jungle warfare would not be a medal winner for him.

A massive oak, that had spread its branches wide and was keeping every other tree at bay, brought memories of my childhood days rushing back. "We must climb it," I delighted, pointing to the wonderful specimen.

My excitement totally baffled and bewildered Tommy. "Climb it. Why?"

"Because..." My foot was already on the first stump of a fallen lower branch.

"Because?" he repeated, still not understanding but nevertheless stepping onto the lowest stump as I climbed higher.

A climber of trees Tommy was not; fences maybe. Then again, he was a few sherbets ahead of me so I guess he had an excuse. I needed to hoist his trembling body up the final few feet to the branch on which I'd decided to perch my bum.

The oak was a real beauty, older than ancient. The first complete branch was thick and strong, and wide enough to walk. Although tempted, with so much alcohol swimming around my brain I decided otherwise and stayed beside Tommy who sat close to the main trunk.

"What a lovely old tree," I said, affectionately slapping the branch upon which we sat.

"This is daft," was Tommy's complaining response, hugging himself close to the trunk, fearful of letting go lest he fall.

"But fun."

"Fun?" he questioned, beer in one hand, his other still clutching the trunk tightly.

"Not scared of heights, are you?"

"Hell, no. But this is… different."

"You're shitting your pants, you fibber. And we're only fifteen feet up."

"Already done that." Tommy lowered his head and glanced earthward, fear written all over his delightful face. "It's how the hell I get back down that's worrying me."

"How d'ya think? Jump."

Tommy took a hefty gulp from his can to calm his nerves. "You reckon?"

"Sure. Just remember to bend your knees when you land."

"Shouldn't I have a parachute, then?"

"Oooh! Oooh!" An owl called, far above our heads.

I felt Tommy jump. I must admit I did also.

"What was that?" asked my troubled friend.

"Tree spirits. They don't like you to sit in their tree unless you ask permission first." I stifled a laugh. "You have to call back to them, then it'll be all right."

"I didn't hear you say it," whispered Tommy, drunkenly taking the bait.

"Oooh yes I did. Before I started climbing."

"Ooh," whispered Tommy.

"Louder, Tommy. They're a bit deaf."

"Ooooooh!" he hollered, loud enough to scare the biggest of tree spirits.

"Ooh dear. Who's lost the plot?" I gave him a gentle nudge, unsettling him further.

"Stop taking the piss, Sandy. How the fuck do I get down from here?" he snapped, still doing his balancing and drinking act, still too afraid to let go of the trunk.

Trees are funny old buggers if you don't know them. They are far easier to climb than they are to get down, as many a cat will tell you. I knew I had Tommy. Knew he wouldn't be able to get down without my help. Knew, too, I could reach into his bell-bottoms, pull out his cock and have a good play. Even give him a blowjob. He'd be putty in my hands.

"Got you now," I cunningly tormented when I moved closer. "You're all mine."

I unzipped my fly and pulled out my cock.

"What the fuck you doing?" Tommy desperately wanted to wriggle his bum away but he'd become paralysed to the spot.

I slid closer still. "Wouldn't you like to know?"

"Stop taking the piss, Sanderton. It ain't funny," He used my surname for extra clout.

Before he jumped from fear of what I might be about to do to him, I let go my pint of pent up pee, sending the golden arc earthward. "I'm not taking the piss out of you, Tommy," I laughed, "I'm taking it out of myself. Do you mind not looking."

Tommy made a desperate attempt to thump me but was still unable to let go. "You bastard!"

"Temper, temper."

"Fuck off, Sanderton!"

I shook my dick and tucked it away. "As you wish." Rolling onto my belly, I slid my tummy over the branch. With a dextrous swing, I got a foothold on the stump below. I used his legs as handholds and worked my way over his lap.

"Jesus, fuck!" cried Tommy, letting his treasured can of booze fall to earth when his body took some of my weight. "You trying to kill me?"

I scrambled down the branch stumps. I looked up at my frightened mate who was still hugging the tree like a baby koala. "I'm fucking off now, Tommy. Just like you told me. See you back on board."

"Don't leave me, Sandy. Help me down. I didn't mean it. I'm sorry. I'll do whatever you want."

"Will you now?"

"Anything!"

"There is something you can do for me."

"What's that? I'll do it. I promise."

"You can tell me what the fuck happened in the club. Did the guy touch you up... come on to you? I'm not going to help you down until you tell me. I think you owe me that."

"No, he didn't touch me up. Get me the fuck down from here and I'll explain."

"Promise?"

"I promise."

I began my accent of the tree. On catching sight of Tommy's solemn face, I felt like a right bastard. I began to guide him down. It was with some relief we reached the main fork with only the trunk to go. Standing on one of the branch stumps, I guided his foot onto the one level with my waist. It was a cautious and slow journey back to earth. So unsteady was he, on a couple of occasions he almost slipped through my arms.

His cute bottom pushed into my face when he gingerly stepped onto the final stump. I just couldn't resist. "Nice arse, Tommy." Tommy didn't reply.

His legs were actually trembling when he set his feet back on solid soil. Without a word, he bent and picked up his dropped can. Giving it a shake, he sank the droplets that hadn't escaped.

Pulling one of my three remaining cans from the plastic ring, I handed it to him. I was now feeling guilty for what I'd done. "Let's go back to the ship, Tommy. You don't have to tell me anything."

Tommy thanked me for the beer with a friendly slap to my back. "It's me who should be apologising. I fucked up our run ashore. You're right; I do owe you an explanation."

That was more than generous of him and I loved him even more for it. "Come on. Let's get out of these woods."

"Good move. This place gives me the willies."

I laughed. "Twelve-inch ones, allegedly." Tommy laughed along with me; that gorgeous, wonderful laugh that would brighten any sailor's day.

We backtracked to our entry point and began moving southward. If the dockyard were anywhere, then that direction would be the most likely. Again I remained silent, allowing Tommy to tell his story when he felt ready to do so.

Within ten minutes of walking beside flower and shrub-filled beds, orange road lighting appeared when we crossed the brow of the hill. Pleasingly, on the horizon, the familiar sight of ship's masts and dockyard cranes were all lit up and spread out for miles and beyond those, mile upon mile of empty sea.

"Home," I said, pointing to the sailor town where our berthed frigate sat on Number One jetty.

"Yep, for the next year and more," sighed Tommy. Again, I sensed something in his tone that indicated he wasn't totally happy with the prospect.

I tried to cheer him. "Be great when we're abroad. You'll just love it."

"Many shags?" Tommy gave me a nudge. "Girls, I mean."

"They'll be coming at you like Cruise missiles."

Tommy grabbed his cock. "Shouldn't that be the other way around?"

"Twelve-inch Cruise missiles, now there's a frightening thought for the enemy."

As we moved ever closer to the railings and the road, Tommy pointed to a shelter off to our right. "Come on let's pop in there. I promised I'd tell you what happened in the club."

I jumped in front of him and rested my palms on his shoulders. "You don't have to. It's forgotten and in the past."

He smiled but his eyes were sad. "I want to." It sure was a day of mixed emotions for him, a lot to do with the booze I reckoned. Already I sensed yet more doom and gloom on the horizon.

"You really don't have to, Tommy."

Tommy headed for the shelter.

We sat in the shelter facing the dockyard and the road, the traffic lights controlling imaginary vehicles as they constantly changed colour—red, amber, green, and red. In the distance, steam was rising from the funnels

of several ships, their boilers fired up and made ready
for an early morning sailing. Our frigate was among
them, a departure time of midday.

"Drugs," began Tommy.

"Never take them," I said, not really paying attention, my thoughts in Singapore and Madam Foo Foo's

"He was a drug dealer... the guy I smacked."

I turned toward him. "So why did you smack him?
That shit goes on all the time in clubs. You just tell them
you're not interested and they usually fuck off."

Tommy nodded as if agreeing. "You don't understand, Sandy." He paused as if wondering whether to
continue. It was obviously a bit more than that. "They
fuck kid's lives up. I know." His voice became more agitated. "Shit, don't I know?"

"What, you had a drug problem way back?"

"Not me. My kid brother."

"Oh." I braced myself for worse to come.

"They're fucking bastards, Sandy. They get young
kids while still at school and give them free hits until
hooked. Then it's too late." Tommy's head bowed. "Even
kids as young as eight."

"Kids like your brother?"

Tommy nodded. He took a good gulp of beer. "We
didn't even realise he was on the shit; had been for about
a month. He's fourteen." He took another huge gulp
from his can. "Those fucking arseholes ruined his life!"
It was a horrendous way to finish our run ashore, but it
was a torment best aired.

"What happened?"

Tommy's hand trembled when he took another swig
from his can. "Six months ago I was on leave. It was
about ten at night. Friday. Ben hadn't come home on

time. He often pushed his luck. Mum told me that she thought he'd been acting a bit strange when he came home from school. She looked real worried." Tommy wiped his eyes. "About ten minutes later the doorbell rang. It was a couple of coppers, with serious expressions on their faces."

I knew there were tears rolling down Tommy's cheeks so I looked out toward the dockyard so's not to embarrass him. I think I also did it to take away the pain I was feeling for him.

Tommy brushed his finger beneath his eye. "Ben was in hospital. The silly little bastard had been playing 'dare' by jumping in front of cars. Thought he was Superman. Indestructible." Tommy paused. I could see he was fighting with his emotions. My guts went all tight as I waited on the outcome of his kid brother's fate. "The stupid little bastard got knocked down." Tommy's tears began gushing. "Cops said he had enough drugs inside him to fly to Mars. Broke his back, the stupid sod. He's in a wheelchair now and can't walk."

Tommy's head sank to his knees as he sobbed uncontrollably. I moved closer, put my arms around his shoulders, and gave him a comforting hug. "I'm really sorry, Tommy. But it's not your fault. You must understand that."

"No, it's the fucking drug dealer's fault," he yelled and sobbed. "Yeah, and Ben's, I suppose… for taking the shit." He rubbed his palms into his face, smoothing away his embarrassing tears. "Now you see why I hit that fucking cunt! If those bouncers hadn't got on top of me when they did, I'd have killed the fucking bastard." Tommy smacked his fist against the side of the shelter.

"And those fucking bouncers are just the same as the dealers. They're the ones who control the shit!"

I squeezed Tommy real tight and gripped his fist. "Come on, Tommy, deep breath. Calm yourself. I know it's a real shit thing to happen, but revenge and anger ain't the way forward. You have to come to terms with it. And you certainly shouldn't blame yourself, or Ben."

Tommy sniffed and rubbed his runny nose on the back of his hand. "I guess something positive came out of it cos Ben don't do drugs any more. He can't fucking walk but at least he won't turn out to be another smack head lying around in some squat and shooting up all day. At least he's still alive."

I stuck my hand inside my pocket, pulled out a handkerchief, and handed it to my distraught mate. "And he's able to tell other kids not to get into that kind of shit. And you've not got to think that his life is over, cos it ain't. There's a lot he can do and probably will. It's no help to him or yourself if you feel sorry for him and get upset all the time."

Tommy attempted a laugh. "Yeah, you're right. Shit, I'm sorry for unloading all this crap on you. Christ, I've really fucked up our run ashore."

"Wipe your eyes and blow your nose," I said, all motherly, giving him a real matey hug. "You haven't spoilt the run ashore. Next time when one of those pricks offers you a fix, don't hit the bastard just walk away. Promise?"

Tommy returned my soggy hanky. "Promise." He managed a smile. "Thanks for listening, Sandy."

"That's what mates are for." I rubbed his head. "Anything else bothering you? You know, on board?" Tommy shook his head.

"Right. Let's finish this booze and get back on board for some kip."

Tommy bent toward me. His peck on my cheek was a real surprise. "You're the best, Sandy."

"Don't you forget it." I returned his kiss with one of my own as we set off down the slope.

"Shit, Sandy, I've got a real boner coming on." He gave it a familiar squeeze for proof.

I gave his bum a pat; my gaze fixed on his expanding cock. "Wanna go back to the shelter?"

Tommy laughed a deliciously naughty laugh. "I was thinking about Sharon's tits. Not you, you bandit!"

"Guess I'll have to have that boob job after all."

Tommy pinched my tit and rushed down the slope. "Make sure it's a double D cup."

THE EARLY BIRD…

There were only two mess decks on board that contained juniors, each with a Leading Hand to wipe their bottoms. One of them was up forward, the other down aft. The one Tommy and I were billeted in was the mess down aft. I was more than thankful ours was at the arse end of the ship. In a force-ten gale, up forward could be like riding a roller coaster that was ploughing through a brick wall every hundred yards, each time the bows crashed through the onslaught of waves crashing into them. That said a decent swell and a stern sea could produce a similar effect down aft. Only that was as if you were being tipped arse over tit every other second as the fifty-foot waves hit the rear end of the frigate, lifted the stern out of the sea and pushed the bows downward. A very unpleasant sensation especially when you've just polished off a breakfast of cornflakes, runny eggs on toast, sausage, beans, bacon and fried slice, only to find some young sailor who hadn't yet found his sea legs regurgitating a similar menu over the table, you, or both.

Some older sailors might have thought I was unfortunate to be billeted with baby sailors—me being only months away from being promoted and entitled to bunk in the Communicator's Mess. Not so this gay sailor. The reason was obvious. Billeted thus, the naked bodies of the young skins and an endless bounty of pert bottoms and smooth torsos would surround me daily. Sexy and nectarous little neophytes, most of who were still virgins, would tempt and torture me each and every day of the week. Scrumptious skins, the likes of young Freckles, would no doubt drive me to the point of drooling when I nightly destroyed my dick beneath my bedding.

It will come as no surprise, then that when I joined the ship I'd managed to bunk myself just below Freckles. It will also come as no surprise before rising each morning I would usually lie motionlessly in my bunk until he'd climbed from his. It gave me the opportunity to lust over that six inch cock, eight when fully aroused, knowing that with a simple forward movement of my head I could have the whole damn lot slipping between my lips and sailing down my throat. Predictably, I usually climbed from my bunk with a raging boner, especially so if I waited for Tommy to turn out as well and see what he had to offer for breakfast.

"Lash up and stow. Lash up and stow. Hands off cocks, on socks. Don't roll over, roll out." It was the regular call to arms from the far too jolly Bosun's Mate, who had been up since four in the morning; only hours after Tommy had arrived back on board from yet another of his heavy-drinking runs ashore, this time without me.

I knew there would be the usual rush for the heads and showers; the aft showers only capable of accommodating about twenty naked bodies huddled together at any one time. It wasn't that long a wait though. Very few lads hogged a shower or sink—God help them if they tried—and almost every seasoned sailor I'd ever encountered could shit, shave, shower and shampoo in seconds; some two at the same time.

Well before the neon lights came flickering on around the mess, sailors were throwing their bodies from bunks and dropping tiredly to the deck. Most of them were totally naked but a few of the shy young skins did have underwear of various breeds covering their favourite bits. Without exception, not a single lad wore pyjamas. No way would he ever live that down. Almost every youth had a lazy lob swinging free, or a fully blown beauty bursting forth and looking decidedly succulent. Most were not embarrassed by their various states of excitement but several, including me, were more than pleased to be party to such a delightful parade of palatable and proud pricks. It also goes without saying, a good few of those pretty pricks were still dribbling delicious after-come or, those caught midstream, pre-come.

My own cock was pretty sticky, as was my tummy. I guess some lad like clubbing Simon or Freckles might have crept into my dreams somewhere during the night. It might have been any gorgeous sailor though, surrounded as I was by more than enough delicious and tender flesh to fill my days and nights with an endless assortment of similar fantasies—with any luck, realities.

The sight of Freckles' semi-hard cock slipping by my face this morning—a sliver of stickiness apparent— soon had me *rising* and heading for the showers. As always, the bathing system worked with its usual efficiency without ever choreographed. Men and youths religiously soaped and showered naked bodies of all shapes and sizes while others shaved or brushed teeth at sinks. After one cleansed body moved from a shower another that had been shaving at a sink moved beneath the spray, while yet another took up that free sink station, the rotation continuing until each body had been cleansed of its sins and taken through the exit.

Sometimes during these bathing baptisms, a bit of horseplay took place. Often a sexy virgin would be dragged into a shower and a pretend fuck enacted by a beefy sailor. The evenings or when we were preparing for a run ashore, and feeling decidedly randy, were the usual times to witness such pleasant goings on. But it was in the mornings, when a host wet-dream stiffies were in abundance, which I found the most rewarding.

Often when shaving, my attention focussed on an array of mirrored cocks getting savagely soaped, or a pair of delicious buttocks with bubbles trickling between the fuckable cheeks. A familiar bloodied nick on my face my usual reward. This morning was no different and my neck had a fine ribbon of red below the Adam's apple.

As soon as the youth who my attention had been focussed upon vacated the showers, I took up his station beneath the tepid spray. Beside me today, the naked torso of another delightful lad, whom I didn't know, was being erotically eradicated of nightly sin. His soapy palms were smoothing up and down his hairless legs and over his pert little buttocks. With his delicate, soap-covered bottom offered to me so invitingly, it took every ounce of control not to brush my cock against those delectable cheeks and pretend to fuck him. Such was my arousal I'd already lathered my cock to within an inch of reaching a fully blown boner.

He acknowledged my presence when he came upright, smiling innocently and shyly, throwing his head back beneath the spray and running his soapy hands over jet black locks, smooth chest, tummy and finally cock. Only I was aware of my thoughts at the sight of that, my imagination turning innocent bubbles into globules of spunk as they dribbled over his stiffening cock. But mine were not the only eyes to scan between his tender young thighs and witness the heavenly body that had reached an angle that any astrologer would agree could only be deemed as rising.

His body cleansed of imaginary spunk, a blue-eyed gaze again met my own. I don't know if it was just in my mind but a charge of electricity seemed to pass between us at that precise moment, sending a spark of instant recognition that earthed in my groin.

A knowing sparkle glistened in the lad's eyes while our minds remained fused together. He gave another groin-grabbing grin for extra confirmation. I rewarded him with one of my own before I again brought my attention back between his legs. His own gaze fleetingly scanned my own cock but was only detectable to the trained eye.

"You two lovebirds finished?" questioned a beer-bellied, hairy sailor; our two-minute bathing time already breached.

"I'm done," I replied, brushing his comments aside but reluctant to break eye contact with my boy-beautiful whose face had begun to colour.

I moved toward my towel. The youth hastily headed toward his. Our naked bodies collided, cock brushing cock. His face beamed brighter than the reddest of roses, his body smelling even sweeter as it pressed into mine.

"Sorry," I apologised, resting my palm on his silken shoulder when our faces came kissing close.

"Ain't you going kiss him goodbye," sang Beer Belly, who must have been keen to embarrass us further.

"Kissy kissy," chirped a couple of fellow bathers waiting to enter the shower, their lips puckering as they pretended to kiss one-another.

A towel flicked out and stung the lad's backside as he made a grab for his own. His face became as red as his bottom with embarrassment. Quickly he wrapped the towel around his slender waist and covered the reddened mounds.

I sensed he wasn't sure of how he should react in such a situation. I decided I should help and gave my bare bottom a wiggle in the direction of the laughing lad who'd just flayed his tender flesh. "What a about mine?" I camply asked, fluttering my eyelashes, knowing that playing the game was always the best response. "My botty not good enough for you?"

"Need a torpedo to fill that slack hole," joked a stunning salt standing bollock naked beside the shower.

"Whoops! I've dropped me soap," came the familiar cry from another sodden sailor who was washing his body.

"Ooh! Let me pick it up for you," said the guy who'd stung the youth's backside, then promptly bent over.

Instantly another sailor was behind and pretending to fuck him. "Sorry, roll of the ship," he chortled.

"Thought it was a roll of salami," came the punch line as an incredibly hairy bush pressed into his rear.

The lad saw his chance to escape, but still took flak when he made his exit. I soon followed in his wake, camping it up and holding my own when a similar assortment of slander met my own ears.

The youth was nowhere to be seen when I stepped into the Burma Way. I suspected he'd legged it back to his mess. When I reached the heads, I wondered if he might have popped inside because of his embarrassment. I knew too well how a fresh young sailor on his very first ship could take queer jibes far too personally when they certainly weren't meant that way. I decided I'd pop inside in case he was hiding and all upset.

There was only one occupied cubicle inside the heads when I entered. I moved into the adjacent one. For a while, I listened for the sound of sobbing. Happily, there was none. A familiar tingle began to stir my cock, my thoughts moving from a youth with his hands smoothing away tears, to one smoothing away at his solid truncheon.

All cubicles on ships had a foot high gap between deck and partition. Cautiously, I lowered my head toward the deck. Already I was getting a good stiffy, a natural reaction for me when visiting such accommodation, even for genuine use. Bare feet with flip-flops greeted my eyes, bare calves too. Whoever occupied the other cubicle, they must have just left the showers or been on their way to them.

My fingers had encircled my cock, again quite instinctively, when I caught sight of the smooth white flesh. My cock went rigid in my palm when those cute feet slipped forward and rested on the heels, the toes twitching excitedly. He was definitely tossing.

Heart pounding excitedly, I bent lower, my forehead almost touching the deck. Dare I move my face closer to the partition and peer upward? Dare I reach in and stroke that slender ankle? Dare I just shove me whole head right through the gap!

Excited gasps and pants began to slip through the thin Formica bulkhead and toward my eager ears. Urgently, I began to pump my own cock when visions of the cute little bottom I'd witnessed in the shower flashed into my thoughts. Yet more visions of his slender fingers pumping that delicious cock saw my face move closer to the gap, keen to discover if indeed it was my shy young lad pumping his cock on the other side.

My excitement reached fever pitch, my cock already oozing pre-come as I thrashed it. No longer could I be tortured, I just had to find out who was tossing himself so obligingly and delightfully as I dutifully did likewise.

I brought my face closer to the gap and peered inside. My heart began beating excitedly as the youth's toes twitched wildly, his calves trembling as he bent and stretched his legs with each thrash of his cock.

I needed to stretch out in order to get my head through the gap and allow myself a better view. The lad's eyes now tightly shut; I managed to view all of his face, sheer pleasure written over his cherub cheeks as he slaughtered his solid cock between clasped fingers. So fast was his foreskin flashing over the sticky bud, it was nothing but a blur to my hungry gaze. Far from being an upset little bunny, as I'd previously thought when he'd rushed from the showers, he now appeared to be a very happy bunny indeed, his ecstatic expression a joy to behold.

Although in an uncomfortable position with my bum pressed against the stainless steel bowl and my back arched painfully, I managed to get in sync with his tossing, thrashing my own cock for all I was worth. His climax imminent, I allowed myself a brief downward tour of the superb young body before he shot his whack, taking in his smooth chest breathing heavily; his long, hard cock dribbling profusely; his hairless, grape-sized balls, tight and compact, and filled with spunk and ready to spill; finally, his slender thighs and calves shaking in uncontrollable spasms. It was a remarkable sight just before breakfast.

I returned to his splendid cock and held my attention there, waiting for the burst of fresh morning spunk to explode, but not before a quick exploration of his flat tummy and tiny navel as they tightened and twitched with every tantalising tug on that fantastic flesh as he pleasingly punished it.

A slowing hand and flickering eyelids heralded the arrival of his first deluge of scrumptious teenage juices. Gently teasing the foreskin upward over the bulbous bud, he tentatively drew it back down the shaft as if the sensitivity were too much to bear. A desperate gasp saw two hairless spheres rise out of sight before they sent a single spurt of delicious spunk sailing toward his gaping mouth and clean over his shoulder.

Rolling the foreskin back over the sticky head, then jerking it down again, his second spurt landed on his tummy. A third quickly followed, sailing skyward and splattering over his mouth. Enviously, I watched the teenager's fleshy tongue lap the lot away. On seeing his spunk-covered tongue, my own whack came gushing out of my cock and splashed over the deck.

Horror! He caught sight of my peeping face.

Relief! With a delightful grin, he swiftly dropped to his knees, bringing his cock to my face.

I almost broke my neck when I shoved my head further into the cubicle and turned my mouth upward and opened wide. Pushing his solid and sticky cock close to my lips, the teenage sailor continued to pump fast and furious.

The next sensational spurt of spunk soon sailed forth. It seemed to hang in the air before it finally fell, splashing over my lips and lapping tongue. His legs trembling, the final droplets landed on the deck beside my head. Gladly I would have lapped it up as well.

Smiling wickedly, my naughty sailor wasn't done yet. He scooped the spunk from his tummy and pushed his fingers deep into my open mouth. Like a kitten desperate for its mother's milk, I sucked and lapped them spotlessly clean.

The door of the heads opening stopped any further activity. I decided I'd leave first and quickly wrapped my towel around my waist. My face was beaming joyfully when I made my exit, the taste of his spunk fresh in my mouth. It would seem my young lad must have been turned-on by the sight of naked youths showering, even got off on the occasional slap to his cute little bottom. I knew I'd be more than willing to oblige him with a gentle spanking of my own should the occasion arise. I couldn't wait for the next time we met in the showers.

Tommy was fully dressed when I descended the ladder into the mess, my feet not touching a single rung as I rested my elbows on the smooth handrails and slid down. The lazy sod hadn't even bothered to bathe and looked about as happy as any lad should whose head had spent the night under a road hammer.

"Morning, butch!" I greeted. "Hangover?"

"Don't," he said, ignoring my question and offering me a sip of orange juice as he rubbed his sore head.

I gave him a wink. "Already had some juice, thanks."

Tommy gave me a brief once over. Quickly drawing to the correct conclusion, he raised his eyebrows. "Shit, Sandy," he whispered, pulling me close. "Don't tell me you've..."

I gave him a wicked grin and poked his tummy. "Know what they say? The early bird that catches the sperm."

Tommy swallowed hard. He looked as if he was about to puke, his face white when he screwed it up. "Spare me the details... please!"

I gave his bum a friendly slap. "Wouldn't say that if it was your juice I was swallowing."

A GAME OF PATIENTS

Later than advertised on Daily Orders the command came over the Tannoy for Special Sea Dutymen to close up, for all watertight doors and hatches to be closed, and condition Zulu established. It was also a fortnight on from our last days at sea, a gremlin in the engines the culprit.

I was on the flag deck when the order bellowed throughout the ship, sending sailors scurrying to their posts, had been all morning. Already I'd organised the flags indicating the ship's call-sign, and the Hotel flag, informing all other vessels we had a Pilot on board, was ready to be hoisted. Likewise, my watch-keeping buddy was up on the forecastle ready to lower the Union Jack the moment we lost contact with the shore, the White Ensign being the only flag flown when underway.

Both Tommy and Freckles were also at their respective stations; Tommy on the forecastle; Freckles, his big blue eyes wide open and pressed against binoculars, doing bridge lookout and only a matter of feet from me.

"Let go forward. Let go aft," issued the command from the Captain some fifteen minutes later.

Thick hawsers dropped into the sea and began to vanish magically and professionally into the bowels of the ship, the party of seaman scurrying around like worker ants as they did their work. On contact lost with shore, I hoisted both my signals, the flags fluttering wildly when they met the strong wind coming from the West. At the same time, the Union Jack was yanked down and vanished into the arms of my watch-keeping buddy and was speedily unclipped and raced back to the flag deck, the both of us then standing to attention and facing the dockyard piping party.

"Pipe the still!" The command from the Master at Arms bellowed after the final hawser had left its bollard and dropped into the sea, releasing us from our shore side captivity, and we began to move. Obediently and smartly, three seamen standing on the port side let loose single a single shrill note in unison from their Bosun's whistles. The air filled with their orchestral masterpiece but was quickly captured by the strong wind and made the joint effort more a high-pitched warble than a clear still.

Whilst officers saluted on both the upper bridge and ashore, a similar shrill note of recognition came from the Bosun's whistle of a solitary seaman standing on the dockyard between a pair of bollards. It received the same contempt from a relentless wind that had no respect for this ceremony, which took place on every arrival and departure of a naval vessel.

"Carry on," was the next command for the piping party, sending a different sound into the air, again swiftly eaten up.

The journey was slow to the final buoy indicating the end of the shallow channel, which ran from sea to dockyard. My Hotel flag and call sign signals came down as soon as the pilot had stepped into a very bouncy Pilot's boat, heading back to the safety of shore. Already I sensed it was going to be a bastard of a day, weather wise.

"Special Sea Dutymen Stand Down," sang the welcome order over the Tannoy, sending most of the seaman who had scampered to the upper decks for sailing duties scurrying below decks for a welcome hot cuppa. But for Tommy, Freckles and me this wasn't the case. This was our proper watch so we were required to remain at our stations until sixteen hundred. Didn't make much difference during the daytime though, everyone worked during daylight hours unless they had done the middle watch, in which case they would get the afternoon off, a Make and Mend.

For seaman, the likes of Tommy and Freckles, their tasks could be any mundane job from cleaning toilets to repairing equipment, painting bulkheads, chipping paint and the like. Only when they did their proper watch did they do their special jobs—radar operators in the Ops Room, gunners, etc. A seaman's lot was not an easy one.

In normal weather conditions, the Zulu status would be stood down and upper deck doors and hatches opened. Due to the state of the worsening weather, today all outer doors and hatches remained shut, bringing us to a relaxed state of Zulu. Also, in normal weather conditions, you wouldn't find green-faced sailors hugging their bellies and throwing up all over the place. That said I'd known quite a few sailors who began throwing up the moment the ship got into motion, some as soon as the engines fired up. How I felt for those poor buggers, having never been seasick myself.

This was Freckles and Tommy's first ship, and their first time at sea in rough weather. With an even more severe weather forecast already flashed to the fleet, the prospect of both ending up in a similar sickened state was looking increasingly likely by the minute, especially so for Tommy who I knew had one bitch of a hangover to contend with from yet another drunken run ashore.

Already I could see him staggering from side to side as he worked on the forecastle, desperately trying to keep his feet fixed firmly on the slippery deck. Meanwhile, on the port bridge wing Freckles' head was wobbling uncontrollably from side to side as the bows dipped deep into the ocean, rose again, and sent an ever increasing amount of spray toward his already sodden and sad body. Having witnessed this situation before, I was left in no doubt his dinner was about to be regurgitated. Sensing a shower of chunky bits, I quickly stuck my finger skyward and checked the direction of the wind.

We were well away from the shore and battling through the tremendous sea at a reasonable fifteen knots. Visibility decreased rapidly as heavy rain joined in the affray, making lookout duty a complete waste of time and the most miserable job on the planet. With no other Navy ships to send or receive signal to and from, I decided I'd duck into the bridge and keep warm and dry. For the record, the only sailors allowed on the bridge were the Officer of Watch, duty signalman and the Captain. And if you wanted to enter the bridge you had to ask permission, and that included officers. We signalmen were a privileged lot.

As I headed toward the port wing, where Freckles was doing his unpleasant duty, I spotted his knees begin to buckle. Before I'd reached the poor little bugger, he was down upon them, retching for all he was worth. I think I saw his meals came back in the reverse order they'd been eaten—dinner, breakfast. It was an unpleasant sight but I was pleased he'd eaten something. An empty tummy and seasickness is a not good thing. Always put something inside you to throw up was the general rule, good advice for spewy hangovers as well.

Freckles had completely given up by the time I reached his side. Now flat on the deck and groaning, his knees were curled up toward his tummy, spew being washed away by seawater as it swirled around him. With every dip of the bows and roll of the ship, so he retched even more, retched to the point of busting his little gut.

When you are that seasick there are no comforting words a mate can say to take away your discomfort, but sometimes knowing there's help at hand can lift one's spirit. "Come on, Freckles. Sit yourself up," I urged, slipping my hands under his arms and pulling him into a better position, although the one he was already in was probably more to his liking. "Soon have you below decks and all tucked up."

Another tasty helping of spew, this time over my shiny boots, was the reward for my concern. Undeterred, I raised him halfway to his unsteady feet. With our bodies pressed tightly together, I began to reassure him again.

This wasn't supposed to be a romantic act but when his soft cheek fell against my face and his panting chest pressed into my own, an inexcusable stiffy began to develop beneath my waterproof trousers. By the time I'd managed to get him fully erect, so was I.

Pulling a handkerchief from my waterproofs, I smoothed it over his lips and wiped them clean. It was a wasted effort and his next salvo of spew went over my shoulder and began to run down my back.

"I wanna die," Freckles kind of cried. I wiped his kissable mouth clean a second time.

"I might get arrested for indecent assault before you do," was my thought when my eyes continued to feast on those soft lips and my stiff cock pressed even harder into his body as I held him upright.

I was struggling to open the bridge door while still holding Freckles upright with my other arm. "Don't worry, you'll live," I told him when the ship continued to roll and drive our bodies intimately and dangerously close.

Whilst I had Freckles pinned seductively to the bulkhead Tommy came lurching toward us, his body swaying from side to side with the roll of the ship. I briefly wondered if he might have thought the pair of us was actually getting it off right there in to open.

As he passed us by I noticed he too looked as green as any lush meadow I'd ever seen. "Fancy a pint?" I hollered into the howling wind, unable to resist the temptation to torture him.

The briefest of scowls was thrown in my direction. Almost immediately, his body bent over the guardrails, his waterproofs drawing tightly into his delicious bum and outlining their shape delightfully. With a gut-heaving groan, his spew sailed from his gaping mouth, first curling around his face before sailing behind him and in our direction. Before it reached the back of Freckles' head, a gust of wind mercifully caught it and it went sailing out to sea.

A solitary finger shot skyward as Tommy continued on his journey aft. My mouth curled into a cruel laugh. "Another time perhaps!"

My Freckles patient was still retching against an empty tummy when I finally forced the bridge door open against the relentless wind. The Officer of the Watch and a couple of ratings on cleaning duties sheltered inside its warmth and comfort, the Captain and the First Lieutenant now snugly below decks.

"Man down, sir!" I called to the officer, using a term seldom used by us sailors and certainly not by me. 'Man going down' being the one I was most familiar with.

The officer gave the pair of us the briefest of glances, his attention elsewhere. "Who is it, Sanderton?"

"Junior Seaman Wilkins, sir."

Another brief glance ventured in our direction. "Feeling bad, lad?" asked the busy officer, his attention still on charts.

"Ye... yuuwrrk," gurgled the vomiting reply from Freckles, this time without any solid evidence to support his statement.

I think the officer did have a little concern for Freckles' sorry state but didn't really show it. "Take him to sick bay, Sanderton. Jenkins, find me another lookout... pronto!" he barked his order, before once again focussing on more important matters, this time the radar screen that would tell him what other unfortunate ships were in danger of bumping into us during this little dance across the ocean.

My journey with Freckles along the Burma Way and toward the sick bay was not the jolliest of trips, at least not for Freckles. Hardened sailors who had already found their sea legs were not sympathetic when it came to seasick baby sailors. "Fatty pork chops and greasy chips for supper, son," was just one tummy tingling teaser from one old salt to help my lovely lad on his way to a full recovery. And the guy who gobbed a pretend greeny into his palm, then sucked it back into his mouth might have been rewarded with a three course meal had Freckles anything left inside his tummy to throw up at him.

I gave the sick bay door a sharp tap when we arrived. Mo our medic was already getting his happy domain prepared for such emergencies, the likes of which I was now delivering. With a jovial, "Come!" He bade me enter.

Being a signalman, I would meet almost every person of importance on board when I did my daily rounds and distributed their respective signals. Mo was usually on the list, medical results and the like his normal quota. "What's up, doc?" I did my Bugs Bunny routine as I entered.

"I hear you were," my very pleasant medical man greeted as soon as he recognised me. "What you got for me today, besides a dose of clap?"

It seemed the jungle drums were working well and my run ashore with Tommy was now common knowledge. I expect Tommy had beefed things up a little and his version of events had the pair of us shagging a couple of fillies with the biggest tits in town. No way would he have let on that a pretty youth had been gnawing on my cock and that he had bugger all.

I escorted Freckles into the medicine-smelling room. "No signals today, Mo, just one walking wounded to deliver."

Mo came straight over to Freckles and placed a comforting and healing palm onto his forehead. "First day on the big bad ocean, son?"

Freckles nodded; his arms wrapped tightly around his aching tummy.

Mo smiled warmly. "Picked a good day to find your sea legs. Don't worry we'll soon have you back on your feet." Freckles smiled back, his first since he'd collapsed on the bridge wing. Already Mo's bedside manner was making him feel better.

"Don't worry, Freckles. Mo can cure anything. A right old witch, if ever there was."

Mo laughed and moved over to his medicine cabinet and began to prepare a magical concoction. "Hubble, bubble, toil and trouble," he sang, pretending to stir a fermenting pot.

"Eye of frog, leg of toad..." I played along.

Freckles watched intently. "What you giving me, doc?" he asked, his expression a trifle concerned.

Mo turned and gave another warm smile. "Take no notice of that old slapper, son. I'll soon turn you into a round-the-world solo yachtsman."

"He'll turn you into *something*," I continued to tease, doing a Frankenstein monster impression.

Mo came back over to Freckles and handed him a purple mixture. "Here, get this down you. After a couple of hour's kip you'll be able to swim the channel."

Freckles shot me a glance and managed another smile. Obediently, he gulped the remedy down. I had no idea what he'd just been given but I was sure it would work. A tasty looking placebo was my own medical thoughts. It was a common belief among hardened sailors there was no real cure for seasickness. Old salts that had been sailing the seas since man discovered it could swim always claimed a good tot of Navy rum was the only true cure. I'll drink to that!

The ship did another of its bungee jump, western roll, submarine dips on the next wave. Freckles gripped his tummy tightly, desperate to keep the magic potion down. I moved to his side when he doubled over, cradling his sickened body in my arms. "Don't puke or you'll have to drink another one."

Freckles swallowed hard, hand over mouth.

Mo picked up the buzzing phone and listened intently. "Got to go, Sandy. Emergency. Suspected broken arm." Replacing the phone, he grabbed his medical bag. "Would you like to get the lad into bed?"

Did I want to get Freckles into bed? You bet, along with half the bloody gay lads on board.

Now let me tell you something about young Freckles. His sea-blue *come to bed* eyes were big, sexy and seductive, each iris a darker blue and alluring. He was sailor shag of your dreams, a young Adonis. A youth whose hair was golden rather than blond, and longer than most. Dirty buggers like me suspected they knew the reason why he had such a lovely head of hair.

Not a single spot or blemish trespassed upon his angelic face. The small cluster of freckles that did sit below those incredibly sexy eyes, decorating each cheekbone, only complimented his facial features, creating an innocence that was simply irresistible. Indeed, his face was so pretty you almost wanted to cry because of its beauty, cry because you wanted to kiss and caress it, and plant your desperate mouth upon his.

Skin as white as snow, Freckles was a slender youth who stood at a mere five foot five in all his glorious nakedness. His tiny torso had the softest skin imaginable, also without blemish or even the slightest dusting of body hair, discounting his mousy-brown pubic bush.

Below his narrow and tiny waist protruded a deliciously fuckable bottom even the most straight of sailors would be unable to resist after a couple of shagless months at sea. They had a strength about them that was simply mind-blowing. Their constant flexing sent many a sailor's cock into firing mode, making them wonder if those delicate mounds were just crying out for a cock to be cruising between their tightness and into the small tight hole beyond.

Just in case you hadn't been bowled over by such a bounty of beauty, Freckles also had one gift of a dick. Most of the day it hung pretty close to creeping below the leg of his boxers, when lazy, but most definitely peeped through when happy and on the rise.

Quite simply Freckles was the kind of lad you used drool over at school. The lad you longed after in the shower, desperate to lather every inch of his sexy skin, desperate to lasso that limp and lengthy cock with your longing tongue. The youth that filled every second of your day with thoughts of sex, and at night filled your bedding with wanking stains too numerous to mention.

Freckles was also the lad you somehow never got to know because you were too nervous of his beauty, too afraid you would lose control and leap on him, and fill his pretty mouth with cock as soon as it opened. Too afraid you would devour every morsel of his heavenly body if you were alone together. But, worse than this, too afraid of being rejected by him.

Yes, Freckles was your dream shag come true. The youth who tortured your very soul, the youth you would have swum the seven seas just to sniff his underpants, the youth whom I desired even more than Tommy.

"I'll make sure he bunks down, Mo," was my dignified reply.

"Cheers, Sandy. Cot number one, if you please."

Freckles smiled. "Cot number one," he mumbled. A strange glow filled his cheeks and a sparkle glinted in his eyes.

"Right, Freckles, let's get your kit off," I suggested, trying to disguise my keenness to do just that, and not even considering he might wish to do so for himself. Far from complain, Freckles just grinned. It was a dangerous and seductive grin, a cruel grin for a person of my limited restrain.

Freckles waterproofs came off first, working shirt next. That delicate chest with its familiar dark nipples was the next thing to greet my lusting eyes. Lower down, embedded in a soft tummy, his tiny navel tormented me further.

After a long, lustful and lingering look at his naked flesh, I brought my excited fingers to the waistband of his trousers. "I can do that," giggled Freckles, his fingers foraging around the fly.

"Thought you were dying?" I questioned, defending my actions.

Freckles fell into my body with the next roll of the ship. "Okay, then," he giggled kind of drunkenly, raising his arms high above his head. I had a sneaky suspicion he knew exactly what I was about.

After unfastening the belt, I popped the top button of his trousers open. The remainder of the buttons swiftly followed. His trousers came down quicker than a skier off-piste.

White boxers greeted my lusting eyes. A seven-inch helping of rising cock, much bigger than the sausage I'd eaten for breakfast, surprised me when it suddenly popped from the fly. Even in his sickened state Freckles' brain remained connected to his cock.

I didn't exactly fall to my knees on witnessing his wonderful rising sex, but my face was hovering conveniently at crotch height.

The bows of the ship hitting another forty-foot wave brought Freckles stumbling forward again. This time his hands fell upon my head when he steadied himself. I was unable to avoid contact with his cock and my lips pressed firmly into the thickening shaft.

"What a big one," I said, referring to the wave and reluctantly pulling my mouth away.

Freckles' cock grew until all eight inches stood proud and rigid. His cherub face stared down at me, his expression so seductive it was sinful. He began to giggle again. "A real big one."

The wave moved amidships and lifted the stern high. The ship did a lethal roll to starboard. Freckles held onto my head to steady himself. He fell sideways, dragging me. With a gentle bounce, we both landed on the cot.

My face was lying next to his solid cock, my lips resting on his balls. Freckles began to giggle even more.

"Another big one," he said, his demeanour that of a drunken sailor who'd had a rum too many.

I quickly realised Mo's potion was something more than a tummy soother. It must have contained some kind of sedative too. I was no saint that was for sure, but knew I'd have to resist opening my mouth and devouring that delicious cock. "Beddy byes time, me thinks," I said, somehow resisting tucking his cock back into his boxers.

I lifted his legs onto the cot and threw a blanket over his tormenting torso. "A real, real big one," Freckles said with another giggle just before his eyelids flickered and finally shut.

I couldn't believe I'd let the opportunity to have sex with the most beautiful youth on the ship slip me by. I folded his kit and placed it neatly on the chair beside the cot. Unable to resist just one touch of my slumbering sailor, I bent and stroked his locks, then gently kissed his forehead. "Sleep tight my lovely lad," I whispered, pulling the curtain around his cot.

"How's my patient?" sang Mo when he pushed open the sick bay door.

"He's doing just fine, Mo. Sleeping like a baby."

"Don't worry, Sandy. Soon have him up again," chirped the ever-cheerful Mo.

Memories of how close I'd come to sucking that eight-inch beauty were still fresh in my mind. I wondered if Mo was right and I would indeed get Freckles up again. "Sure hope so, Mo. Don't like to see a young lad down for long."

Mo smiled and nodded. He was on my case for sure.

NIGHTMARES

Months had flown by, months of exercises, months of misery. We'd done damage control, fire fighting, man overboard, gunnery and missile drills—firing at every thing that floated or flew. We'd chased submarines, been buzzed and bombed by aircraft, been attacked by terror-ists. We'd pretended to break down, get towed and the reverse. We'd fought imaginary fires, while Mo had re-paired damaged bodies both imagined and real. About the only thing we hadn't done was abandon ship, the of-ficers fearing we might not come back once over the side. Worse than all of this, we'd been tortured and tormented by visions of seaside towns, all lit up invitingly in the dis-tance, but not once calling into any port for a well-earned shag. Quite simply, we'd gone to bloody hell and had yet to come back.

The rough weather had left us behind a couple of days ago and we no longer needed big waves to get us tossing all over the place. So many guys had reached the point of sexually bursting they were doing that for themselves, relentlessly thrashing their sex-starved cocks. I myself was up to five wanks a day and Tommy wasn't far behind, torturing himself regularly with glossy tit and pussy pages, his hungry lips pressed against a juicy pair of melon mounds on most nights.

'A happy sailor sails on full stomach' so it was said by the chefs of the sea. How wrong they were. A happy sailor sails on a satisfied sex life. If by chance he could get a damn good meal before or afterwards, better still. And it was obvious by the gloomy look on many a frustrated sailor's face we were getting neither.

As for Doc's magic potion, that had done the trick for Freckles all right. Already he was as good as any veteran sailor who had sailed the seven seas. He too was just as guilty as the rest of us, playing with himself like some dirty demon, the disgusting little devil. And it didn't fail to go unnoticed by other drooling sailors who adored his delightful body that young Freckles appeared to walk around the ship with a permanent stiffy bursting inside his trousers. If nothing else, he'd at least discovered his middle sea leg, the horny little fuck-bunny.

Sadly, Freckles still hadn't managed to find *my* middle leg. With Action Stations being sounded on a regular basis there just wasn't the opportunity to make a move on him. I was aware of one thing though; he was the biggest tease I'd ever met.

It had become more than apparent whenever Freckles descended from his bunk first thing in the morning his delightful body seemed to linger a good deal longer when his cock reached the level of my face. Often he would rise a good ten minutes before the lights came on—making sure he woke me in the process—and leave it lingering there all longingly. Invariably his scrumptious teenage sex would be fully erect and only inches from my mouth. I was certain he was waiting for my hot mouth to slip down the thickened shaft so I could send his balls spinning in sensational spasms when my lips hit the base and buried into his pubic bush. Delicious and desirable though that would have been, it was too dangerous a manoeuvre to engage in when surrounded by slumbering sailors. That said it would have been one worthy of getting a discharge for. As I said, he was a bit of a tease.

I was two hours into the Middle watch. The moon was high and bright. The sea flat calm, the moon's reflection glistening on its surface. I was on the flag deck scanning a merchant ship sitting far off in the distance, right on the horizon, checking to see if it signalled us. Merchant ships didn't usually signal Navy ships, although we would often challenge them when on patrol.

Ambling along the starboard bridge wing, from the corner of my eye I spotted a solitary silhouetted figure puffing on a cigarette. My attention moved away from the merchant ship and back on board. I thought I recognised the slouchy walk of the approaching figure as that of my lovely Tommy.

"That you, Sandy?" I heard a voice whisper well before the figure had reached me. My willy gave a little wiggle inside my boxers when I recognised it.

Like the rest of us randy boys Tommy hadn't had sex in an age, even on our last run ashore. At least I believed he hadn't. Maybe, just maybe, if I played my cards right I might be able to give that beautiful big bone of his a real good blow. Better yet—my imagination going wild—get him to bang my bum into sensational submissive oblivion while he had me tied to my twenty-inch signalling lantern.

I flicked the switch on the smaller ten-inch lamp and flashed a quick beam of light into the silhouetted body to check if it was indeed my sexy straight buddy. The illuminated sight of Tommy's beauty bounced instantly back at me, sending my bone bursting in eager expectation.

"Who goes there, fuck or foe?" I challenged with a laugh.

"Piss off, you second-hand shag." Tommy was covering his eyes when the beam of white light almost blinded him.

"Call your sister a second-hand shag would you?" I whispered, dowsing the light before pulling a ciggie from my pack, the sight of him smoking sending a nicotine surge throughout my own body. It also brought my cock even higher, but that's another fantasy.

Tommy laughed and puffed a smoke ring that would just about fit over my cock into my face when he reached my side. "Come to think of it, you do look like my sister."

I doubted he was into incest but the thought did do something for me, especially so if it was his teenage brother he was shagging. I rubbed my stiffening cock. "Bet you wished I was that sexy cousin of yours? The one with the big tits you're always talking about. Bet you'd give me a shag then?"

He puffed a bigger smoke ring at me. "You're a perv."

I spotted the rolled-up girlie mag in the pocket of his waterproof jacket. I had a sneaky suspicion he was searching for a little hideaway in which to perform a bit of sensational salami slapping.

I set the slanderous play in motion. "If you ask me nicely I'm sure I could look like one of those cheap tarts you usually shag. Just give me a couple of secs to slip into something sexy and seductive, and put on some slap."

"Told you before, when you get a nice juicy pussy and a big pair of knockers you might be in with a chance." Tommy rubbed his crotch, then cupped a pair of imaginary breasts for effect.

I was about to suggest he probably did shag his cousin but thought that might be going too far. I gathered my nuts into my palm. "What d'ya mean, I've already got a nice big pair of knackers."

Tommy gave me the finger, a new gesture of his that I didn't like. "Balls!"

I grabbed the offending digit and gave it a painful backward bend. "That's what I said, didn't I?"

Tommy winced and cursed. He stuck his top half over the low bulkhead that surrounded the lamps. "What you up to, then? You got Freckles behind there giving you another blow?"

"And why would he be doing that?"

"'Cos you and him…"

"Well, you're wrong and we didn't," I interrupted. "And he's not gay." I thought I would defend Freckles' sexuality. After all, Tommy had no proof we'd done anything together, which we hadn't. I rubbed my cock. "Or maybe you're just jealous and wished he was, wished he was blowing you?"

Another figure gesture almost followed but was speedily withdrawn. Tommy grinned, like he thought I was lying. "Piss off, you powder puff."

I leant forward and plucked the girlie mag from his pocket. His hand reached out to grab it back but was too late. "Off for a little bit of *studying*, are we?"

"Yeah. A subject you wouldn't know anything about, you bandit."

I turned to the centrefold. The picture was easily visible in the moonlight. "I see. It's a geography map you're studying." I ran my finger over a pair of mountain breasts and scratched my head. "Let me see now... I think I recognise these. They're the Alps, aren't they?"

Tommy raised his eyebrows, as he always did when annoyed or embarrassed. "Very funny."

"Could be the Rockies, I suppose? Rock-hardies even?"

He made another snatch for the mag. "Gissit back."

"Hang on, I wanna learn more." I held the picture up for him to view and ran my finger over the spunk stained furry pussy. "Tropical forest, eh? Endangered species." Tommy looked unbelievably embarrassed. I giggled when he struggled to get the mag from me. "Isn't this the place where strapping lumberjacks find their... woodies?"

"Come on, Sandy. Stop pissing about." He was becoming agitated; his tossing time ticking away.

I decided I'd test the water. "Fancy a blowjob? Better than some dull old wank."

Tommy shook his head, his eyebrows dancing on his forehead. "Blow yourself."

I closed the mag and handed it back. "Here you go, you sad old fucker. Go and have your boring wank."

Tommy scratched his head and laughed a kind of hurt laugh. "'Spect you could only cope with Freckles' little knob anyway, not a big cock like mine."

"Hark at Mr Butch, here," I went for his ego. "I've had bigger cocks than yours for breakfast. You're just jealous I can get sex even when we're at sea. You just wait until you've spent another shagless week without shore leave; you'll be begging me for a blow."

"Wouldn't want a blowjob from you if you were the last person on earth."

I moved closer, my teasing not done. "Wouldn't you now? Just think of it, Tommy, my soft lips slipping and sliding over your cock and going right down to the base, and into your pubic bush." Tommy was almost drooling. "And my tongue, all hot and pussy soft, swirling around that swelling spunky head of your rampant cock." I checked his expression. "You fucking my face, fast and furious, before shooting your whack down my throat, and me swallowing the lot."

Tommy wasn't aware of it but his hand had been rubbing his cock while I was detailing his potential blowjob. For one delightful moment, when I saw it begin to stiffen, I thought he was wavering and was about to let me oblige.

"You need help, Sandy?" was his disappointing response, after he'd stuffed the dirty mag back into his waterproof jacket, before walking away.

"Know your trouble?" I called after him. Tommy looked back. "You're thinking with your brain when you should be thinking with your cock."

"You're definitely sick, Sandy. You should go and see the Doc and get an injection or something."

I gave a real wicked laugh. "Would that be a *meat* injection you'd be recommending, sir?"

Tommy couldn't help himself from laughing. He pulled the rolled-up girlie mag from his pocket, pushed it into his mouth and began sucking upon the phallic length. "Delicious!"

"But so small."

We hadn't fallen out or anything and were only playing. I still hoped one day he'd succumb to my advances and let me suck on his delicious dick, or maybe he'd give me the fucking of my life. There was still plenty of time and I was a master at waiting.

As I watched Tommy walk away, his pathway was suddenly blocked by a senior rating who had ascended the ladder from the boat deck below. I didn't catch any of the one-way conversation that slammed into him, but it was clear Tommy was getting a right old bollocking. I certainly couldn't believe my eyes when I saw his girlie mag fly into the sea, now divided into squares by the senior rating. A finger pointing in the direction of the forecastle followed it.

Tommy's arms rose in protest. Seconds later he came stomping angrily back toward me.

"What's up?" I asked when he came level.

Tommy didn't even look at me. "One day I'm gonna kill that fucking bastard! You mark my fucking words!"

I'd been party to my mate's anger on several occasions. This time, however, I found it quite scary. The threat was more than believable. "Right," was all I could muster.

The object of Tommy's discontent moved closer as he casually followed in his charge's wake. As he did so, he was constantly looking around my flag deck as if searching for other seaman from whom he could bite the head. He was also giving me sneaky glances; sickening glances at that.

"All right, son?" he asked when he reached me, releasing a quirky and decidedly spooky smile when he leant upon the low bulkhead surrounding my safe domain. If it was an attempt to be friendly, it wasn't working.

I recognised the senior rating as Acting Petty Officer Purdy. I didn't pay him much mind and merely nodded. The reason? Purdy was one of those senior ratings to whom I had taken an instant dislike the moment I'd first set eyes upon him. Why? I can honestly say I had no idea. Just call it intuition, self-preservation, or whatever. The Navy had a way of making you aware of hidden dangers, aware of arseholes both civvy and service.

It is possible my dislike for Purdy could have been his ever-sweaty armpits and the stale body odour that constantly wafted from them. Then again, it could have been because he was fat and short, and had a plump piggy face. More likely, however, it was his spookiness and that quirky smile he gave whenever he tried to get friendly. More truthfully, it was because he nearly always had a pretty youth in tow. Not a happy youth who gave the impression that he had a caring father figure at his side, but a very sad youth, one who appeared as though he was being used, bullied, or worse. Whatever it was, I hated him.

Being a little more sailorwise than Tommy, I thought I'd test the water with Purdy. I knew that if I went too far it would be very unlikely that he'd make anything of it, unless I was really out of order with my play. There was an unspoken rule in the Navy, we kept most events that deserved disciplinary action within branches—seaman disciplined seaman; stokers, stokers; chefs, chefs, and so on.

"Tommy do something wrong, Hooky?" I gave him my innocent look.

Purdy moved smelling close and gave me that disturbing smile. "You want to stay away from that one, lad. He's a bad sort."

I pretended to be on his side. "Really, Hooky? I had no idea."

He pulled a ciggie from his packet and lit it, giving me the impression he planned to linger for a while. "Always skiving off, that one. Playing with himself in the heads most of the time." Purdy informed.

"Reckon we all are. Bet you are, too." I grinned cheekily. "Been some time since we've been ashore."

"Mark my words, lad, he's the type who'd catch a dose when he does get his end away. Doesn't care who he shags. Bad influence on the younger lads, he is. Seen plenty of his sort before."

I got the gist of that statement but had a feeling Purdy was telling me more about himself than of my mate. "Like that, is he?" I continued playing his game.

"Sure is; the disgusting little perv."

I noticed Purdy had another odour present when he spat that venomous information at me—rum, a good deal of rum for him to be so careless with his talk, him being of rank as well.

I thought I'd try a bit of sarcastic humour. "Can't have all those innocent Skins looking at smutty mags, can we now?" I laughed. "Might give them dirty ideas, not to mention dirty bedding."

Purdy coughed—a guilty cough if ever there was. Another sickening grin swept over his rum-reddened face. He reached over and pressed an unwelcome palm onto my hand. "Better go and find out what he's up to now. Probably corrupting some young lad."

He squeezed the back of my hand before peeling the sticky palm from it. "Bye!" I said, as friendly as I was able and hiding my thoughts.

"Might see you ashore one night. Buy you a pint," suggested Purdy, another smile oozing from his face like sickly puss.

I forced a smile from my mouth and simply nodded, thinking, "In my nightmares, you prick!" It was clear Purdy had it in for Tommy big time and I would have to warn him.   As Purdy walked off, I rubbed my palm against my trouser leg, cleaning it. Before I brought my attention back to the horizon, I watched the slime ball sink safely out of sight, down the ladder, and onto the forecastle below. My flesh was crawling. I had to get the feel of his sweaty skin from my own and moved over to the seawater tap situated on the bulkhead. I ran my hands beneath the cold water, then swilled some over my face. "Yuk!" I grunted, my whole body shuddering.

I resumed my duty, checking both port and starboard horizons for any ships that might be signalling. Predictably, there was none. A fleeting visit to the bridge was my next port of call. All was quiet so I gave a quick shout over our intercom to the Main Signal Office below and checked with my opposite number to see if anything was happening. Again, all was quiet.

Moving back onto my flag deck, I sleepily scanned the horizon a final time. Although I still had another hour on watch, I'd reached that point of tiredness that often came around at about three. Pulling out the small swivel stool fixed beneath the metal signal desk, mostly used during action stations, I plonked my bottom down. Although it was risky, sleeping on watch a punishable offence, I decided I'd grab a catnap before going off watch. Folding my arms, I rested my head and drifted into slumber.

DREAMS

One hundred and ten degrees was my guesstimate of the sweltering heat. The temperature of the smooth white sand was even hotter, too hot to walk upon with bare feet. I left a trail of small sand hollows as I walked beneath coconut palms and toward a sea, which was as blue as the sky above and so clear you could observe the colourful fish swimming beneath. Purposefully, I'd chosen a beach void of people. I wanted to bathe nude, bathe in the most tranquil of settings in order to rid my body from weeks of Action Stations and the like; rid myself of all things Navy.

My snazzy Bermuda shorts came off first. I sent them flying into the sky like some sexy stripper. A not-so-loud T-shirt followed; a similar stripper routine going through my mind when I tossed it onto the beach. I smiled to myself suspecting there might have been a drag queen hidden somewhere in my persona.

Settling back in my idyllic setting, I ran my palms over my chest, abdomen, and crotch. "Paradise," I sighed, sinking back onto a beach towel, allowing my body to absorb the rays of scorching sun.

For a brief moment, while my fingers caressed my horny cock, I did think it would have been nice to have had someone like Freckles with me, someone to caress, cuddle, and make passionate love, someone to relieve me of weeks of sexual frustration.

About ten minutes into my bronzed body routine, it became all dark. Opening one eye, I glanced toward the sky for the offending cloud. Seeing nothing but blue I opened my other eye and began to lower my gaze. Before me—looking as delicious as any dark chocolate—stood a very tall, very handsome, very muscular and very masculine black man.

I suppose I should have jumped at the awesome and somewhat threatening sight. Perhaps I did. Rather, a vortex of hormonal activity started to whirl inside my brain, with the force of a tornado. Immediately, my randy little hormones began to hurry back and forth, rushing from my brain to my cock and back as they happily passed messages of pending sexual activity. Blinded by any other possible scenario other than sex, the only message my hormones were giving was clear. "Sandy, your shag has arrived!"

My cock bolted upright and began to ooze oodles of pre-come in anticipation of a well-earned shag. Simultaneously, my willing hole tightened and twitched excitedly, before relaxing and making it ready to receive. I beamed a welcoming smile. "Hi!" I excitedly greeted, my fingers subconsciously tossing my cock.

"What you doin on my beach, boy!" thundered the mountain-of-a-man, his threatening tone instantly cutting all hormonal activity between my cock and brain.

My cock shrank back into my body like a frightened tortoise's head. I was speechless and my body remained motionless. I couldn't say the same of my gaze. That was all over the place, taking in every inch of this formidable creature.

Though decidedly nervous, I continued on my journey of discovery. Avoiding the handsome angry face, though it warranted more attention, especially the full lips and reddish-brown eyes, I began to study the remainder of this incredible man-shag, starting with those biceps, which were the size of cannon balls.

It was clear his arms could easily hug me into submission had they wrapped around my chest and passionately squeezed. Clear they had the strength to raise my hips until my cock was level with that large mouth. Clear they could do anything to me they wanted had he desired it. Once more, I offered a seductive smile. Again, it was met with an expressionless beauty that was both threatening and provocative.

My attention moved to my man's amazing hands, hands that were so huge they could have gone halfway around a basketball, halfway around my waist. I knew they would have been more than capable of engulfing my small buttocks as they raised and lowered my light-weight body over what I hoped would be an enormous black cock. I knew that one of his thick fingers could work wonders on the soft walls of my tight hole when it probed and played. My cock began to stiffen and my willing hole pulsate with the thought of such pleasure.

Although I was keen to glimpse my man's huge cock, I returned briefly to the handsome face. A full set of pure white teeth had now appeared between those pinkish lips when my gaze met his. Disturbingly, the smile beaming on his face was threatening rather than one of possible seduction. Daring not to linger, I quickly moved onto his superb torso.

Glistening with sweat, a concrete chest on which you could crack coconuts, calmly rose and fell as my man deeply breathed. I watched in envy and awe when the most powerful pecs I had ever set eyes upon became more defined. With each intake of air, the darker nipples adorning each appeared to harden, becoming as firm as black peppercorns. Still drooling with excitement, I wondered if this guy knew how desperately I wanted to bite those firm studs and frantically chew upon his tits, while he drove his dick deep into my submissive body; drove it up to the hilt and beyond, drove me wild!

A whimper of excitement escaped my lips but still my man didn't blink.

Those massive hands moved either side of my man's waist and clasped behind his lower back. The sudden movement caused my tummy to tighten and a bead of sweat to roll from my temple. "What you doin' on my beach, boy?" his voice barked again.

I was startled and nervous. I didn't look up and couldn't answer. Instead, transfixed by his magnificent beauty, I continued on my journey of his superb body, this time drawn to his strong abdomen, which had now tightened, the muscles defined with his new stance.

The tight knot caught my attention next, larger than your average navel, not really an outy or an inny, more an inbetweeny. Like his nipple studs, I knew I would love to get my teeth into it. Love to try to untie it with nips and nibbles.

A fine ladder of tightly knit black pubics took me lower, to the top of his mini-length sarong. Wrapped loosely around his tapered waist, tucked in and not tied, I knew a swift tug would see it fall to the sand on which his bare feet stood. How much I would have loved to have done that became even more apparent when I spotted that much sought after prize of prime meat tenting the sarong and protruding a good six inches from his body, even in its softened state.

My gaze quickly sank to the bottom of the sarong. I was sure the bud on that massive bone would be peeping from beneath, the eye dribbling and waiting to be lapped clean of pre-come. Sadly, I was not to be rewarded.

Just as I was about to avert my eyes, a kindly breeze gusting between his ebony strong thighs caused the brightly coloured material to briefly flutter. Delighted, I caught the briefest glimpse of the monster. A gasp of air rushed from my lips. Boy was I going to have trouble swallowing that amount of a cock when it was fully erect.

My man spoke again. His voice seemed a little more kindly but his expression did not change. "You have to pay if you want to use my beach."

I slipped my palms down my naked thighs as if pushing them into pockets. I gave my shoulders a shrug and offered yet another smile, accompanied by a flutter of my eyelashes. I looked suggestively at his hidden cock. "No money," I whispered, hoping he'd get the message.

My man actually smiled, a wicked yet provocative smile, but said nothing. Feeling decidedly aroused I wiggled my bottom into the sand and parted my legs, allowing my balls to fall between them. With no help other than his glorious presence needed, my cock once more began to spring into life and became fully erect. There could be no doubt I was his for the taking.

"You white boys have never got any cash," said my man. "Don't matter. You'll still have to pay…" He grinned wickedly. "Or face the punishment."

My eyes sparkled. Had he looked deeply into them he would have seen they were full of desire, windows to my soul, indicators of my willingness to please, a pathway to my payment.

I raised my body onto my elbows before sitting upright and bringing my face level with the massive mound hidden teasingly beneath his sarong. "Punishment?"

He released a deep laugh, a suggestive smile, then a more serious expression, but no words. I heard his knuckles crack behind his back. Another uncontrollable rush of sexual excitement exploded throughout my torso. What could this wonderful punishment be?

My mouth was slightly agape and my lips moist as I continued to study the tenting sarong for any evidence of movement lurking beneath. My fingers began to twitch, desperate to disrobe him. My own cock was still totem pole stiff, eager for another notch to be carved upon it. Dare I make a move? Dare I send my head beneath that sarong and devour his succulent flesh.

The flash of light was almost blinding when the silver blade of the machete caught the sun as it lifted above his head and sailed toward me. Heart pounding fearfully I fell back onto my towel, my eyes closing tightly when visions of my head rolling from my shoulders and falling into the sand rushed my brain.

"Aaaahhh!" I screamed, my hands covering my eyes when the blade swished over my crotch. In my terrified state, the dull crack that followed sounded more like a thunderbolt crashing to earth than that of a machete slicing the top from a coconut.

Hearing cruel laughter, I tentatively withdrew my palms from my face and opened an eye. A wickedly amused expression greeted my gaze; the voluptuous lips poised on the rim of the decapitated fruit. "That's not funny!" I murmured, before beginning to laugh somewhat hysterically.

The devilish red-brown eyes were staring into mine as my man slurped on the cool contents of the coconut, allowing come-like dribbles to run over his lips and chin. My heart was still racing wildly as several droplets dripped onto my cock and tummy making it look like I'd just shot my whack.

I rubbed the clear liquid into my abdomen, brushing my hardened cock in the process. Desperately I wanted to grip my dick and thrash it like crazy. More so, after observing an extremely long tongue lap the globules of juice from around his chin, imagining he was lapping the come from around my cock.

"Uhm," sighed my satisfied man, like he'd just sunk a stein of delicious spunk.

"Uhm," I sighed at the thought of that, albeit under my breath.

Black Beauty—I just had to give him a name now we'd become acquainted—held the coconut toward me as if offering some of the refreshing nectar. Before I'd risen onto my elbows and accepted his offering, the remaining contents were somewhat seductively poured over my chest, tummy, and finally crotch. I couldn't help my excitement and my cock gave such a hearty jump it caused the foreskin to roll back over the head. A decent helping of pre-come to spurted from the eye and min-gled with the juice.

My excitement increased. What was he planning to do next? Was he planning licking my entire body clean, planning on playing that long pink tongue playfully up and down the length, planning on swallowing my dick deep into his palate until I'd given him an even more nourishing liquid meal? I could hardly contain myself as I motionlessly awaited my fate—my glorious punish-ment.

The sarong fell to the sand. My gaze went from face to cock in a nanosecond. I was wrong, Black Beauty wasn't *his* name but was most surely the name of the eight inches of glorious black flesh that arched tantalis-ing away from his body and toward my own, the weight of the gigantic circumcised bud barely able to bring it back between his thighs in its semi-erect state.

My eyes, those windows to my soul, didn't exactly pop from my head on witnessing such a wealth of weap-on, but sparkled so brightly even a blind man would have been dazzled. Yes, the bastard wanted his enor-mous cock sucked, wanted it badly. Although champing at the bit to oblige, I patiently waited.

With so much excitement to contend with my mouth had begun to dry. I knew I'd have problems swallowing such an incredible amount of cock. I think Black Beauty might have sensed this too. Feeding his massive black cock into the shell of the large coconut, he began to curl it away like some snake charmer putting his favour-ite pet to bed. When next the black mamba emerged, lubricated in white coconut jelly, to my sheer delight rigormortis had undeniably set in. What had once been and eight-inch scrumptious semi-softie was now a thirteen-inch, extremely thick, incredibly appetising, rigid and robust ramrod of a beauty. What's more it was all mine, every glorious, juicy, gigantic centimetre.

It was payment time. Boy, was it payment time! Without even being invited, I lunged forward, knelt in the sand, and grasped his thighs tightly. My mouth wide open I headed for his coconut-covered cock. Before he could protest, not that he should, the sticky head had vanished between my lips.

I detected a manly grunt above my head and watched Black Beauty's abdomen tighten when I twirled my tongue around the enormous black bud and cleaned away the coconut cream. Like a contented boy sucking on his favourite Popsicle, I played my mouth around the succulent bud bringing it almost to the point of bursting. Pants of pleasure greeted my ears as I continued to gorge on the juicy plum, occasionally going deep upon the lengthy shaft.

With one palm pressed into his muscled abdomen and toying with his navel knot, the other cupping his hairy balls, I pushed my lips toward his knit of black pubic hair. I felt my throat stretch to its capacity and beyond when I started to feed the colossal head under my tonsil tag. Keen to feed more of his cock deep down my throat Black Beauty planted his huge hand onto the back of my head and impatiently pushed.

Although I wanted his cock badly, I just couldn't take it all. This was no chipolata I was devouring this was a jumbo sausage of unimaginable proportion. No way could I manage the lot in one sitting.

I heard a curse of complaint. My man's other hand clamped onto the back of my head, his grip frighteningly strong. His muscled abdomen tensed and his buttocks tightened. Sensing what was coming I took a deep breath and relaxed my throat the best I could.

With one powerful thrust, all thirteen inches of thick cock vanished down my throat. My eyes began watering like Niagara Falls but I sure wasn't crying. My lips were now buried into sweet smelling pubics; my nose pressed into a solid abdomen. Amazingly I could still breathe. Don't ask me how.

Deciding I'd give him some of his own medicine I gave his balls a painful squeeze and tugged them hard. A squeal of pain did escape his mouth, but rather than withdrawing that massive cock, he just loved the roughness and merely pulled the bud back as far as my lips before ramming the lot back down my throat.

I released his balls, cupped his smooth buttock cheeks in both my palms, and began caressing them passionately. I felt the mounds flex and relax as he began to thrust and withdraw—slowly at first, then faster and faster. A quick jab of my finger deep into his hairless hole saw him move up a gear. Two more probing fingers pushed deep into the musty darkness and he was fucking my face full throttle, forcing me to gorge on his cock with the passion of some crazed carnivorous animal that hadn't eaten meat in months.

Gasps of pleasure puffed from my man's mouth. His palms left my head and began to work on his defined pecs, rubbing them excitedly while pinching his tits.

He suddenly stopped thrusting into my face. Surely, his energy wasn't spent already. "Eat my cock, boy! Eat the lot!" he panted his command, urging me into action. Although his frenzy of animal lust had been fantastic, I was more than happy to take control

Withdrawing his throbbing cock until the big bud bulged in my mouth I began to work passionately upon the head, nibbling on the defined ridge that separated the shaft from bud, while licking deep into the sensitive slit. Black Beauty relished the ravenous attack. I was pretty much relishing it myself.

Alternating my actions, I spent several minutes sucking around the thick head before doing some tip to base stuff. Finally, I did some deep throating, allowing his cock to stay down and my swallowing actions to massage the thick shaft. As an extra treat, I also licked beneath his balls or sucked both together, tossing them around my mouth like some skilful juggler.

After ten minutes of glorious feasting, I felt the head of his cock fatten and firm. Cupping his balls in my palm, I began to stroke the sac. Excitedly they rose when the loose flesh tightened. Sensing an imminent eruption of succulent sweet spunk, I sent my mouth deep over the shaft before returning to the expanding head.

Frantically feasting on the exploding flesh, I wasn't to be disappointed and a small jet of thick cream hit my tonsils. Greedily I gulped it down ready to receive the main course.

"Stop!" gasped my man. Grasping my head, he began pulling back.

"Uhm! Uhm!" I whimpered my complaint, gripping his buttocks tightly and pushing my mouth back to the base, desperate for the rest of his spunk.

"Stop!" barked my man a second time, shoving me forcefully backward.

"You bitch!" I snapped back at him when my back hit the soft sand.

Black Beauty's brow was dripping beads of sweat in the searing heat of the afternoon sun, his torso glowing moist. "Bitch, eh?" he grunted, his fingers squeezing the bulbous head of his thirteen-inch cock in order to stem the flow of delicious juices. "I'll show you who's a bitch." Falling to his knees, he angrily parted my legs.

Why didn't he just tell me he wanted a shag, the silly man?

I decided I'd make things more exciting for my hunk and began thrashing my arms and legs, pretending to fight him off. Black Beauty grinned, loving every complaint.

His palm pushed firmly into my abdomen and held me down while the other began dipping fingers into the coconut shell for lubricating jelly. Scooping a decent handful from the hairy container, he pushed my thighs further apart with his knees and began to ladle the slimy liquid into my hole.

"Oh no!" I yelped, desperate to make it sound like an emission of protest rather than one of joy.

I was right about those large fingers, it was mindblowing what they could do to a sex-starved youth when they pushed deep, then played on that magic spot just inside the hole. "No!" I gasped again, still trying to make it sound like a statement of protest but relishing every probe and penetration.

For a few minutes, his fingers continued to forage deep, curling around my hole and tease the soft wall within. All the while, his mouth was drooling with delight as he worked the digits deeper, his eyes sparkling hungrily, his cock as solid as a ship's steel mast. Yet more yelps of pleasure and false protest emitted from my mouth.

As I continued to wriggle, thrash and complain both my legs were placed upon my man's powerful shoulders. An unexpected worm of worry suddenly wriggled its way into my brain when I realised I hadn't taken a thirteen-inch cock before. As I recall, twelve and a half was my guesstimate of the massive cock I rode when making the porno film, but that delicious dick was never as fat as this one. I could only imagine what damage another half-an-inch of shaft and a cock head almost as large as an avocado pear might do to my poor little hole. On the other hand, what pleasure it might give. Biting my lip, I braced myself.

Black Beauty brought the massive head to my hole and began to push. I screwed up my eyes and bit my lip ready to receive it. The pressure and pain was almost unbearable when the head slowly parted my cheeks and penetrated. My legs began to tremble but I managed not to scream. This cock wasn't massive, it was bloody monumental.

The big bud vanished with a *pop* when it disappeared. This time I did scream. I actually did. The pain was unbelievable. I now knew what it was like to give birth, albeit in reverse. My only thought: I needed an epidural.

Several deep breaths filled my lungs in an attempt to relax my hole. I knew there was no point in asking my man to take it easy. This was a straight man fucking me; no way was he going to stop. No way, either, was he going to let me kiss his gorgeous mouth to help ease away the pain. Not to be denied, I threw my arms over his broad black shoulders, slammed my lips onto his and sucked that enormous fleshy tongue deep into my throat.

It did the trick. I felt my hole relax. My brain switched to pleasure mode, keen to take the whole length. "You arsehole!" I cursed, feigning anger and firing him up.

Black Beauty's buttocks tightened and his abdomen knotted in a ripple of hardened muscle when he sent thirteen inches of throbbing cock up to the hilt in one almighty thrust. He pulled his tongue from my mouth. "You love it. Don't you, you bitch!"

"Yes," I gasped, biting into his beefy neck and clawing on his broad shoulders when his cock rammed home.

With each withdrawal of that lengthy cock I felt my insides contract as the bud pulled back toward my hole, then the reverse, the fleshy wall sucking around the slippery shaft and accentuating every ridge and ripple of the tremendously thick cock when it was ruthlessly rammed deep again.

My man was fucking me hard and fast now, his cock thrusting relentlessly back and forth, his big balls swinging free. Powerfully he drove his dick deliberately deep as chest rubbed against chest, mouths locked on mouths, and tongues darted excitedly between them.

I wanted to toss my own cock while Black Beauty was fucking me to oblivion and beyond, but he now had my wrists pinned to the sand. Had I managed to reach it though, I knew I would come instantly. The friction of that fantastic cock spreading my hole wide was causing such a surge of pleasure throughout my entire being it would have been impossible not to.

On his next deep thrust, Black Beauty pulled me upward, wrapping his muscular arms around my back. His biceps squeezed me hard, almost crushing the life out of me. When his teeth sank into my neck, I whimpered from the sheer pleasure of being eaten alive, my nails tearing into those broad shoulders. His fantastic fucking was relentless but my hole was relaxed and receptive now, only the occasional twinge of pain mixed with an indescribable pleasure on each penetration.

Effortlessly he raised my body from the sand when he stood. I sent my legs around his waist and my arms around his neck, clutching his body tightly. Cupping my buttocks in both large palms, I couldn't help but scream with delight when Black Beauty began raising me clean from his cock before slamming-dunking me back over the bulging bud.

A groan and then a grunt escaped Black Beauty's mouth. His arms began squeezing me in a vicelike grip. Those thick and luscious lips smacked back onto mine once more, his tongue diving deep into my throat. Even more ferociously, I fucked his cock, my own rubbing against his hot and muscled abdomen. Such was the incredible euphoria erupting in my head I almost cried at the triple pleasure of mouths sucking tongues, his cock driving deep into my hole and my own cock slipping and sliding against his sweaty body.

Joyously impaled, I began driving my buttocks down upon his mammoth cock. My man rewarded me with simultaneous thrusting. "Fuck me good and hard," I excitedly encouraged. Black Beauty willingly obliged.

I could no longer hold back my rising spunk. "I'm coming!" I gasped. Raising my buttocks clean from the sticky bud, I slammed them back to the pubic base.

My cry of delight sparked my man into more urgent action. His hands gripped my buttocks tightly and began driving me over his cock. Oodles of pre-come ladled onto his abdomen as my cock rubbed against the solid muscle. On his next mighty slam-dunk, my cock discharged its creamy load, shooting salvos of scrumptious spunk between both our steamy bodies.

Seeing my tasty spunk dribbling invitingly between his pecs, a gasp of pleasure rushed from my man's mouth. I felt his mammoth cock swell inside of me when he slammed my buttocks down again. With several desperate thrusts, the mammoth cock began to siphon spunk into my twitching hole. I ran my fingers over Black Beauty's shaven head and sank my teeth into his broad neck as he began to empty his balls.

Scooping my spunk from his chest, I pushed my fingers into his gasping mouth. "Like that, bitch?" I asked as he sucked them clean.

"Yes!" was his only cry of pleasure when the final flurry of spunk spilled from his pumping cock, then siphoned into me.

"Jesus!" I gasped when another unexpected salvo of spunk sailed from my own cock and splattered over his chest and abdomen.

The hand on my shoulder caused me to jump. I refocused my eyes when the dawn light burst into them. "Jesus, Tommy, you scared the shit out of me."

"Sleeping on watch, eh? You'll get a spanking for that."

I rubbed my eyes. "Is it four already?"

Tommy tapped his watch. "Quarter after. We're off watch. You going down?"

I knelt on the deck, grabbed his thighs, and moved my head toward his cock. "Thought you'd never ask."

Tommy pushed me away. "In your dreams, slag."

I stood up and rubbed his head affectionately. "Believe me, Tommy. You don't wanna know what was in my dreams."

Tommy spotted the stiffened cock tenting my trousers. "Think I've got an idea. Sticky wicket, have we?"

I gripped my zip and pulled it down, my hand diving inside my spunky boxers. "Hang on, I'll show you."

"No thanks!" yelped my alarmed buddy, before nipping down the ladder and heading toward his bunk.

"Coward," I called after him, rubbing my wet dream spunk into my tummy.

BOY'S NIGHT IN

I thought I'd better give you a brief tour of our beloved mess, seeing it's where we spent more than half our lives. Situated right at the stern of the ship it runs across its entire width. You reached it by way of a ladder leading down from the Burma Way. At about twenty foot square, it billeted thirty of us.

The first thing that greets you when you descend the ladder is a bank of highly polished silver lockers stacked back to back. A kind of obelisk right at its heart that you can walk all the way round. Except for the aft bulkhead, thirty bunks ran around the perimeter; three bunks being situated one above the other. The bottom and second bunks become a settee kind of feature when the second bunk folded down.

Adding to the comfort of this less-than-inviting living area are four large tables, running from port to starboard, situated on either side of the obelisk. And either side of them, benches that could seat six bottoms, or seven at a push. These exciting features were bolted down but could be removed for Action Stations. The only other creature comforts were a fridge for milk—or booze, more truthfully – and an ironing board with steam iron slotted into a special brackets. There was also a Tannoy on the aft bulkhead plus extractor and fresh air fans. In addition, a host of wires, pipes, cables and hooks and other not so attractive decorations completed the clutter, not a picture, telly, pot plant, or any other homely comfort in sight.

When at sea every night was a boy's night in, and the delightful setting I've just described is where we spent them. When not on watch, and after we'd fed our faces, we usually found ourselves gathered around the tables and making our own entertainment by playing games. If this were too demanding, then we'd swap gossip or make up sordid stories and have a damn good laugh. Booze often accompanied these sessions, not too much though. Illegal booze, you understand.

The weather was on the turn again and a swell brewing. The ship was rolling from port to starboard with an occasional pitch thrown in for good measure. The weather wasn't so bad that we needed to lash things down, or hold on when moving about. A few tummies were beginning to turn. I suppose it felt a lot like being drunk as we swayed from side to side, but most of us were used to that

Freckles, Tommy, Chad and me were playing Ludo—'Uckers' to us sailors. We were playing doubles, the players sitting at opposite corners playing as a team. Also at our table, a couple of lads were playing crib, while two decidedly camp, intellectual types were battling away at chess—queen against queen, if I was to be cruel.

Over on the port side four more lads were playing Chase the Pisser on their bunks—sorry, just another card game—while a couple more wrote letters to family, girlfriends, maybe even boyfriends. The remainder of the lads lay on bunks—some reading, some relaxing and listening to the music coming from the Tannoy, but a good few sleeping before their watches began. Anyone missing was probably already on watch, showering, tossing in some darkened hideaway—alone or otherwise—or just wandering around the ship and maybe visiting another mess deck. Oh, there was a lad enthusiastically ironing his kit—Yuk!

A pair of boots came clomping down the ladder, the half-drowned body following. "Raining?" asked the youth, who was lying in the worst bunk in the mess.

"No, it's tropical up there. I'm just sweating, you pillock," the guy grunted, before sending droplets of water shooting all over the youth's naked chest, with a sharp shake of his cap.

Tommy threw a double six, ignoring the sodden guy, and moved one of his counters from the starting grid and onto the first square. The other six he used to move a counter already in play, zapping one of Freckles' when he landed on top of it, sending it back to start all over again.

"You jammy bugger," my partner complained, placing his counter neatly over the vacant white circle next to the rest of his counters that still sat there.

"Skill." Tommy laughed, shaking the dice in his fist a second time, before sending them clattering onto the table, doubles giving you another throw.

"Double six!" excited Chad when the dice had settled.

"You got golden bollocks, or something?" I complained. "Fuck me, Tommy."

Tommy grinned, moving another counter from his starting grid. "I hear most guys in Pompey already have. That right, Freckles?" Freckles lowered his head, embarrassed. Well, he was a quiet and shy lad most of the time and easily baited.

"Only those who've paid me enough money." I played along.

"How much was that, a quid?" Chad joined in. "Can't be bad."

Tommy moved his second counter. "Yeah, but he gave fifty pence change."

Freckles laughed loudly, his cute cheeks beaming bright red. We each looked at him, sensing a rare quip. "One pound fifty change," he spluttered, his face blushing bright when he became even more embarrassed from tossing in his one-liner.

Both Chad and Tommy doubled up with laughter. Freckles' face almost exploded, his palms covering his embarrassment. "One pound fifty," Chad repeated the joke between laughs. "Nice one."

I gave my lovely lad a pretend glare of disapproval. "I'm on your side... *remember?*"

Tommy was still laughing at the thought of me giving more change back than the punter had given me. "Like it on your side, do you?" he said, bringing the subject onto sex. "I prefer *doggy* myself."

"Not surprised. Having seen your last shag *doggy* is about right." I hit below the belt.

"Meow!" squawked Chad, passing the dice back to Tommy for a third throw.

The dice came up two and one. "No justice," complained Tommy, adding them together and moving one counter.

Snowy, the lad who'd been soaked, began to ascend the ladder, now dressed in waterproofs. "Don't get wet," teased the lad on the bunk.

"You'll know wet when I come back down and piss on you when you're fast asleep," Snowy threatened.

Tommy turned and faced him. "Do us a favour and piss on this one," he said, pointing at me.

"He'd really enjoy it," said a lad wrapped in a towel and heading for a shower.

Snowy looked over his shoulder. "Piss on Sandy? No chance. I heard the bitch charges too much."

Chad laughed but not at Snowy's jest. He gripped my hand when I was about to take my turn, stopping me from throwing. Games were often interrupted and regularly didn't see completion. "This slapper picked me up in Pompey," he began. "Boy, was she a boot."

"One of Tommy's regulars, eh," Freckles bravely interrupted.

Chad laughed. "I didn't have no rubbers. She was so damn ugly no way was I going to poke her without one. So I told her so."

"You told her she was ugly? You nasty bugger," said Tommy.

"Idiot! I told her I had no rubbers. She already knew she was fucking ugly." Several laughs erupted around the mess. "Anyway, the bitch was desperate for dick…"

"Christ, she must have been desperate if all she could get was your dick." My turn to enhance the story.

Chad continued, unaffected by my interruption. "She takes her boob band off and her huge tits flop out.

Then she kneels down and whips out me nine inches."
Several laughs of disbelief could be heard. "I think she
ain't been fed for a week, cos she sucks me dick so fucking hard I nearly had two more balls in me sac and none
in me head."

"That makes three, then," tossed in one of the crib
players.

Chad continued through the laughter. "After about
five minutes of me dick being devoured, me last two
pints of beer have worked their way down to me bladder
and it's swelling up like fuck." He squeezed his tummy,
recalling the discomfort. "I'm busting for a pee. I wanna
tell her to stop cos I can't hold back. Problem was I was
just about to shoot me whack, so no way am I gonna."

"Should have peed anyway. You already had your
dick in the head," came a remark from another eavesdropping lad.

Chad looked around for the voice, and laughed. "I
decides I'll shoot me stuff first. Right?"

"You bet," said the same hidden voice. A few mum-
bles of agreement supported him.

Chad began to fondle the friend growing inside his
briefs, his excitement increasing as he thought about
his story. I would gladly have done it for him if he'd
asked. "Stop playing with yourself and get on with it,"
I urged.

He left his palm covering his cock and continued.
"Anyway, she pushes deep on me knob and keeps her
mouth there, gobbling like a good un she was. Lipstick
all over me pubes," he goes into detail, his hand moving
inside his briefs. "I've been holding back for ages but
now I have to let me whack go cos it's so damn great."
Freckles became all ears, loving the juicy bit. "Me knees

give and me tummy relaxes ready to fill her mouth." He took a deep drag on his fag and puffed a cloud of smoke toward the extractor fan. "In a massive gush me spunk shoots out. Boy, did it fly!"

"And?" urged the other crib player.

"Then it happened."

"What?" said several anxious voices.

Chad laughed like he was kind of embarrassed. "The two pints of piss I've got backed up chases the fucking lot out."

"No!" exclaimed Freckles, his voice going all high-pitched and girlie, his hands going to his mouth to hide the fact.

"Great!" delighted a partially hidden face secreted under blankets.

Chad clasped his head as if in pain. "Shit, her face was so red I thought she was going to bite me fucking bell end off cos of it." He rubbed his locks as if disbelieving his own story. "But what does she do?"

"What?" excited the partially hidden face, now peeping higher from its bedding.

"The tart gulps down a gallon of me piss along with me come." He raised his hand stopping any further interruptions. "And if that weren't bad enough, she pulls her mouth off me cock, then lets the rest spray all over her face and over her big tits, rubbing the piss all over them like crazy."

"Wow!" exclaimed the lad peeping from the blankets, obviously turned on by such an event.

Chad checked out our expressions. "Truth."

Freckles lowered his head onto the table and held his tummy. "I think I'm gonna puke." He added sound effects.

"It's raining men," sang a youth climbing onto his bunk.

"That it? That your story?" mumbled Tommy, disappointed. He was obviously hoping for something a good deal more sordid.

Chad gave him a scowl. "What you want for nothing? I ain't Barbara Cartland, for fuck sake."

"But you sure look like her," chirped Tommy. The whole mess erupted in jeers, whoops, and a host of slutty comments.

"Sounded great to me. Got her number?" requested the partially hidden face that had now risen fully above its blanket.

"Ring the Sewage Department," suggested another lad.

Chad adjusted his subsiding cock; a little peeved his story wasn't good enough for Tommy. "Roll on the fucking weekend. Boy, do I need to get me end away."

"You and the rest of us," agreed Tommy.

"Come on boners," I said, rolling the dice in an attempt to get the game underway again.

We got back into the swing of the game, blobs and mixy-blobs getting hit on a regular basis. Chad and Tommy were well in front of Freckles and me both with a couple of counters on home base. I think my problem was more to do with too many distractions to contend with rather than bad dice throws. One distraction in particular, a lad who'd taken station at the ironing board putting regulation creases into his bell-bottoms.

Dressed only in tight white briefs, his matching torso was just crying out for a dirty bugger like me to be slipping and sliding all over it. Just to add to my frustration he was receiving regular visits from his youthful buddy, whose skin was also snowy white, but who found the need to troll around the mess deck totally naked. Naturally, I couldn't fail to be drawn to the long, thin cock that was swinging freely, noticing it appeared to have even less pubics sitting above the slender shaft than Freckles had under his armpits.

Constantly I was wondering whether either had had the pleasure of the other's lips buried over their respective cocks, whether one of those dainty bottoms was getting a decent fucking on a regular basis. For the time being, I had to be content with imagining that was the case. I promised myself I would do my best to find out at a more convenient time.

Tommy polished off his second can of strong lager. "I couldn't half knock back a decent bottle of vodi. This beer's shit."

"Let's send Frecky out to fetch some," suggested Chad.

I've no idea why Freckles looked so worried. I suspected he might have been pretending and playing along. "We're at sea, Chad," he reminded.

Tommy winked and jumped from the bench. He stuffed his arms under Freckles' armpits and clamped them around his chest. Pulling him backward, he started to lift him. "Come on, Freckles. You can swim, can't you? It's not far to the offy."

"Come on, Sandy, let's toss the little sod over the side and send him for some sherbets," urged Chad, grabbing a pair of legs. Freckles struggled like he thought it was really going to happen, his hands tugging at Tommy's arms in an attempt to free himself, his mouth issuing obscenities.

"Fetch a bucket, Sandy," said Tommy, pulling the lovely Freckles off the bench, causing his naked tummy to pull taught and his tiny navel to wink when exposed from beneath the boxer's waistband. The action also revealed a neat bush of pubics when his boxers began to ride over his thighs.

"Bucket?" said Freckles, looking puzzled.

"Yeah, you'll need something to bring the booze back in," said Chad, whose hands were dangerously close to Freckles' cock.

Tommy rubbed Freckles' locks. "It's not for the booze. It's to stick over your fucking head, you ugly little runt. Don't want you scaring those pretty lasses in the offy, now do we?"

It was clear Freckles was enjoying the close contact fun, his body writhing delightfully. Sadly, just as his rising dick was about to become fully hard and bounce free from his boxer's waistband, the authoritative voice of the mess deck Leading Hand called for them to keep it down.

"Shush," whispered Chad and Tommy, both returning their bottoms to the bench, leaving a somewhat disappointed Freckles to reclaim his tenting boxers and hoist them back over his cute little bottom.

"I've had some wicked hangovers with vodka," said Chad, adjusting his own cock, which had gotten all excited during the play.

"Got to tell you this one," I said, butting in, Chad's recollection sparking a memory of my own.

"Is it about sex?" Freckles excited, his face still flushed from his body on body fun and the alcohol taking effect.

I shook my head. "Back on my last ship I had this mate called Shells…"

"You had a mate? That's a first," Tommy interrupted.

"A real one!" I silenced him. "Anyway, Shells was a great guy but real piss head, hence his nickname, Shellshock or Shells, cos he nearly always had the shakes." Tommy paid more attention, handing out fags from my packet. I slapped his fingers and continued. "Shells had been on a right bender the night before. I can't remember ever seeing him so shot away as he was when he climbed from his bunk that morning. Shaking like he was doing a knee-trembler in mid winter, he was."

Tommy lit two fags and passed one over to me. He sent his body into a sexual shiver. "Been there."

"I hear all your shags are a bit shaky," Chad took a swipe at him.

"Probably shaky because they all draw their pensions," laughed Freckles.

I took a couple of puffs on my ciggie and got it going while I waited for further quips. "Shells is standing there waiting to get to his locker, eyes like a couple of setting suns; his hands deep inside his briefs and scratching his nuts." I took another puff. "Standing beside him and foraging in his own locker was Boxer, who was also a bit of an early morning boozer and usually had something to drink hidden away." I took another drag on my ciggie, my audience silent and receptive. "Having found what he was looking for, Boxer turns around and faces Shells. He's holding a tumbler of clear liquid. Shells' eyes suddenly light up when he spots the tumbler. 'Just what I fucking need!' he says, grabbing

it from Boxer and downing the lot in a single gulp."
Tommy and Chad both laughed. I laughed myself, and
continued. "Shells' face changed colour. It looked like
he was about to throw up. 'Jesus fuck, Boxer, this stuff
tastes like shit!' he curses." I paused for effect. "'And so it
should, you stupid fucking bastard,' yells Boxer. 'You've
just downed my fucking contact lenses!'"

Chad shook his head in disbelief. "No!"

Tommy let out a yelp of laughter. "You're joking?"

"As sure as my grandmother gives good blowjobs," I
said, taking a deep drag on my ciggie.

"Desperate, or what?" said Tommy.

"I expect *you'd* still let her give you a blowjob,"
laughed Chad, who was quick to twist words.

"Do you keep contact lenses in vodka, then?" asked
Freckles, totally missing the point.

"Oh dear," said Tommy, rubbing Freckles' thigh. "A
tad too much booze, me thinks."

"Not enough. How far is it to the offy?" bubbled
Freckles, falling backwards, which had nothing to do
with the motion of the ship.

"Did Boxer get his contacts back?" asked Chad,
smiling at Freckles increased drunken state.

I gave him a poke in the tummy and laughed. "No.
But I hear there's some octopus swimming around with
twenty/twenty vision." Tommy and Chad laughed.
Freckles started giggling like a little girl, his body swaying as he tried to light a fag.

Chad nodded to Freckles. "I think this one should
have got them. I reckon he's blind. Blind bloody
drunk!"

"Ain't," said Freckles, falling sideways into a crib
player when the ship gave a gentle roll to port.

"You sure it wasn't a crustacean that got them?" one of the chess players offered a late response.

Tommy's eyebrows wriggled. He ignored the far too clever 'shell' joke, his expression speaking volumes. "Give us another one, Sandy. Tell us about the Far East. The last one was great."

This was the first time at sea for nearly all the juniors. Tales of far off places was something new so they were always keen to hear them—true or otherwise. Because of this, I'd become a bit of a mess deck storyteller. "Name your subject," I said, trying not to sound too big-headed.

"Give us a real funny one," requested Chad.

"Yeah, one with lots of sex," slurred Freckles, sitting up from his slouched position and almost falling from the backless bench.

Tommy glanced at both Chad and myself, and winked. "So what do you want the story to be about, Freckles. What turns you on? Big juicy jugs? Pussy licking? A bit of spanky panky?" he listed a few of what I suspected to be his own favourites.

Freckles' face fired up, going all tomato again. "Erm..."

"What you reckon, lads.... Reckon young Frecky here ain't never dipped his wick?" suggested Tommy.

Chad laughed, his palm diving excitedly toward his briefs. "Probably never had any of them, not even a blowjob. Cherry, if ever there was."

Freckles laughed, kind of shyly. His eyes fixed into mine. I wondered if he was toying with the idea of telling the boys that he'd almost had a blowjob from me that morning in the sick bay. I was sure he was still going through a phase that youths often go through when they just didn't know who or what they were sexually. The only thing they knew—they wanted sex.

"Tell him, Freckles, with a dick as big as yours you can blow yourself. You don't need some lass to do it for you," I said, rescuing myself from possible danger.

"You bet," he proudly agreed, gulping down more liquid happiness and still giggling.

I caught Chad's reaction. His expression said it all. He was clearly intrigued by my revelation that Freckles could suck his own cock, even jealous. He glanced down at his own decent helping of dick, no doubt visualising his mouth slipping down the shaft. "I wonder if I can suck mine?" he asked himself.

"You'd need to be a bloody contortionist to get your mouth down on that tiny dick," said Tommy.

Chad ignored his remark, his head bending slightly. "If I can, you can bet your swinging bollocks my head will be buried between my legs every other morning."

I gave him a nudge. "From what I can remember, Chad, it often is... but you're usually throwing up."

Tommy decided he wanted to continue with the game. It could have been the subject was too close to gay sex. He handed Freckles the dice. "Your turn."

Freckles chuckled as he fired the dice across the table. They rolled off the edge and landed on the deck. I couldn't help notice his cute little bottom when he bent to collect them, his boxers tightening around the cheeks, the seam sinking between the small mounds when it plunged into his virgin hole. I really hoped he would be into guys. The sight was far too scrumptious and inviting for a randy bugger like me for that not to be the case.

Freckles threw his legs over the bench and sat back down. It was obvious Chad had been studying the impressive length of soft cock sitting in Freckles' boxers as he did so. I had a sneaky suspicion he was still toying with the idea as to whether such a scrawny lad like Freckles could actually perform that miraculous act and suck his own cock. Although I'd made the whole thing up, I was even beginning to wonder myself.

"Problem with your bones?" Chad asked Freckles, a little double entendre irresistible.

"No way," giggled Freckles, then unexpectedly boasted, "I can suck my balls into my mouth at the same time as I suck my cock."

"I'll believe that when I see it," Chad prompted, his keenness to witness the act a little too obvious.

Tommy bent and grabbed four more cans he'd secreted under the table and passed them round. He clicked his open and took a swig. "A blowjob's fine, but that ain't as good as fucking or sucking a juicy pussy."

Chad clicked open his can and took a good slurp. "When you come, do you swallow your spunk?" he asked Freckles, his mind still on the merits of self-sucking, eager to remain on his original tack.

I quickly checked Freckles' reaction. This was a tricky one and I wondered if he was up to it. I knew what my answer would have been.

"I gulp the lot down. Loads of calories. Tastes great!" he quickly responded. With a gorgeous chortle, his lovely little tongue began lapping the come-like froth from his freshly opened can.

It was clear the alcohol was working wonders for Freckles' confidence; bless him. It was also clear Chad was contemplating stuffing his head between his own legs and having a go at sucking himself in the not too distant future. I just hoped he wasn't to be disappointed. I knew I was when I first tried. Still, a boy has to experiment.

Tommy swallowed hard. "Drinking your own spunk. God, that's gross."

"Gross eh? But not when one of your old slappers is swallowing your juicy whack," I challenged.

"That's different. And they ain't slappers. My birds are the best. Tasty," Tommy went on the defensive.

"But don't it make you wanna puke?" Chad continued to quiz Freckles, still unable to get sucking himself off the agenda.

"Pussy..." Tommy butted in. "D'ya know how to make a pussy twitch? I bet you don't."

Freckles gulped down a decent whack of lager. He burst out laughing. "Kick it in the knackers," he merrily spluttered, his mouthful of booze spraying over the Ludo board. Chad laughed so much I thought he was about to pee himself, several lads lying on their bunks and sitting at tables joined in.

"Brilliant!" praised a very pretty youth; his peach smooth face barely visible as it peeped from around the bank of lockers.

"Kick it in the fucking knackers," repeated another, causing yet more laughter.

Young Freckles didn't know it yet but he was about to get a moment of fame. His little gem of a joke would be all over the ship by morning and repeated throughout the week until it had lost its sparkle.

A light went out behind Chad. "Keep it down, guys. Trying to get some kip here." It was a complaint from a lad who had an early watch.

"And how you going to manage that when you're still thrashing your cock?" asked Tommy.

"Go blow yourself," was the reply.

"Freckles already can," said Chad, determined to keep his cock sucking fantasy going.

"What's all this about problems with blowing yourself?" Tommy asked Chad. "Shit, you're black. All black guys can blow themselves, can't they? Anyway, didn't you tell us you had a nine-incher?"

I spotted Chad's palm engulf his cock and give it a stroke as if testing the length. "'Course," he replied, boastfully. "I just ain't never tried sucking it before."

Tommy squeezed Freckles' thigh. "For fuck sake show him how it's done, Frecky. Then perhaps we can talk serious pussy."

With a tipsy giggle, Freckles' baby face bent below the table and between his thighs. Several sleepy youths opened eyes, fully or in squints. I spotted Chad's cock gain in girth and begin expanding his briefs, his palm encircling the thickening shaft and gently squeezing. A couple of lads lying on bunks close to our table dropped books into laps and stopped reading. Shuffling sounds came from other bunks as a few more cocks were rising in anticipation of watching Freckles blow himself.

"Uhm! Uhm!" Freckles' muffled cries of pleasure issued from below the table; his golden head of hair barely visible as it bobbed gently up and down.

The temptation for Chad to bend below the table or run around and have a bloody good look was almost unbearable for him. I glimpsed his cock. It was now as stiff as it could possibly get, tenting his briefs and forcing them upward. My own cock was rising too, and keen to be thrashed, but that was more to do with Chad's happy cock throbbing beside me than Freckles' head bouncing up and down.

Tommy had the best view of the proceedings, though the guy on a top bunk just above Freckles might have had an equally good one.

"Jesus!" sang Tommy, a smile spreading over his face, his head bending toward Freckles' bobbing head. "How the fuck do you manage it?"

"Fucking hell, Chad. You should see this," marvelled the lad lying on the bunk just above Freckles.

"Can this boy blow," confirmed another lad, his body hanging precariously over the edge of a top bunk to get a better view.

Chad could barely contain his excitement and frustration. He was fidgeting like a little lad who desperately needed a pee. "Is he really doing it, Sandy?"

"Reckon so. Told you he could. Right down to his pubes from what I hear."

More muffled moans of pleasure rose from beneath the table as Freckles' bobbed his head ever faster. "Oh, yes!" he gurgled, his hand slapping the tabletop.

The sudden cry of joy almost caused Chad to jump from his skin. "My god!" he gasped, his bottom leaving the bench as he rose to view the proceedings, rose to witness Freckles coming in his own mouth.

A wickedly cheerful face suddenly popped up from below the table causing Chad to sit back down. "Delicious!" delighted Freckles, his lips covered in spittle, the dribbles rolling over his chin and making it look like he'd just swallowed his own spunk.

Chad's eyes were wide open and agog at the sight of it. To everyone's amusement it must have taken him several seconds to realise he that was on the receiving end of brilliant prank and it was spittle dribbling over Freckles' lips, and not spunk. "You little prick," he cursed, becoming all embarrassed when the lads began to rib him.

"Gotcha!" chirped Freckles, taking a swig from his can, his face red from exertion and a little self-induced embarrassment.

"Hook, line and sinker," I agreed when Freckles' appreciative audience jeered at Chad and delighted in the brilliant deception.

Chad sprang from the bench as if a firecracker had just exploded under his bum. "I need a pee," he mumbled, forgetting his cock was pushing his briefs way out in front of him and was in urgent need of attention.

"Break a neck," teased Tommy when Chad charged up the ladder in order to escape the barrage of barracking wreaked upon him.

"Swallow, don't spit," was the last taunt to redden Chad's ears as he raced away.

What can I say? This is what made being a sailor such a wonderful experience. Discounting all the pomp and ceremony, the meaningless tasks we had to perform, the hard work and the authority crap we often had to endure, it was a sailor's humour that made life fun and the whole thing worthwhile.

Where else could you find guys who were constantly tuned-in to being able to improvise, play along with a joke and turn it into entertainment of the highest quality, whatever the subject? Be able to approach a thing like giving yourself a blowjob, or somebody else for that matter, with such an open mind. Not only that, do it without any offence being taken and only a bit of short-lived embarrassment for the guy who got baited. Nowhere, as far as I was aware.

I winked at Freckles. "Nice one, Frecky. You're on form tonight."

Freckles laughed, pleased with himself. "Nearly got a hard-on pretending to do it."

"Chad did!" Tommy enlightened him. "Gone to try for himself."

Freckles rubbed the back of his neck. "Better fetch the doc, then. It doesn't half hurt. Thought I wouldn't get back up again."

"So you can't blow yourself, then?" Tommy asked Freckles, sounding somewhat disappointed.

Freckles gave me a *come to bed* wink. "If I've got a stiffy I can. No problem when it's reached its usual eleven inches."

"Knew a lass called Harry who could lick her clit." Tommy changed the subject, probably because he couldn't blow himself and knew he didn't posses eleven inches.

"Was she a tom?" asked Freckles, attempting a cat joke.

Tommy appeared preoccupied and nodded to a bunk far in the starboard corner, the small light illuminating the occupant's serious face. "The Pope's still at it," he whispered.

"Poor bastard," I said.

The Pope was Junior Seaman Spencer, the saddest and loneliest lad I'd ever come across. A Catholic, he'd spent his life in a home run by priests. Before sleeping, each night he would wade through his bible. Mercifully, he didn't get the piss taken out of him more than any other lad. Worse, I suppose, guys often ignored him.

I felt deeply saddened for the lifetime of guilt the priests had left him with. Even the mention of him tossing himself would fill him with anguish. And any talk of sex with girls before he'd wed them 'for better or worse' would almost bring on a panic attack.

"There's still a chance he might get saved," I said. "A year with us lot should do it."

"A good run ashore, ten pints of scrumpy and an hour shagging some Pompey slut should cure him," was Tommy's recommendation.

"Perhaps we should take him ashore with us," Freckles suggested.

"You what?" gasped Tommy. "It's bad enough with a little runt like you tagging along."

"You're just jealous cos the girls are always drooling over me," Freckles hit back.

"That's cos they think you're a poofy little poodle with that haircut."

"I expect it's because he's got an eleven inch dick and can blow himself," I defended my favourite lad.

"Too true," agreed Freckles, looking down at his crotch and checking, beginning to believe it was indeed the truth. Tommy didn't respond.

Most of the lads who had been sitting at the tables ambled to their bunks, switching off overhead lights and turning on their small bunk lights before they bedded down. I scanned their bottoms, bodies, and crotches as they did so. I could never resist having a good gander at what sexy smooth skin might be available for some later date. Invariably I would make a mental photocopy of one body for my evening tossing fun. This time of day was always a good time to observe their gorgeous bodies, as most boys would be clad only in underpants and

be bare-chested. Better yet, totally naked. Often there'd
be a decent stiffy tenting a pair of boxers or held tightly
in skimpy briefs, the owner keen to get beneath his bedding for his own nightly toss.

Our game had long since dwindled to a halt. Chad
still hadn't returned from his pee. I was beginning to
wonder if he'd found himself stuck in an embarrassing
position, still having failed to give himself that illusive
blowjob, and was now sitting in the heads with a dislo-
cated neck and waiting for help.

Breaking the silence, I stupidly decided to ask a
question that had been on my mind for some weeks.
"So what's this thing with Purdy?" I asked Tommy, my
voice low.

Tommy's eyebrows danced like crazy. His face reddened. He looked angry. "Go on, spoil the fucking
evening, why don't you."

It seemed like I'd pressed one of his *destruct* buttons. "Sorry. I was just curious as to why he's got it in
for you."

"Let's just say the guy's sick. Mark my words,
Sandy…" Tommy took a deep breath and finished off
his beer. "One dark night I'm going to smack him over
the head with a brick."

"A brick? On board a ship?" I tried to make light of
such drastic action.

Freckles stood. It was clear he didn't like the subject
and didn't wish to be party to it. "Gonna crash, guys,"
he said, gathering his empty cans and walking to the
bin; his face now drained of all its earlier humour and
looking tired.

"What the hell's going on?" I pushed Tommy for an
explanation, still whispering, the subject delicate.

"Leave it, Sandy. It'll get sorted." Tommy thumped me in the arm real hard. "I can take care of myself."

I gave my bicep a rub. "Don't I know it... but Purdy has got rank and you'll end up in cells if you smack him. Worse, if you hit him with a... brick!"

Tommy was listening but not really paying attention, and didn't respond. I blew him a kiss and winked, making light of it. "Come on. Tell your old mate. Problem shared and all that."

Tommy began stowing the Ludo and clearing the table of dirty ashtrays and empty cans. "I'm gonna crash now, Sandy. Going ashore the weekend?" The subject was clearly dead in the water.

"Sure. We'll beat up Purdy," I sarcastically replied.

"I'll look forward to it," was his last remark for the evening.

I grabbed a wet cloth and cleaned the table before turning out the top light above it. Pipe Down was due to sound at any moment, though a good few of the lads were already fast asleep. After turning my bedding down ready for my own kip, I slipped my feet into flip-flops and headed up the ladder and toward the heads from whence Chad had yet to return.

'Course I wasn't going in search of Chad to help him with that illusive blowjob. A boy's got to clean his teeth last thing at night, hasn't he?

FOR WHOM THE BELL TOLLS

Saturday and I was on the First watch, a great watch to have before we entered port in the morning and went ashore at midday. All being well, it meant I'd be bunked down just after midnight and be able to get a good night's kip before Harbour Stations. In the morning, there would only be the entering harbour routine and the hoisting of the Union Jack on the jack staff for me to contend with. Come lunchtime I could get myself all tarted up and go in search of some long overdue sex. To this end, I still hadn't decided whether I'd go ashore with Freckles or Tommy, or just myself, a visit to the gay pubs and clubs foremost in my mind. Anyway, Tommy was still at war with Purdy and getting more manic by the day, so I doubted I would be ashore with him.

Apart from standing on the flag deck and signalling ships or doing other Bunting Tosser stuff, we *Tactical* signalmen had many other duties to perform during a watch. We were also required to type-up signals before and after they'd been sent or received. Then, if not snowed under with other tasks, distribute the same to whatever officers or departments those messages related. And that is precisely what I was doing now, trolling all over the ship with a CONFIDENTIAL signal that I needed to place into the hands of the Diving Officer, who also happened to be the Engineering Officer (EO).

I loved doing distributions. It was the perfect time to check out the available talent. Even an opportunity to arrange for secret sex sorties. It also gave me the chance to meet loads of different guys I wouldn't normally meet, or meet regularly, and partake in snippets of conversation. A chance to get the gossip, gossip such as which were the good pubs to visit, or the real juicy stuff like the antics the lads had been getting up to during their last run ashore. If *really* lucky, discover who'd been shagging whom on board. Naturally, the important information, like whether we were off to fight a war, in line for some gruelling exercise or brilliant trip abroad, or any confidential information about a member of the ship's company, only we communicators would know. Consequently, we were the hub of the grapevine.

It will come as no surprise, then, if something was in the air and rumours were rife, bribes of every species would be coming at us signalmen like prostitutes in a popular port of call. It was a great way to get extra fags, rum and favours when guys, keen to get the low-down, went overboard to please. Yes, a signalman was a respected and sought after person on board any ship and practically everyone would know you by name. Not surprisingly, distributing signals could be a real pleasure. At best, it was a bit like going on a refreshing cruise.

There weren't that many guys to chat with at this time of night as I went in search of the EO, just those on watch and a few who were moving from mess to mess, or visiting the heads and showers before bunking down or preparing for their watch.

'Tinker' Bell was the first guy I happened upon when I came down the ladder, having just stuck my head inside the Wardroom to check if the EO was knocking down a few slugs of pink gin before retiring. As usual, he was dressed in a pair of blue overalls, splattered in a variety of multicoloured blotches of paint. As usual, he held a paintbrush and was refreshing lettering above a fire hydrant, sign-writing one of his fortes. Playing practical jokes was another of his fortes, many of which I'd been the victim. Moaning at just about anything and everything, especially the ship, was another.

"Hi, Tinks!" I greeted. "Reckon those overalls would be priceless if they were hung in the Tate and not draped over your shagged-out scrawny body."

Tinker laughed his gruff laugh. "Hi, Sandy! How's it hanging? My bloody draft come through yet?" He had a smiling face, all red and weather-beaten from years of working on the upper deck in every kind of condition imaginable. Reddened also from the rums I suspected he'd sunk before starting his watch.

As I said, Tinker was prone to a bit of moaning while he worked, always telling everyone that he wanted off the ship. Truth was he loved the old bucket, and the guys with whom he worked and played. No way did he really want a draft.

I studied the signal on my clipboard and raised my eyebrows teasingly. It was my turn for a bit of practical joking. "Funny you should ask, Tinks. Looks like we're finally getting shot of you. Got your draft right here."

Tinker wiped the back of his hand across his mouth, leaving a red lipstick streak behind. He resembled a dishevelled drag queen with his crop of girlie, curly hair. "You're joking!" A look of stunned surprise spread over his face.

I studied my clipboard again, flicking the corner of the signal up and down, my face serious. I shook my head. "Nope. Toss and boat your oars time, darling."

"Damn and fuck!" he exclaimed. He dropped his quarter-inch brush into a pot of red paint with a plop, then rubbed his cheek with the back of his hand, adding rouge to his make-up. "Where they sending me, Sandy?" There was a little concern in his tone.

I held back my laughter. It was a good start. He'd taken the bait.

"Thought you hated this tub and was desperate to be drafted to foreign parts, sunning your scrawny body on some exotic beach and showing off your tats to all those foreign lasses?" Tinker didn't speak his expression one of doubt. I gave his ribs a poke.

Tinks grunted, his concern still apparent.

"Guess I was wrong," I said, rubbing it in. "Missing me already, are you?"

Tinker knew I had him on the ropes and needed to save face. His expression immediately changed to that of a cheerful cuddly teddy. He rubbed his paint-covered palms enthusiastically down the legs of his overalls. "Show us, Sandy." Stepping closer, his hand reached out for the signal.

I kept the clipboard tantalisingly close to my chest and averted from his gaze. "No way." Shaking my head, I added a few warning tuts for good measure.

Tinker's excitement mounted as the thought of being drafted to some exotic place began taking over. He resorted to fantasising. "They sending me abroad, Sandy? Sending me to Singapore or Oz? Boy, I just love Oz. A smashing Sheila to screw on every corner."

I wanted to laugh. I was witnessing a grown man turn into an excited little boy before my very eyes. "That so?"

"Let's see, Sandy," he repeated his request, his grimy fingers again reaching toward my clipboard.

I pulled the board back into my chest. I was really enjoying this torment. "Sorry, Tinks. You know I can't do that. Shouldn't even be telling you. Up to my neck in it if you let on."

"Shit, Sandy, you know I won't drop you in it. Just a peek. One teeny-weeny peek."

I shook my head again. "Sorry, Tinks. No can do."

"A pack of smokes," he bargained, tapping the twenty in his top pocket and moving his paint-stricken body closer to mine.

I stepped back, not wishing my kit to resemble his. "Now let me see…" I began feigning interest. Tinker smiled as I pretended to consider his offer. I decided I'd deflate him further and told him he'd have to do better than that.

"What you want, then?" he sort of snapped.

I gripped my crotch and grinned wickedly. "How about a good old blowjo…"

"Two!" he said, butting in and upping the ante, purposefully closing his ears to my sexual bargaining.

"Two blowjobs! Sounds goo…"

"Stop pissing about, Sandy. I'll give you two packs of smokes." He shoved out his grubby hand to shake on it. "Deal?"

"Sorry, Tinks. You'll just have to wait until your DO tells you your draft. You know how it works."

Tinker's chin hit the deck. Boy, was I enjoying this.

Tinker became frustrated. He drummed his fists up and down like a spoilt young boy who was desperate to know his present before his birthday. Mercifully, he wasn't stamping his feet. "Give us a clue, then," he pleaded, nuzzling close and squeezing my bum, which was no substitute for a blowjob. Two packs of smokes and a tot of rum were the increased bribe.

I pressed a finger to my lips, looking thoughtful. It was time to reel him in. "Tell you what, Tinks..."

His eyes sparkled, sensing a result. "What?"

"'Cos you're a mate I'll give you three guesses. Only three, mind."

"Hong Kong?" he blurted excitedly, picking his first choice, him being partial to Chinese lasses in sarongs. Tinker was partial to all things Chinese, especially food, and always ordered number sixty-nine from the menu regardless of what might end up on his plate. We all knew what he was hoping would end up on his plate.

I told him it was too far.

Tinker decided he'd better take his time. He rubbed his chin thoughtfully for a few moments, spreading more make-up over his face. The Persian Gulf was his second guess.

I fanned my own face, made puffing sounds, and told him it was too hot.

"Aust...." he began to go for his final guess.

I raised my eyebrows to torment him.

"Singapore?" he hurriedly changed his mind, making his final stab.

"Wrong," I said, turning away. "That's your lot."

Tinker grabbed my elbow but quickly released it fearing he might have put paint on it. "Come on, Sandy. Don't be a bitch." He thought for a second as I continued to walk away. "Hang on, I've got it… Mauritius? Where else is it nice and hot and full of frisky fillies?"

I turned around and released a wicked laugh. "Who said anything about nice and hot?"

"Three packs of smokes and my tot," he pleaded, reverting to bribery.

How could I be so wicked? Easy. When he was duty Bosun's Mate his last prank had me cycling across the dockyard in the pissing rain at the dead of the night, searching for some non-existent officer who supposedly had an urgent signal for the Captain.

It was time to be even more wicked. "Imagine this…" I began setting the scene. "The sun's shining brightly in a clear blue sky. Beautiful whales are slipping by, their tails gracefully rising above the waves, waterspouts spurting high into the air. You're lying there, drink in hand."

Tinker's expression became serene from the peaceful picture. "Yes," he sighed, his face beaming contentment, his imagination taking him to who knows where.

"You're supping on that tall drink," I continued. "There's ice beside you to cool your lips." His expression was one of utter bliss. "Plenty of ice!" I said; a sharpness in my tone as my eyes fixed into his.

Tinker's expression changed slightly. "Plenty of ice?"

"I mean *plenty* of ice," I said, my expression cruel.

His face began to freeze over. He'd sensed all was not what it seemed. "What you saying, Sandy? Where they sending me?"

I gave his shoulder a slap. "How does Fishery Protection sound, Tinker me old buddy? You've been drafted to a frigate on Icelandic Patrol. Plenty of ice there, me thinks."

Tinker fell against the bulkhead; his freshly painted lettering printing onto the sleeve of his overalls as it smudged. "Tell me it's not true, Sandy. For fuck sake tell me you're pulling me pisser."

"'Fraid so," I said, desperately holding back my laughter. "Emergency draft. You're off as soon as we've docked in Pompey. Better start packing your kit."

His palms covered his face. "I hate fucking penguins!"

"That so. I hear they're pretty tasty with chips." Tinker didn't laugh. I gave him a nudge and winked. "I'm not sure about *fucking* them though."

I almost felt the pain myself when he banged his head against the bulkhead. "I ain't going, Sandy. No way. The fucking bastards!"

I rubbed his shoulder as if consoling him. "Don't suppose you've seen the EO, have you?" I tapped my clipboard. "Got this signal for him."

Tinker shook his head, his expression sulky. As I walked away, the penny suddenly dropped. "Hang on a bit. What you want to show the EO my draft for? He's not my DO."

I licked my finger and stroked it downward through the air. "Hook, line and sinker."

"You witch! You wicked fucking witch!" Tinker began laughing loudly, a relieved laughter. He slapped his own face. "Nice one, Sandy. Shit, you had me going there."

"Let that be a lesson, you miserable old bugger. Stop moaning about wanting off the ship. Next time it might not be a piss take."

A nod of agreement and an offer of a gulp of his rum were Tinker's last comment on the matter. I suspected it wouldn't be his last complaint about the ship though, it was just the way he was—a loveable moaner.

"Nice and slutty. Just how I like my women," was the camp comment from a guy who was approaching. I left Tinker to deal with the state of his make-up and continued to make my way along the Burma Way in search of the EO.

RUBBERED UP

I glimpsed my watch. It was getting late. It was more than likely the EO had bunked down. It wasn't wise to enter an officer's cabin late at night unless a signal required an immediate response. Although urgent, the one in hand could wait until morning. As a final thought, I decided I'd check the Engine Room and then the diver's haunt before returning to the flag deck, on the off chance he was loitering in either of them.

I could hear the engines hammering away when I approached the heart of the ship. They were driving the propellers at full throttle as they sliced us speedily through the sea and toward Pompey, and our much-deserved run ashore. A shaft of hot air punched into my face when I bent over and peered down the hatch for someone to ask if the EO was below. Without ear defenders, it wasn't wise to wander around the engine room searching for someone, the noise excruciating. But on a wintry and wet bitch-of-a-night the top of the ladder was a good place to get warmed up, the unbearable noise less deafening.

As I peered down the hatch, I spotted a head bobbing about as its owner worked below. Sweat was seeping through the lad's hair, captured by a red rag tied around his neck, preventing if from slipping down his spine and between the cheeks of his backside. The youth had his ear defenders hooked around his neck. There was a chance I could get his attention.

I began tapping my metal clipboard on the top rung of the aluminium ladder, the clanks barely audible against the noise of machinery. His reddened face eventually looked up. I asked the cute and chunky boiler room boy whether the EO was about. It took a while to lip-read his negative reply. I mouthed *thanks* in return; leaving him to play with his cocks, reminding me I would very much like to play with some myself.

The Boiler Room accounted for I began to move toward the aft offices and mess decks, to the quarterdeck beyond where the Diving Office was situated. As I did so, the main lights along the Burma Way began to be extinguished and replaced by the warm glow of the red nightlights. Almost immediately, Pipe Down sounded throughout the ship, the Bosun's voice low so's not to wake those already sleeping.

Just before the Stoker's Mess, the Burma Way took a sharp ninety-degree turn to port before taking another ninety-degree turn and continuing aft. As I was about to turn the second corner and continue on my journey aft, I spotted three bodies beside the hatch leading down to the Stoker's Mess. The two older guys appeared to be engaged in what I can only describe as some sort of confrontation.

The guy giving it all the verbals I didn't know, but he was big, very big indeed. Dressed in a boiler suit, he was obviously a stoker. He was also of rank, a Hooky, the blue anchor on his sleeve clearly visible against its white background. Facing him, the one on the receiving end of his cursing, I'd recognised immediately. His short plump body was all too familiar. It was that of Purdy.

Slotted between Purdy and the stoker, a forlorn and apprehensive looking youth stood silently. He wasn't 'Adonis' pretty but did have a wonderful body and shagable bum. Half-naked and dressed only in a white towel, the material defined his shape quite nicely as it draped over his hips and buttocks, and pressed against his thighs. I didn't know him but would have been more than happy to do so

I froze in my tracks and ducked out of sight. Not wishing to miss the action, I decided I'd wait and see what developed, my face peering gingerly from around the bulkhead.

For a few moments, my attention remained on the youth rather than the ongoing argument, but soon my ears were open wider than any secret listening post, desperate to catch just a word that would make good gossip for a later date, words I might use to cheer Tommy when I next saw him.

Eavesdropping proved difficult; try as I might I was unable to grasp a single juicy word that wandered in my direction. With the noise of the engines not far behind and that of the fans gushing warm air from above, each sentence was being gobbled up or pushed further away. Undeterred and desperate not to miss any of the action though, and hoping I might suddenly be gifted with lip reading skills, I continued to study the heated scene.

I've no idea why but butterflies began flitting excitedly around my tummy. I suspect the cause was the expectation—hope—that at any moment a fist might fly forth from the big stoker and send the fat arsed Purdy bouncing over the deck. More realistically, my fantasies of what the masculine stoker and the half-naked youth got up to in that hot and sweaty boiler room during their long and lonely nights together was the culprit.

The scene was mesmerising, unbelievable. It was practically unheard of for two guys of rank to square up like this, especially in such a public setting. I could only guess something very serious must have happened. Purdy must have done something way out of order. But what?

The stoker's mouth continued to work angrily, his spittle flying toward Purdy. A wagged finger from the stoker was followed by clenched fist. A poke in Purdy's ribs, then a gentle rub of the worried youth's locks. A sickly smirk filled Purdy's face. Another clenched fist from the stoker. Another smirk from Purdy. A finger poked harder—into Purdy's chest this time—then another. Yet another poke, this one causing Purdy to stumble backwards. More verbals, both this time. A silent youth watching, an even more silent me, apart from my heavy breathing, also intently watching as the situation reached boiling point. Still I caught not a single word, my own frustration also reaching boiling point.

For a good five minutes, the mostly one-way argument continued to rage.

Then it happened. No, not that fist smacking into Purdy's porky face, which I was so desperately awaiting, but the advance of a Petty Officer. With the presence of an approaching Rank, the argument came to an abrupt halt. Sadly, Purdy's smug face was still intact.

A glare and another nodded warning from the big stoker was the final assault on Purdy. Then, with a comforting rub of the lad's locks, and a reassuring slap on his back, both man and youth vanished into the Stoker's Mess below, the lad now smiling and looking a good deal more relaxed.

The Burma Way was silent and still, the Petty Officer ascending a ladder. I remained hidden at the corner, my mind toying with what had just gone down. What was amazing was the stoker was of a lower rank. Purdy was an Acting Petty Officer and could have had the stoker up on a charge before I'd even had time to whip the towel from the young lad's cheeks and kiss his cute backside. I could only imagine Purdy had no choice but to take the flak.

It was driving me nuts not knowing what could have been the cause of the incident. It obviously involved the youth. Maybe Purdy was bullying the lad, like he did Tommy? Maybe he was trying to steal him away from the big stoker, the youth possibly being the stoker's bit of *skin*. I just didn't know and perhaps I never would.

I couldn't wait to tell Tommy of the scandal. I'd try and tell it as it was and not tart it up. With any luck, it would put him in a good mood for shore leave. It was a pity there was no juicy black eye or broken nose to report. That would have really got him chirpy.

I poked my head back around the corner to check if the coast was clear. Purdy was almost on top of me, heading in my direction. He was wobbling from side to side. It had nothing to do with the motion of the ship and more to do with his drink habit.

For a split second, I began toying with the idea of discreetly asking Purdy what was up and what the

argument was about. I suddenly remembered his sug-
gestion that we have a drink together next time shore
leave was due. No way was I going to give the slime ball
the opportunity to make that offer again. Without even
knocking I threw open the door of the Switching Room
beside me and darted inside.

"Fuck!" yelped the dishy electrician when the door
knocked him backward and I almost scared the pants
off him.

"Diving Officer… EO… Signal," I hastily asked the
delectable youth, waving my clipboard, noting he was
indeed worthy of having his pants scared from his backside.

A sarcastic smile was my reward from the young
lad, who simply pointed to his electrician's badge and
raised his eyebrows, questioning whether I'd just arrived
from some alien planet.

"Long watch," I apologised, feeling stupid. "Don't
suppose…"

A voice hidden deep behind hot and humming
equipment, the owner obviously doing a quiz to wile
away his watch, helped save my stupidity with a timely,
"How many bones in the human body, Willy?"

"Only one that matters," the laughing lad quickly
and cleverly replied. He grabbed the appendage that
matched his name and gave it a decent squeeze, wound-
ing me with his *I bet you'd love to suck on this* seductive
smile.

Unable to resist making a comment on any subject
deemed sexual, I chucked in my own pennyworth. "And
the most sought after," I said, delaying my exit, eager
for a suggestive response while I contemplated what

size the bone attached to Willy's sexy body might reach when he'd made it sucking solid.

"Hope you find your man," was the purred response through pouting lips as Willy began to close the door on me. Well, if that wasn't a pick up line... the randy little tease. I added the Switching Room to my list of compartments with shagable occupants.

Willy had gotten me horny again. "Cute lads shouldn't tease like that," I whispered to myself as I adjusted my rising cock. I laughed when I suddenly occurred to me that being an electrician he'd probably be able to give an AMPle amount of cock. Even take one if he was a hOHMo. Yeah, I know it's sad. Months of watch-keeping can often curdle the brain.

Back on track, I continued on my journey down aft. I couldn't wait to get bunked down and have a damn good toss. In my fantasy, I'd already planned to have Willy and Freckles in bed together, me sandwiched between the pair. My cock rose even higher as I strolled along and mentally prepared the script.

A couple of half-naked, tattooed, muscular sailors popped out of the shower room as I approached. I suspected they were hardworking seamen with such magnificently bronzed torsos. I couldn't resist checking their towels for evidence of naughty goings on. Both were only slightly tented, their cocks hanging semi-hard from being adequately soaped. Having a disgusting mind I still managed to picture the pair fucking each other against the shower bulkhead, spunk splattering from what I suspected would be huge cocks with massive balls hanging below. My own cock almost burst my trousers apart when each gave me a knowing smile. They knew what I was thinking all right. Yes, they'd been up to something, I'd bet my bollocks on it.

I needed a pee—a wank, to be honest—so I popped into the heads. I did a quick check of the cubicles for multiple activity, after I'd sprayed a face on the wall of the stainless steel urinal. All were vacant. I'd expected they would be. It was too dangerous to perform in a cubicle together even when desperate. I managed to refrain from having a premature wank. One thing was for sure, it was going to be one hell of a bollock-blower when I finally got around to it.

Back in the Burma Way, I resumed my lonesome journey down aft. When I reached my own mess, a quick bend of the head saw me peer down the hatch to see if anyone was up and about. The lights were off, the lads slumbering, their body odour filtering upward. The smell wasn't in the least arousing so I moved on.

A few more yards and I'd arrived at the metal door which led to the quarterdeck. Once in the fresh air, I did a couple of left turns and headed forward.

On the starboard side, adjacent the Captain's launch, I stopped in front of the door marked DIVERS. I knew it was very unlikely the EO would be inside at this time of night, but decided I'd check anyway.

I gave the door a couple of sharp taps with my clipboard. As I did so, the ship gave a gentle roll to starboard. The clips weren't fastened properly and it swung toward me. Giving it a tug, I opened it wider until I could see inside.

The room was in total darkness apart from a glimmer of light to my left when I pushed my head through the doorway. Whispering, but I don't know why, I announced that I was the Duty Signalman and that I had a signal for the Diving Officer. Hearing no response, I stepped inside the dimly lit room to investigate further.

I'd never seen inside the diver's den before. I discovered the light was coming from behind another door within. It too was slightly ajar. When my eyes had become accustomed to the darkness, I noticed the diving paraphernalia decorating the bulkheads. There was a chart with hand signals; various types of breathing apparatus and rubber suits; a first aid chart and another with examples of useful knots. On the aft bulkhead hung an ancient looking, highly polished, brass, diving helmet—a piece of history and prized treasure belonging to the Diving Officer no doubt. Also, a variety of ropes used by divers and swimmers were either coiled on the deck or hanging on hooks. A selection of lethal knives had been locked in a reinforced glass-fronted cabinet for safekeeping. Disappointingly, there wasn't a thing to keep my state of horniness going, not even a dirty mag floating about. As for a naked swimmer, no such luck. Oh, there was a rubber diving suit hanging from the deck head. It made me jump when I thought some diver had topped himself.

I've no idea why I did it but I pulled the outer door shut, fastening several of the storm clips to prevent it from reopening. As I did so, the ship gave a sudden lurch to port. The diving helmet clanked metal against metal when it rolled against the bulkhead. It caused me to jump. Briefly, I began to question what the hell I was doing inside the den but continued to nose around regardless.

With the sudden movement to port, the inner door had opened wider. To my surprise, I heard intriguing groans and moans coming from the other side. They were similar to those of someone having sex. My cock began to rise as thoughts of discovering some naughty goings on stirred in my mind.

I couldn't help myself and began to press a finger on the door. Easing it open, my heart increased in pace. My excitement mounted further when the expectation of finding a couple of teenage swimmers engaged in the art of *deep throat diving* began to ravish me.

The figure of a youth greeted my lusting eyes when I'd finally opened the door wide enough for me to peer around. With his back to me, the pair of arms wrapped around his shapely body, the fingers fiddling with the zip, quickly had me aroused. If I was right, and I hoped I was, the mystery young swimmer was in the process of being stripped naked and mercilessly ravished by his lusting buddy. What's more, it was about to happen before my very eyes.

It must have taken me a good thirty seconds before I realised it was the youth's own arms that were embracing the top half of his body, his own fingers that were doing the fondling, and not some amorous buddy preparing to strip his buttocks bare and shag him senseless. Shamelessly, my right hand had already been working my cock, preparing for some serious synchronised sex with the lusty young swimmers.

I suppose I should have introduced myself straight away. Instead, I just stood there, taking in this wonderful vision of a rubbered up youth. Creating even more fantasies to torment and tease my sex-starved brain before I reached my bunk and had that inevitable toss.

Just for the record, I was partial to swimmers. The Olympics had brought about many a wet dream fantasy or brilliant TV toss as a boy. I loved the way the lads casually talked about shaving each other's bodies before a race. I could only imagine how sexy that would be. I'd often wondered whether they shaved each other's pubics as well. In my yet unwritten *Swimmer's Guide to Breast and Bonestroke for Cute Bottomed Beginners* they sure did. What an event shaving a teenage swimmer while he was tossing you or giving you that blowjob of a lifetime would be, one that just had to be worthy of a gold medal.

I cannot say I'd ever been turned on by a youth in full diving gear though, but I was sure beginning to see how easily I became aroused by one wearing nothing but a skin tight wet suit, now that I had the very same standing within fucking distance. It was as if someone had taken this delightful creature, dipped his naked body in a rubber solution and then allowed the film to dry. Every mouth-watering mound, muscle, gully and gorge of this tantalising teenager now perfectly detailed. Every delightful hillock and crevice highlighted. Quite simply, he resembled a living liquorice just waiting to be devoured. Boy was I hungry, hungry enough to swallow every delicious morsel of this Bassets Liquorice boy.

I continued to study the glorious vision that I'd yet to greet. Starting with his dainty feet and ankles, I brought my gaze over his developed calf and thigh muscles, before finally settling on his incredible bottom. This was my favourite kind of bottom, protruding invitingly as if he was purposely pushing it out and preparing for a fucking. The firm mounds looked unbelievably inviting where the rubber squeezed them tightly together, defining the virgin crack that separated the cheeks.

Like a black marble statue of David, the voluptuous young buttocks rounded toward the base of his spine, meeting a tapered waist. Strong and muscled, yet soft when relaxed, I knew those buttocks would be a dream to fuck. Already my cock was so stiff I knew I would have no problem sending it right through that protective rubber and deep into his hole. My cock began to dribble profusely.

Broad swimmer's shoulders filled the top half of the lad's wet suit. They were supporting a longish and thin, slender white neck. With the zip pulled partly down, the watertight neckband was open allowing me a view of the nape and the first few inches of spine. How much I longed to be biting into that delicate skin while passionately fucking him. How tender his flesh would be against my lips.

Even from the back the youth looked adorable, with his hair cropped extremely short at the sides, almost to the scalp. It appeared to be a sandy white rather than blond; reminding me of Silversands beach in Africa. The crown possessed a good deal more hair than the back and sides, at least an inch. Strangely, it was much darker, almost ginger in places. Fancy hairdos not being permissible, I guessed the colours must have been natural. Didn't matter to me, just the thought of rubbing that shaven area on the back of his head, while he gave me a sucking of a lifetime, set my entire being alive. Unbelievably aroused, I took a tentative step toward those inviting buttocks.

My cock was almost busting my bell-bottoms apart as it pressed against my fly. I knew it wouldn't fail to go unnoticed by the lad. Even so, it was time to get the teenager to turn around. A timely cough did the trick.

"What the..." yelped the youth, his voice high from the shock, his palms pressing against his pounding heart when he took in extra air.

I raised my clipboard in a gesture of apology and to indicate that I wasn't a threat. "Signal for the Diving Officer."

It took a matter of seconds for me to take in the detail of the youth's frontal features. My eyes focused on his face first. They usually did. Angelic, simply angelic, was the only way to describe it. Pale, longish and narrow, it was almost flawless. A slender nose decorated the centre of the youth's face, a nose that suited him perfectly. His thin eyebrows matched the cropped part of his hair but were so fine they were almost invisible. Not to be disappointed, magnificent blue eyes sparkled as they stared into my own, not a piercing blue but a blue that was soft, comely, captivating. Eyes that simply begged the question: Am I stunningly beautiful, or what?

His fullish and pale, pouting lips were slightly parted, the lower lip glistening. Between them, a set of baby like teeth smiled without him actually doing so. The gap that separated the front teeth was simply delightful, inviting you to place your mouth on his and allow your tongue to toy with it. Completing the facial masterpiece, petite ears protruded slightly, both begging to be licked and nibbled as you gently made love.

There was a blemish on that choirboy face. A fading spot sat close to the corner of his mouth, his tongue occasionally darting out, nervously licking. Even that became invisible to my gaze after I'd mentally kissed it better.

I briefly scanned his upper torso, my eyes absorbing every detailed hill and valley. His chest wasn't excessively muscled and neither was his abdomen, but his body was strong enough to hold me in a passionate embrace. An embrace that would most surely get stronger as he regularly swam and dived, and developed into a magnificent tribute to the male species.

What would develop sooner than his body, I hoped, was the delicacy that lay dormant beneath the impressive mound of rubber sitting below his tummy. At a guess, it would be six inches of thick and succulent spunk-filled sex when I'd gotten it good, stiff, and ready to blow. At a guess, or rather, desperately hoping, that would happen in about ten minutes.

The last thing to catch my eye was the fluorescent orange lettering sitting above the youth's left breast, indicating his name. It was MATT. What can say? I knew I'd have been more than happy to find him lying on my doorstep, WELCOME HOME stamped on his cute little bottom.

Matt's pale face had begun to flush at the cheeks, his tongue licking more frequently at the tiny blemish. It could have been my silent scrutiny of his exquisite being that had brought his embarrassment about, or perhaps it was due to the predicament he'd obviously found himself in.

"Can't get out of my rubbers," he informed with a shy laugh, the high pitch of his voice replaced by a soft and seductive deeper tone. "Zipper's jammed."

I've no idea what he was doing in his wet suit at this time of night, and didn't ask. However, I was more than willing to help him get shot of it as soon as I possibly could. "Need a hand?"

Matt nodded and smiled. He turned his back toward me, his fingers gripping the problem zipper and giving it a tug. "Can't seem to get it up."

I couldn't help myself. When you're bowled a full toss you just have to smack it out of the park. "That *does* surprise me," I said with a wink, getting all smutty. "Don't have that problem myself."

The youth's cheeks had gone from red to crimson when he turned his head to face me. I spotted his gaze make a brief excursion to my stiff cock. A hint of a giggle escaped his lips but he remained silent. I found his innocence unbearably appetising, his bottom even more so when he backed into me so's I could access the zipper.

With such an important task to undertake, I needed to free my hands. My clipboard bounced on the plastic surface of the four-seater bench anchored to the bulked when I chucked it down. It hit the deck with a clatter when it jumped back off. Matt almost leapt into the air when I gripped his waist at the same moment. Boy was he nervous. What on earth did he think I was going to do to him?

"Sorry," I apologised and patted his waist in an attempt to calm him. "I'll soon have you out of your wet suit."

Matt's cherub cheeks almost exploded again when he turned his head at my remark, and found his lips within kissing distance of my own. "A good tug should do it," he quickly suggested, his voice slightly a tremble, his minty breath wafting over my face.

I knew he was referring to the zipper but my dirty mind suggested otherwise. "Gentle movements up and down are usually the best," I continued with my smutty approach, placing my palm upon his shoulder for extra leverage and squeezing intimately into his developing muscle.

"Okay," he kind of sighed, his embarrassed face turning further toward me, then briskly facing front.

I brought my fingers to the zipper and began to toy with the tiny tag. It was a simple task but concentrating proved difficult. Being the same height as me the nape of his biteable neck was tantalisingly close to my mouth. The urge to place my lips upon it was becoming irresistible.

"Any luck?" asked the youth, interrupting my vampire thoughts, his head turning again and causing his cheek to brush my lips. This time I needed to bite my tongue to stop me from placing my mouth onto his.

The answer to his query, whether I was having any luck, had yet to be determined. I remained calm. "I think there's something jammed under the catch. Looks like cotton."

"Pubic hair, I expect," he casually and unexpectedly tossed at me. "The buggers seem to get everywhere."

I could have spanked him for saying that. How on earth did he expect me to be fiddling with his rubbered-up body and not come over hot and horny if all I was thinking about was his pubic hairs? "Wrong colour," I instinctively replied, my thoughts now well and truly away from the task in hand and loitering just above his hidden cock.

Matt laughed. He arched his fuckable bottom and pushed it suggestively into my stiffened cock. "How would you know?" Another cheeky giggle broke free.

I was sure he was playing the game and was up for it. He was definitely beginning to relax. I decided not to act upon his actions straight away. I might be wrong and it was nothing more than playfulness—a sailor's way.

"Well, it's not one of mine," I said, wishing it were.

He arched his bottom into my cock again. "Never know."

Yes, he was playing all right!

The cabin was dark. I told Matt I couldn't see properly and needed more light. He glanced up to the deck head and nodded toward the brightest light about five steps back. I placed my palm on his hip in order to guide him backward. His hand fell onto the back of mine, steadying himself as I did so. As we began to move, I felt his buttocks flex and tighten beneath the rubber when his bottom pushed into my crotch. My cock gave its usual happy response.

Willing to continue with his playfulness, Matt gave my hand a gentle squeeze. "Fancy a dance?" he joked, shuffling his bare feet backwards and stepping on my toes.

I placed my arm fully around his tummy and began shuffling the pair of us in the direction of the light. "Only if I can lead."

More than ever, I was convinced he was up for some naughtiness. He was getting more daring by the second. I still couldn't take his banter as a green light though. Sailors often just clicked and made even the worst moments on board ship fun. I needed him to be a little more direct before I could dive into his pants. Grabbing my cock usually did the trick.

Matt continued to play. His bottom was wriggling invitingly as we shuffled toward the light and closer to the bench. "You come…"

"Only if you ask me nicely," I butted in before he could complete the dance cliché; eager to feed him more lines he could follow up on.

His own witty reply wasn't completed and replaced by a yelp of surprise when the ship suddenly lurched and sent us sprawling. The back of my knees met the seat of the bench. My legs buckled as the pair of us fell clumsily onto it. Completely off balance, my backside slammed down on the not-so-soft surface. With my arm about his waist, I pulled Matt on top of me. His soft buttocks bounced on my stiffened cock causing me to grunt as if I'd just shot my load. Another grunt leapt from my mouth on his second delightful bounce.

With my hand still on the zipper as we fell, the sudden movement had loosened it. It was now down as far as the crack of his buttocks, a pure white back revealed. More rewarding though, my other hand had slipped inside his wet suit and was now only inches from his cock and pressing against his soft tummy. I couldn't believe my luck, I'd accidentally moved up a base.

Matt's bare back pressed into my chest, his head close to mine and resting on the back of the bench, our cheeks almost touching, my mouth close to that scrumptious neck of his. Again, I was desperate to bite into the tender white flesh. Predictably, my cock was painfully solid and keen to please. He just had to be aware of it pushing into his tasty young buttocks.

The pair of us began to laugh as the ship settled. My right palm was still pressing into the soft flesh around Matt's tiny navel, the other on the outside of his wet suit and dangerously close to the mound of rubber that tormentingly covered his cock.

I gave his tummy a playful squeeze. "Anyone ever tell you you're a crap dancer?"

A huge smile erupted on the youth's delightful face, the small gap between his teeth enriching it. He gently butted the side of his head against mine as if we were old lovers. "What d'ya mean? I thought you were supposed to be leading?"

Although I knew I should push him off, I decided I'd wait a while and see if I was rewarded with the result I'd been searching for. I sensed the lad was more than happy to be sitting on a stiff cock. I for one was completely content with the seating arrangements. For a brief moment, the pair of us just sat and studied one another.

I wanted to move things along, slip my hand deep into his crotch and discover what treat he had secreted there. Momentarily, I toyed with whether I should be forward and ask him what he was doing in the diver's den so late at night, and whether he got off on dressing-up in his wet suit. Ask him whether he fancied a fuck. Problem was I truly believed innocence should find its own way forward.

I gave his tummy a provocative squeeze. "We can get arrested for this."

His face lit up with smiles of joy and playfulness. "You can get arrested for that!" he replied, his bottom bouncing on my solid cock.

"Can't help it," I said, making light of the fact and remaining controlled, but hoping this was the development I'd been waiting for.

"Me neither. Get a right stiffy when I lark about." He looked thoughtful for a moment. "Often get one when I put my rubbers on." His tone was subdued as if a little unsure of his confession.

"'Spect it's because they're tight and rub against your todger," I said, remaining cool, suggesting it was a natural occurrence.

He looked directly into my eyes, an expression of want and desire written on his face. "Got one now," he confessed, pulling his tummy in.

His unexpected action caused my hand to slide from his navel and slip downward. My fingers fell into his small bush of pubics. His erect cock was now lying across my knuckles; a strand of pre-come left in its wake.

His whole body shivered and went all a tingle on contact. "I see what you mean."

Matt continued to gaze into my eyes. For some reason his expression had changed to one of uncertainty, even sadness. Maybe it was suppressed desire. He still looked adorable, though. He would, no matter what.

It wasn't exactly a lunge but it did make me jump. A movement of desperation would be the best description. His mouth was soft against my own when he crazily pressed his lips onto mine, his tongue chewing gum fresh as it darted between them. I felt his cock twitch excitedly against the back of my hand as the blood rushed in and brought it to its maximum length and girth. I remained silent and still, allowing him to relish the moment, to take things at his own pace.

A deep breath suddenly rushed into Matt's lungs when he nervously filled them. He quickly pulled his mouth from mine. "Sorry!" he gasped, his mind filling with doubt and uncertainty. "I'm really sorry."

My lack of response had had the wrong effect. An act of reassurance was of the essence. I cupped the nape of his neck with my free hand, brought our mouths back together, and began to kiss him passionately, gently, lovingly.

Gripping tightly on his teenage cock, I gently squeezed its thickness. Slowly I rolled the foreskin back and forth over the head while my tongue continued to explore the softness of his mouth.

I felt Matt's body relax as he succumbed to the pleasure of being tossed by another guy for the very first time. He was so ecstatically subdued for a brief moment I thought he'd fainted. I soon brought him back to life with strokes of his sensitive balls followed by more meaningful tossing.

Keen to have a throbbing cock in his own hand, Matt slipped from my lap. Swiftly, he sent his fingers down to my crotch and began to toss me through my uniform. It was obvious he was new to wanking guys because he was squeezing far too hard. I knew he couldn't help it, it was his first sexual encounter and he was on fire.

My stifled grunt of complaint caused him to pull his mouth from mine. "Sorry," he breathlessly apologised when he realised his error.

A smile of reassurance from me, and our mouths were soon back together, his fingers tossing my cock less painfully as he continued to wank me through my bell-bottoms. My own fingers were more kind to his cock and oodles of pre-come was oozing over my fingers and onto his soft belly.

I could hardly wait to peel his wet suit from his body and send my mouth over the head of his brilliant cock and suck it to its thick and throbbing base. Suck it until he came. Still I held back.

While we kissed, Matt's clumsy fingers had managed to free my cock. It too was moist, sticky, and dribbling profusely. He pulled his mouth away from mine and apologised for almost breaking the shaft in two when he'd impatiently tugged it through the fly.

Briefly, he studied what he held in his hand. "Wow!" he delighted, rubbing his thumb over the sticky slit.

"Big enough?" I rather boasted. I took his smile as one of satisfaction.

We resumed our kissing, something he appeared to enjoy immensely and was extremely adept. A good deal more tenderly this time, his fingers worked my cock, his thumb continuously rubbing the pre-come around the foreskin and lubricating the head while he tossed.

His whimpers of pleasure became increasingly frequent when I increased pace and brought his spunk ever higher. "That's nice," he remarked, all innocently.

Sometimes the brain can be a right bummer and throw a reality spanner into the works at most unwanted moments. Why mine should remind me at a wonderful time like this that I was on watch, and should have been back on the flag deck by now, I've no idea. I guess it was saying that time was running out and I should ditch the preliminaries and get on with it.

I needed to know exactly how much of that precious time I had but couldn't see my watch, my wrist attached to my tossing hand and happily buried in a wet suit. Not wishing to interrupt our kissing and tossing, I gently turned both our heads and began a search for the obligatory clock that every office had.

I found the miserable machine, all brass and highly polished, ticking on the port bulkhead. "You've got fifteen minutes!" it screamed.

It was a tough decision but I knew we'd have to finish this later. Reluctantly, I pulled our mouths apart. Matt's face was the happiest yet, all cherry-red from excitement and pleasure. He looked like a boy who had just found hidden treasure as he lovingly gazed into my eyes. I took a deep breath, preparing to break the bad news and tell him we'd have to make fresh arrangements.

"Ever been sucked by a guy?" he casually asked before I could open my mouth, his expression keen, his attention focussed on my cock as he enthusiastically squeezed.

I couldn't believe my ears. When I'd least expected it he'd bowled me a googly. I was stumped!

I could, should have told him I needed to return to my duty immediately. I might have told him the truth and that I'd had more blowjobs by guys than he had hair around his delicious cock or under his armpits. Instead, I simply replied, "Never! This is the first time I've even wanked with a guy."

I did a damn good job of looking surprised when he innocently informed me this was his first time with a guy. His keen and unexpected offer to give me my very first blowjob was not helpful to one who was planning to return to his duty. My own sedated invitation for him to go right ahead and give me one, most surely wasn't.

I think Matt might have detected my urgency to get back to my duty. Then again, it might have been my unmistakable desire for him to have his delicious mouth sliding up and down the length of my cock that he'd sensed. Before I had time to make the difficult decision whether I should get a damn good blowjob or return to work, he'd swiftly bent his head and had begun to mouth my cock with breathtaking swirls of his magnificent tongue.

"That's great," I praised, rewarding Matt with gasps of delight and strokes to the back of his neck when the first two inches my cock were gratifyingly consumed by his eager mouth.

"Feel nice?" was his brief interrogation between sucks; obviously pleased he was pleasing me.

Yes, it was nice, incredibly nice after such a long time of celibacy. But it was clear he'd never blown a guy before, the lack of depth the culprit. "Great, Matt. Just great," I praised again, positive things would improve when a mouthful of my spunk was up for grabs.

For the first few minutes, it was more like lollipop licking than a fully-fledged blowjob as he concentrated on the head. I worked ever faster on his own cock to help build his desire to suck me more passionately; suck me to the base. "Deeper Matt. Go deeper," I eventually encouraged, my hand doing a quick excursion to my cock and pulling the foreskin back for extra sensitivity.

I continued to mouth words of encouragement and moans of satisfaction as I sent his foreskin flashing back and forth. Soon his legs were trembling when the pleasure of getting tossed, while sucking on a cock, set his groin afire. It wasn't long before two swallowed inches became three, then four, then four and a bit—his mouth bobbing swiftly and smoothly as he sucked and savoured and searched for my spunk.

"Great, Matt. Fantastic!" I continued to praise, pounding his cock in sync with his sucking.

"Uhmmm," he murmured; his excitement mounting as he slurped and sucked.

I was still craving more depth; wanting to give him all I had. On Matt's next fantastic swallow, I gripped the back of his head and pressed down. An extra inch slipped between his lips. My cock wasn't tonsil deep but he still gagged. Before he had time to complain, I swiftly fed another succulent inch into his fantastic sucking mouth.

With greater enthusiasm, he worked my cock between his lips. Deeper and deeper it sank into his palate. With rapid thrusts, I continued to feed it back and forth into his gorgeous face. Meanwhile, my fingers thrashed ever more frantically on his cock, my thumb working his pre-come around the sensitive bud and bringing it to bursting.

"Take it all, Matt!" I sang, confident he could swallow the rest. Still he held back.

Soon the duel action of me rubbing his cock, while thrusting mine into his angelic face, had him writhing excitedly. Evermore he was whimpering with ecstatic pleasure as his spunk began to rise. I knew it wouldn't be long before his teenage juices splattered over his silky tummy, not long before my own hot spunk ladled over his lavishing tongue.

I continued to bring him to the brink with my tossing, a telltale bubble of real spunk spilling from his cock and over my thumb. More uncontrollable whimpers of delight issued from his mouth and he began to suck more savagely; aroused like never before in his teenage life. It was time to feed him the whole length.

Releasing my own yelp of pleasure on his next downward thrust, I gripped the back of his head and began to push. This time every inch of cock slipped smoothly down his throat, passed his tonsils and beyond. Without complaint, he buried his mouth deep into my pubic bush, smothering them with spittle and pre-come, sucking and savouring every succulent centimetre.

Consumed with lustful greed, I held Matt's head tightly and continued thrusting my cock ferociously back and forth into his beautiful face. I felt my spunk spiralling upward as it prepared to fire. Another series of ecstatic moans accompanied a further eruption of pre-come jettisoning from Matt's tingling cock. I sensed the real stuff—his creamy teenage spunk—was on its way.

I released my hold on his head and surrendered control. Gratifyingly, he feasted, devouring my cock to the base; greedily and gluttonously gorging on every mouth-watering morsel, keen to empty my aching balls into his sucking mouth.

My balls began to tighten with an indescribable sensitivity. I felt the head of my cock swell to capacity when my spunk prepared to let fly and gush down his massaging throat. "I'm coming!" I cried, gripping his head forcefully when his mouth pushed down.

Just as I was about to shoot, Matt's head unexpectedly pulled clear of my cock. I could have slapped the beautiful bugger because of it. Surely he wasn't one of those lads who couldn't swallow *or* spit?

"I thought you were coming? I was!" I kind of cursed.

His fingers began to squeeze my cock to stem the flow of spunk. "Sorry." He sat up; his gorgeous mouth and chin covered in spittle.

"Something wrong?" I asked more calmly.

"I wanna make it better for me." He apologised again, urgently tugging my hand from within his wet suit while gently rubbing my cock.

How could I have been so selfish? It seemed to have escaped my mind he might have wanted to be sucked as well, might have wanted us to come in each other's mouths at the same time. I'd been in such a rush to satisfy my own lust I hadn't even seen any of his body apart from his back and face.

"'Course," I said, giving him a peck on the nose.

Instantly, the prospect of peeling away his wet suit and revealing that treasure-of-a-body became more than appealing. Decorating his smooth and hairless pecs, I hoped to find a pair of tiny nipple buds. How much he was going to enjoy having them licked and nibbled until they became excited and firm. A taught but soft, white-as-baby-talc tummy would be the next wonderful delicacy for me to delight in. Smooth and tender, it would lead me to a bush of fluffy hair where I'd find the masterpiece that I'd been tossing and teasing for the past ten minutes. I already knew how long and thick it was, but seeing it in the flesh and in all its glory was something quite different. My excitement increased and my mouth began to water at the prospect of pushing my lips far over the fat and throbbing length. I could hardly wait to start peeling.

While Matt passionately kissed my mouth, his cock still horny and hard, I began to tease the wet suit from his body, easing it over his shoulders and arms. After I'd managed to glimpse those first treasures—the tiny nipples studs sitting on his white chest—and was on my journey to his soft tummy and juicy cock he again dampened the moment by requesting me to stop.

"What's up?" I asked, my frustration more than evident.

Matt smiled rather shyly. "Can I be zipped up?"

The light in my brain suddenly shone brightly. Hell, I needed to go back to Sex School. It should have been obvious from the start the wet suit was his thing. I might have guessed he probably came here late at night to live out fantasies of having his other diving mates doing all sorts of naughty and wonderful things to him while dressed in it. I dread to think what the inside looked like.

I gave him another apologising kiss and squeezed his cock. "You should have told me earlier." I was more aware than ever the unforgiving clock was still counting down. Keenly, I began redressing him.

Disappointed to see his tender flesh disappear, I folded the wet suit back over his shoulders and around his slender neck. Reaching behind his back, I pulled the zipper up. I wasn't sure if it was a good idea to zip him up, it being the cause of his troubles in the first place.

His treasured torso now hidden from my view, I only had memories of those nipple buds and smooth chest to go on—bad news for me, good news for him, apparently.

Reaching down and fondling the incredible rubber mound still hiding his cock from my hungry gaze, I checked if restricted by the skin-tight wet suit had produced any developments. The answer was a resounding, yes. His cock, now bullet hard, was fighting against the restrictive rubber garment and outlining the thick girth splendidly, especially the considerable head.

I glimpsed the wretched clock ticking away on the bulkhead. Unsympathetically it continued to count down the last few minutes of my watch. "Ready?" I asked keen to get on with it.

Matt's lips parted slightly. He smiled knowingly. His exquisite tongue whipped across his mouth, again licking at the fading blemish. "Am now," he delighted, lying back on the bench, indicating we should take a sixty-nine position

We were back on track. A two-minute sexual mile was about to make the record books. Make a couple of sailors happy.

It was obvious how good the sex was for Matt, his squeals, moans, and whimpers of delight getting louder and louder. Ravenously, he sucked to the base of my cock, as if it were the last thing he would ever eat. For me the excitement was just as fantastic, the torment and torture of his tight wet suit, and the desire to tear it to shreds and feast on his cock, sending me into a frenzy of fantastic sexual frustration the likes of which I'd never experienced.

Crazily I chewed on enormous rubber mound, biting as hard as I could into the restricted cock. Desperately I gnawed on the bulging head and shaft, the rubber making the magnificent beast appear even bigger than it already was. All the while Matt manoeuvred his mouth magnificently, manipulating the head of my cock with his tongue before sucking down to his fingers, wrapped tightly around my balls like a steel cock ring.

Keenly I gripped his firm young buttocks and chewed on his cock while thrusting my own deep down his throat. I knew how desperately I wanted to fuck those mounds of succulent virgin flesh. The thought of that made me even crazier with my carnivorous attack on his rubbered up dick. If I carried on the way I was, he'd need to check for punctures when we'd done.

"I'd love to fuck your arse," I gasped, driving myself crazy as I probed and prodded his buttocks, bringing my spunk to the tip of my cock, eager to send it sailing down his throat.

A muffled, "Toss me," emitted from Matt's cock-filled mouth when he came close to coming.

Obeying my youth, I grasped his cock and began thrashing it like crazy through its rubber prison, my other hand still gripping firmly onto those wonderful buttocks and frantically squeezing. All the while, my mouth continued to gnaw into the enormous hidden cock head, keen to devour the sensitive flesh.

"Oh, God!" squealed my teenager, releasing his cock ring grip on my balls and pushing his mouth hard against my pubics.

I felt his throat muscles tighten around the head of my cock and begin massaging it as he swallowed hard. "That's it, Matt!" I gasped.

Matt didn't have to tell me he was on the brink of coming. His whole body was alive from the incredible thrill of me fucking his face and that of his own restrictive pleasures. Already his thighs had begun to shake and quiver as he prepared to unleash his spunk. A whoop of ecstatic joy rushed from his mouth.

The sound of his excitement fired me further. More urgently than before, I began to bite and suck on the head of his rubbered-up cock. His buttocks began to tighten, preparing to add firepower to his delivery, ready to fill his wet suit with salvos of sticky spunk.

My balls tingled at the thought of him coming. I withdrew the head of my cock back to his lips as I prepared to dump my own deluge of spunk into his sucking mouth. "I'm there!" I gasped.

The first flash of his fantastic tongue around the tingling bud was enough bring me off. Like a speeding bullet, my spunk sailed from the eye of my cock and hit the back of his throat. I felt his own sex expand excitedly against the restrictive rubber when his mouth filled to overflowing with spunk. Savagely I bit into the swelling mound eager to bring us off together.

Shrill squeals escaped Matt's mouth. I felt the head of his cock pumping against my mouth as he siphoned his spunk into his wet suit. Frantically I licked and chewed on the rubber, my mind imagining the delicious spunk splattering all over his hidden tummy. Several more spurts of spunk sailed from my own cock into his sensational sucking mouth. Happy to receive a second helping, Matt's buttocks went into spasm when his own cock delivered more, more and yet more of his own teenage juices.

Exhausted, my teenage swimmer fell away from me, a decent helping of spunk around his mouth. "That was fantastic," he elated, licking his lips. "Simply fantastic."

I quickly brought my lips onto his and helped lick my spunk away. "You come?" I asked, although I knew the answer.

"Come? I never knew I could shoot so much spunk. Be dry for a month after that."

"I doubt it," I said, giving his glorious cock another squeeze, sending him into a sensitive shiver. "Bet I could bring you off right now."

Matt's eyes lit up. "Reckon?"

The unforgiving seconds continued their countdown. I pointed to the clock on the wall. "Got to go."

Matt gave my cock a squeeze before I tucked it away. "Pity."

There was barely time for a quick embrace and kiss, less than thirty seconds for me to get back to the flag deck. We agreed to meet up again. I thought it best and unzipped his wet suit before leaving. I didn't want some other lustful sailor placed in such a wonderful predicament as I'd been.

"I'm off," I said, reluctant to leave and wishing there was time to do it all again.

Matt gripped my wrist as I went to leave. "What's your name?"

"Sandy," I said, sneaking another kiss and a handful of cock.

He gave me his naughty smile. "Sure it's not Spunky?"

I laughed. "Must run, Matt. See you soon."

I stepped back into the adjacent room. Matt called after me as I went to open the door leading to the upper deck. Turning around, the vision of his total nakedness greeted me—his broad shoulders and developing chest; his tight little tummy all white and welcoming; his small tuft of fluffy pubics; finally, that lovely thick cock, still hard and dribbling spunk.

Matt gave me a wink. "Make sure you do." He gave me a wank-provoking twirl. Bending over, he slapped his arse. "Or you won't get this."

My stride was buoyant and my spirit high as I bounced back to the flag deck. Who needs shore leave? I thought. Already I was champing at the bit to have sex with Matt again. He'd just made sure of that. And now that I'd seen that tight little arse... it would be my *cock* rubbered up next time and not his delightful body.

WHIPCRACKAWAY

I suppose I should fill you in on the situation on board ship before I tell you about the fun. Six months on and we are still in Pompey. Tommy and I haven't been ashore together for some while, not since I'd spotted the argument in the Burma Way. He'd turned into a bit of a grump due to his ongoing battle with Purdy and wasn't the best of company. Truth was he could be damn difficult and I was starting to worry about him. Purdy was forever pressganging him into some very nasty chores, punishments for debatable crimes. There's not a lot you can do in those situations, just offer support. You cannot let another sailor's problems affect your own life or the whole, damn ship would be constantly in the doldrums. Usually, if you acted as if you didn't care, the person giving you grief would eventually find another victim. I guess Tommy still had a lot to learn.

I hadn't been ashore with Freckles either, the randy little sod. Some lass with tits bigger than his tasty little buttocks had bludgeoned him senseless with them. Young and impressionable, he was now cock-over-balls in love and was banging her pussy like he was up for the *Fuck Bunny of the Year* award. Regularly he'd be giving her a knee-trembler that would measure 9.5 on the Richter scale, the aftershocks more than evident as he tossed himself tinderbox dry on the nights he couldn't meet her. All was not lost, though. Once we were back at sea and he was pining for her pussy, I could be very formidable when it came to looking fanny faced. If needs be, I could even stop shaving for a week. All things being equal, I'd get my turn.

Matt still hadn't managed to arrange for me to give him the baby he so richly deserved. Even on a small ship, you could go weeks without bumping into someone. I'd seen him sitting on a pontoon, mouth spread invitingly wide with breathing equipment, as he prepared to do a bit of diving beneath the ship. He'd made a circle with his fingers before he plunged into the water. I hoped all his diving buddies weren't fucking him and he wasn't referring to the size of his hole. I'd made the same signal in acknowledgement but improved it by pushing my finger back and forth through the circle. I think a smile issued from his overfilled mouth before he fell backward into the sea.

So, to the fun. Remember how I told you I'd done a bit of porn on my last ship. Well, Dave the porn guru had managed to track me down and had invited me for a day at the races. "A day that would be fun and profitable." And this is where I was now, up on Trundle Hill at Goodwood racetrack, ready to lose my shirt and with any luck my jeans and boxer briefs as well.

Goodwood is a fantastic racecourse. I'd been to others—Ascot, Epsom and a few more besides. On Derby

Day at Epsom, I'd worn my uniform and got as drunk as a skunk before the racing even started. The National Anthem woke me from my stupor, accompanied by a policeman's boot nudging into my back.

As I stood, to my horror the Queen and her entourage were just feet away as they travelled down the turf in their horse drawn carriages. I'll never forget the look on that copper's face when I stood to attention and saluted, my body swaying from side to side as if I was in a force-nine gale. Not the best of ambassadors for the Senior Service, me thinks.

No such thing was going to happen today. For a start, there was no Queen here. Actually, there were loads. Also, I'd dumped my uniform and was kitted out in jeans, T-shirt, and trainers. And, unlike previous race outings, I had some extra cash because Dave had posted me a fifty quid sweetener, telling me it was a gift. Previous experience also told me that he hadn't brought me here for his health, or mine, and more dosh—in the form of wages—would be winging its way before the day was done.

Dave was rich, disgustingly so, profits from his porn empire. Even so, he was a real down-to-earth guy who didn't put on any fancy flourishes of fame to impress others. I guess it was because he was from London's East End and, unlike your stereotypical rich East Ender, he didn't drape himself in chunks of gold to prove the fact. As they say in his part of the world, he was 'sorted'.

It will come as no surprise, then, instead of being in some posh box with waiters and bum-licking cronies creeping all over us as we sank champagne and swallowed oysters, we were up on Trundle Hill with the poorer folk. Cans of lager and burgers in hand, we were having stacks fun drooling and dribbling over the delightful farmer types, almost all of whom would have fitted nicely into one of Dave's disgusting and delightful *Ploughman's Lunch* series of videos.

I bustled my way between a couple of shorts-clad youths that had very spankable bottoms. "See anything you fancy, Dave?" I asked, nodding toward the pair of delightful delicacies who were standing in front of TUSSOCKS bookmaker.

"Fair Trade. Looks good to me," Dave replied, ticking his race card.

I fanned my face with mine. "Can't argue with that. Fair trade as far as I'm concerned. Fancy any of the horses?"

Dave grinned and pulled a wad of fifties from his wallet. "Haven't changed, have you? Still the randy bugger."

I bent toward him and tapped his wallet. "Think they're rent, do you? Reckon you'll need a lot more than that for the pair of them."

Dave gave my bum a crafty squeeze. "Plenty of time for that." He handed me yet another twenty. "Pick a nag. First one's on me."

At least five hundred quid flicked through Dave's and then the bookie's fingers when he placed his bet on Fair Trade. Neither of them batted an eyelid. It was peanuts to both. Not so a sailor pauper like me. I shook my head, almost in disgust, at such an amount of money placed on a single nag.

Trying to look as though I knew what I was doing, I eased my body between the spankable lads. "Twenty to win…" I shot an informative glance toward the youth on my right, "Pretty Boy." With a grin, I temporarily handed Mr Tussocks my cash while continuing to study the delightful face belonging to the cuter of the two bottoms for any response.

A snigger spilled from the youth on my left when I pulled back to Dave. "Fruit," he informed his mate, ensuring I heard his derogatory remark.

I parried his statement with a wry smile. I'd heard a lot worse. Anyway, I knew I could have lashed him to death with my tongue had I wanted to create a scene and make him look as ignorant as he obviously was. Yes, I was a fruit and happy to be one. I also knew that if lovely lad squeezed me long enough he'd get a decent helping of juice all right. Truth be told I could shag him out of sight on a good day and still have some left over for his mate.

The horses were on their way to the start. The race was a three-mile affair and the stalls were way off in the distance. Dave and I walked further up the hill to get a good all round view of the racecourse. "Lend us your bins," I asked, giving them a tug.

Dave laughed when he handed me his binoculars. "Want to see what a pot of glue looks like, do you?"

"Not bothered." I put the glasses to my eyes. "It's the jockey's bums I wanna see."

"Ah, yes," said Dave, his expression teasing. "I remember you saying you had a thing about jockeys. Managed to bed one yet?"

"Only knob jockeys. Do they count?"

"Not if they've never ridden a horse, they don't."

"How about the one who rode me all the way to Malta on my last ship? Boy, could he ride a wave at speed."

"Not even if he rode you all the way to Banbury Cross. Nope, an apprentice jockey is a classy ride you'll never forget, the occasional stable lad too."

I rubbed my cock. "You better stop now or I'm gonna embarrass us both with this beautiful boner I'm starting sport."

Dave patted my bum. "From what I remember you've always been a walking hard-on." He borrowed his binoculars and had a gander at his own horse.

"How about a disc jockey? Took one of them for a spin. Hole was well slack, though. Nearly vanished. A case of Black Hole Syndrome," I continued with my list of humorous shags.

An announcement warning of the start of the race ceased our banter. Some three minutes later a rush of hooves thundering over the turf saw the horses enter the final furlong.

Dave stood beside me as calm as the Dead Sea as Fair Trade began to eat up the rest of the field. Me? Shirley Temple on speed would just about sum it up. I was shouting and screaming for the jockey to shove a bloody rocket up Pretty Boy's arse or get off and push the lazy bugger. It was farther back than last. It was in the previous race.

'Fair Trade' came gurgling through the speakers when it was announced the winner. I ripped my ticket to shreds and let the pieces flutter to the ground. "I've seen a rocking horse run faster!" I cursed my nag, keen to get my gambler's loosing spirit going. "I could have beaten it myself."

Dave shoved his winning ticket into his back pocket without ceremony. "Told you Pretty Boy was a donkey.

Saw them boiling a pot to shove the old bugger in." He gave me a wink. "Not to worry, it's only money."

I butted my shoulder against his, and laughed. "And it's all yours."

Between races, we ambled over the Trundle, me eyeing up possible trade, Dave searching for future stars no doubt. He wouldn't be looking for sex. He had a devoted boyfriend at home. A youth that he was crazily in love with.

I did a couple of trips to the cottages. It was a pointless exercise apart from peeing. They were those Tardis types. Single metal cubicles with no glory holes and barely room enough for one. They were also disgusting and stank worse than some salty sailor's sweaty nix. Even a randy sod like me would think twice about doing a blowjob in one.

Mr Tussocks hung onto another ten quid of my cash on the next two races. Even Dave had lost his touch with only a second and a third. I still had forty quid left to blow without touching my own cash. After tucking into another beer and burger apiece, the pair of us headed down the hill, striding between scrumptious youths bunking school, back to the only winners on the course, the bookies.

"Twenty-four runners in this race." I waved my card. "It'll be a bloody miracle if I find the winner this time."

Dave was studying his race card, but his eyes appeared to be caressing a blond lad who was wearing a pair of hot pant shorts that must have been painted on. "What you got left of that money?" he asked.

I told him I had forty.

"Put the lot on number nine," he said, his eyes not wandering from hot pant boy's bottom.

I ran a finger down my race card to number nine. WHIPCRACKAWAY - JAMIE O'LEARY (A) (7) - 7-10. This told me my jockey was an apprentice carrying seven stone ten pounds. Being such, he had a seven-pound allowance. This was also Whipcrackaway's first race. I suspected it was probably another pot of glue.

I glanced up at Mr Tussocks betting forecast. It was twenty to one. I waved my card at Dave. "You sure?"

Dave touched his nose. "Trust me."

"I'm a doctor," I tossed in the punch line.

Short of sticking a pin in the card, I had no idea of the possible winner. Obeying my man, I reluctantly handed another forty quid over to the ever-smiling Mr Tussocks. Worryingly, Dave didn't have a bet.

We retook our station at the top of Trundle.

"They're under Starter's orders... and they're off!" Bellowed from a barrage of speakers and bounced up Trundle Hill.

With a thunder of hooves, the horses came galloping around the first bend before heading back around the course. Mine was last but one. I studied my horse through Dave's binoculars; my jockey's golden silks catching the breeze as he raced. I couldn't believe what I was seeing.

"My jockey's a boy, Dave!" I complained. Then, more appreciatively, "Dishy little bum though. And a real cutie." I gave Dave a nudge. "Reckon he's got more chance of getting fucked than he has of winning this race."

Dave made no comment.

With my concentration focussed on my jockey's bottom rather than the race, before I knew it the horses were back in the straight. The voice behind the speakers began giving his commentary more urgency as they moved into the final furlongs—submerged in a tub of bath water by the sound of it.

"Sid Snot by a length from Tickle Me Pink. Behind those, all in a bunch, Marry Me, Mr Magic, Vision On and Tittle Tattle. Moving up the field on the outside comes Whipcrackaway."

My jockey began slapping his horse more times than I could count. "He's gonna flog the bugger to death," I alarmed. "The poor thing."

"Bit naughty with a whip, is Jamie," Dave informed.

His comment went ignored, my concentration having become riveted on my ever-improving nag as Jamie continued to belt it. Already it had sped by three horses. Predictably, Dave stayed as. I suspected it was because he hadn't had a bet.

Not so me, I'd gone back into my Shirley Temple on speed routine, this time with greater animation. The only word ringing in my ears was *Whipcrackaway* as it was repeated over and over by an equally excited announcer, and my forty quid began to pass horse after horse after horse.

"Come on, Jamie. Hit the bugger harder!" I heartlessly yelled, visions of my pot of gold coming to the boil.

My body began shaking uncontrollably. You'd have thought I was in the middle of a brilliant fuck rather than watching a bunch of nags. I'd even broken into a sweat from jumping up and down. Dave remained like block of ice.

"Come on Jamie!" I screamed even louder. "Hit the bugger again!"

The underwater commentary reached fever pitch. "It's neck and neck. Whipcrackaway and Beat Me Senseless. Beat Me Senseless and Whipcrackaway." I almost tore my ticket in two with the excitement. "There's nothing in it as they come to the post. Neck and neck. It's..." An unbearably long pause interrupted the manic commentary. "It's a photo... photo between number one, Beat Me Senseless and number nine, Whipcrackaway."

My backside went down on the grass with a heavy bump. "You what? You're bloody joking!" I pointed to the heavens and waved my ticket. "Why are you punishing me like this?"

Dave sat down beside me. "Who's a rich boy, then?"

"No way. I don't have that sort of luck. Not with money, I don't."

Dave nodded to Mr Tussocks who was shouting out odds. "Listen to the betting on the photo. Whipcrackaway's got it all right."

My expression changed to one of optimism. "You sure?"

Dave grinned. "As sure as I am that you're no virgin."

After an eternity, the speakers began to crackle and come back to life. "Result." I gripped Dave's leg and squeezed it hard. "First..." My hands moved to my ears and covered them. "Number nine... Whipcrackaway. Second. Beat Me Senseless...."

The joy of winning was too much for me. I jumped on Dave, sending his ice cream flying into the air. "I'm rich!" I gleefully yelped, kissing his cheek while frantically waving my beaten up ticket in his face. "Good on you, Jamie boy. You can ride my ass any day of the week."

I leapt to my feet and rushed toward Mr Tussocks before the judge could change his mind and reverse the placings. He beamed a big cuddly smile at me when I handed him my ticket. Unbearably, I had to wait until after the weigh-in before he counted just short of eight hundred and forty quid into my palm. I was so excited I even shook his hand. Had he been a youth I reckon I would have kissed him.

I began shoving the notes into my pocket. My fingers trembled with excitement. "I'd have brought a purse if I'd known I'd win so much cash." Mr Tussocks smiled at my camp remark. He'd seen and heard it all before. For sure, he wasn't upset at my big win. With a twenty-to-one outsider coming home, he'd cleaned up.

I waved my race card. "Next race," I sang, happy to start losing money again.

Dave grabbed my arm and dragged me away. "That's your lot, you greedy bugger. Got important stuff to do."

"But there's still five races."

"My grandmother always told me to quit when ahead," warned Dave.

I poked his tummy. "That's funny, mine always told me never to quit when I was giving head."

Dave was still laughing as we made our way through the exit and over to his parked convertible. In a matter of minutes, the smart and expensive vehicle had us speeding along winding country lanes. In less than an hour, we were zipping through a dense wood and along a gravel drive that led to the front door of one of Dave's many farmhouse retreats.

"Get this," I remarked on seeing the enormous and enchanting old farmhouse with its assortment of barns, stables and other impressive outhouses dotted about. "Wanna boyfriend?"

Dave didn't comment. "Come on." Jumping out of the car, he headed toward a mediaeval-looking door that had chunky black hinges and horse's head door-knocker.

As we entered the vast kitchen, I was greeted by a coal-burning Aga, a football pitch of a breakfast table, enough copper pots and pans to start a restaurant and a load of other cooking paraphernalia. I touched my fore-lock. "What, no servants, me lud?"

Dave looked preoccupied. He immediately picked up the phone and dialled out. "Help yourself to booze," he said, pointing toward a fridge-freezer the size of a small flat.

I chose cold beer and cracked a can of ordinary strength ale. I left Dave to make his own choice until after he'd finished his call. I didn't eavesdrop and con-tinued to study the smart room, noting the pictures of tasty lads decorating the walls, strategically placed be-tween strings of garlic and other kitchen utensils. I sus-pected the youths were a gallery of the boys Dave had turned into porn stars—trophies to the trade. Indeed, I'd recognised one lad who was in the last movie I'd made. I recalled he was nicknamed Tippex, something to do with him being good at rubbing things off.

"You can take a shower and then we'll get to it," Dave commanded without actually doing so after he'd completed his call. "I like my boys nice and clean before a shoot."

I gave my armpits a sniff. Fermenting juices from my racecourse excitement were more than apparent. I pinched my nose. "Good idea, boss."

About an acre of highly polished, woodblock flooring led us across the hall, to a matching staircase. Signed photographs of famous people watched us as we climbed. A further bounce on Royal-red, inch thick carpet took us along another passage about a mile long and delivered us outside adjacent rooms. "Use this guest's room," said Dave, tapping on the door to his right. "You'll find everything you need inside."

I chopped off a salute. "Aye, aye, Cap'n."

Dave paused before entering his room. "Oh! There's a pair of shorts and a T-shirt lying on the bed, if you'd like to slip into those after you've showered. I'll meet you downstairs when you're done." Ever the perfectionist, Dave had planned ahead.

I simply nodded in acknowledgement and bade him a temporary farewell as I stepped inside the luxurious room. Let's face it I knew why I was here. That is, I knew I was here to make a porno. With whom, had yet to be revealed. It wouldn't be with Dave that was sure.

Dave was sitting in the kitchen when I strolled in, sipping champagne by the looks of things. He was dressed in Khaki shorts and a sloppy-joe top. Memory reminded me this was his *director's* outfit. "Freshened up?" he asked, his face all smiles.

"And ready to blow," I replied, giving him a quick twirl so's he could see the effect of the tightest pair of shorts on the planet he'd kindly asked me to squeeze my bottom inside. The torn white T-shirt was quite revealing too, a nipple showing through, the hem sitting sexily around my midriff at about two inches above my navel.

Dave filled another glass with champagne and handed it over. "To your win," he toasted.

I clinked my glass against his. "Talking of winners… where did you get a tip like that?" I shook my head, still unable to believe it. "Twenty-to-one and all."

"Easy," said Dave, his eyes sparkling.

"Well?"

He gave me a knowing grin. "I own Whipcrackaway. She made me a tidy little nest egg today, bless her." He pointed down the hall to a cabinet filled with silverware. "And another trinket for my box."

"Whipcrackaway," I toasted, taking a good gulp of the bubbly stuff, sending it fizzing up my nose. I raised my glass again. "Not forgetting the juicy little Jamie jockey, bless her."

Dave glanced up at the kitchen clock. He grabbed a bucket, opened the refrigerator, and began filling it with ice from the automatic dispenser. Withdrawing more champagne from the cooler, he stuck one bottle in the bucket and handed the other two to me. "Fit?" he asked, selecting another champagne glass to add to the one we each held.

"For what?" I asked, feigning innocence.

"To make a great movie, of course." He gave me a concerned look. "You are up for it… aren't you? You must have guessed why you're here?"

I reassured him with a smile. "'Course I know why I'm here. Just teasing. Me refuse a fuck?"

"Great. Thought you couldn't resist. Five hundred okay?"

"Five hundred fucks?"

Dave laughed. "Five hundred quid, you slag."

"What? I'd screw a cage of gorillas for that amount of cash."

"Good. Let's get them apes rolling then." I knew there was a primate joke in there somewhere. Obviously Dave did too.

AWAY IN A MANGER

A saunter into the sunshine saw us bypass a row of thatched buildings, until we reached a disused stable where Dave had already set things up. Several lamps were pointing in the direction of the main filming area and ready to illuminate the set. Four remote controlled cameras had been strategically placed between them. Another handheld job lay on his chair. Dave would use this for his close up sucking, fucking and come shots. Other items of interest included half-a-dozen straw bales forming a bed-like structure; a saddle slung over several more bales, plenty of protection and lube, and paper sheets that I took to be the script. The only thing missing was the rest of the cast.

"You sure know how to spoil a boy," I quipped, attempting to bounce on the makeshift bed.

"Sure do." He sat beside me, working a champagne cork from the bottle. *Pop* it suddenly went, missing a camera before bouncing off a lamp and causing me to duck when it flew over my head.

Dave poured my drink. I then twigged there was only one extra glass. If my assumption was correct, this wasn't going to be another of his *Ploughman's Lunch* farmer orgies as previously thought, but a fantastic one on one, with good old me as one of the ones.

A surge of enthusiasm gripped my cock and sent it springing upward. "Who am I fucking?" I keenly asked.

"Patients, dear boy, patients," was Dave's cruel reply as he went about checking his equipment. I had no need to check my own equipment. That was now completely up but not yet running.

Ten minutes of minor adjustments and Dave was happy with his angles, lighting, and other photographic whims. A flick of a switch and the lighting was temporarily doused. No sooner had he sat back down and picked up his drink, when a car could be heard crunching on the gravel drive. The slamming door caused me to spill champagne all over my face. Unlike me, first night nerves were taking hold.

I rose nervously to my feet. Dave indicated that I should stay put. I glanced up at him, seeking reassurance. He gave me a crafty wink as he headed toward the door to greet his mystery guest, again gesturing for me to stay where I was. For reasons known only to him, the rotten bugger wanted me to suffer in silence.

My heart was pounding against my ribs like a pneumatic drill. There was no reason at all why I should be so nervous. It wasn't the prospect of performing sex in public, so to speak. Rather, the unanswered question as to what delightful creature I would be performing it with. I refilled my glass then emptied it in a single gulp when I suddenly thought, "Stable! Surely it won't be a horse? Whipcrackaway."

Dave's pleasant voice could be clearly heard as he returned to the stable. Between his deeper tones, a much softer and sweeter sound occasionally intervened. My trained ear told me that it belonged to a youth. My heart changed gear and began to skip and dance in excited flutters. My date was approaching. More importantly, it had two legs.

Dave's tall and broad torso darkened the sunlit doorway first, his face grinning wildly. Walking behind him, and hidden from my view, was his mystery guest. Still delighting in teasing me, they remained that way until both stood just a few feet from my trembling self. It was only then that Dave reached back and invited his guest to the fore.

I almost came in my pants! It must have been a good thirty seconds before I breathed again, the shock so great. At Dave's side—looking boyish, innocent, and so adorable that he'd make Freckles look like an old man—stood a stunning, sexy and unbelievably seducible youth ever. None other than my hero of the day, the golden-silked, five foot figure of my teenage jockey Jamie O'Leary.

"Jamie, meet Sandy. Your sailor boy supreme," Dave introduced, somewhat over-egging my popularity pudding.

I tried to stand and introduce myself to the youth but my legs had ceased to work. Before I had a chance to stick out my hand, a pair of extremely strong arms quickly wrapped around my body and began to hug me tightly. Surprising me further, his unexpected intimacy was then followed by a pale-lipped mouth pressing against my own. It seemed to kiss me longer than your average formal greeting.

"Hi, Sandy," spoke the soft and sweet voice after our mouths separated "I've always wanted to meet a real live sailor."

When Jamie stood back up my lusting eyes immediately fixed on the incredible bulge snaking down the inside leg of his extremely tight riding breeches. Predictably, my cock exploded inside my shorts. Stunned like a rabbit in car headlights I failed to answer and simply coughed.

"And Sandy's always wanted to meet a real live jockey," Dave answered for me, giving my head a playful rub, more than aware of the wonderful state of shock he'd placed me in.

Dave suggested we sit, and sat in his director's chair, for camp rather than superiority. Lying down would have been more appropriate. Jamie took his place beside me, intimately placing his hand on my knee. Several A4 sheets were handed to the pair of us after our glasses had been filled with bubbly. Dave told us to help ourselves to booze as required. It was often a good way to relax inhibitions.

As I'd predicted, the sheets of A4 were the proposed script, a list of the major points of activity and where they should take place. Dave told us we could say whatever we wished when Jamie pointed out the lack of dialogue, reassuring us that it could be dubbed if unsuitable. He also suggested we could improvise when it came to the sex if we felt we could enhance a scene. His main objective was that the whole thing came across as sexy and raunchy, that it looked natural.

I already knew the way Dave worked. Perhaps Jamie did too. His movies were certainly believable. Often he'd approach good-looking youths on the streets—straight or gay—and offer them good money if they were prepared to make some gay porn. This way he'd get guys who really wanted to fuck each other, and not be pussyfooting around with expensive professionals and the artificial sex scenes they often produced, not to mention their regular ego tantrums.

To be honest, on paper the movie didn't appear that exciting for Dave's potential punters. According to the script, I would soon be giving my heaven sent jockey a seven-furlong fucking of his life, and him me. There was no doubt in my own mind the event most surely would be fantastic. I was so damn horny I may well have fucked Whipcrackaway had it arrived instead of Jamie.

For half an hour we supped champagne, ate nibbles and mulled over possible dialogue and the shots pertaining to them, the booze calming our nerves and evaporating any inhibitions that might be present. Jamie appeared to be showing a temporary disregard for his weight as we giggled, cuddled, drank, and ate. Didn't matter really, there would be a lot more calories sailing down his sweet young throat than a couple of glasses of bubbly and a few nibbles by the time I had done with him.

What a lovely lad Jamie was; the fuck of your dreams. He'd easily pass as a boy with his delicate lightweight body, schoolboy haircut, and bonnie innocent face. Although appearing less than barely legal, he most certainly was legal. Dave would never touch a minor. How the punters perceived the lads in his movies... "That was their affair".

"It's all above board and legal," was the first thing Dave always told his boys.

Dave stood and gave a stretch. "Right my beauties let's make a movie." He flicked a switch, practically blinding us with the strong lighting when the set was illuminated.

Jamie and me speedily cleared away the glasses and champagne and placed them out of shot. I felt my cock rise at the prospect of the wonderful sex that lay ahead. Jamie's fine helping of cock also appeared to have grown in stature, now more than ready.

A chicken suddenly scampered from a far corner and dashed through the doorway. "One of your props has just escaped," Jamie joked.

"Not mine. Don't do animals," laughed Dave.

"You wanna bet," I said, giving Jamie my first intimate touch when I pinched his bum.

Dave picked up his hand held camera and put on his serious face. "Okay, boys… know where we're going with this?" We both nodded. "Let's get to it then."

To look at him you wouldn't think it but Jamie sure was the brazen one. His hand went straight to my cock and gave it a good grope. "Give me all you've got," he whispered. "I want to remember this."

Jamie would remember it all right. Be able to watch it as much as he wanted. "You will," I said, steering my thickening cock down my thigh so it would be visible against the tight white shorts.

"Places!" sang Dave, still serious.

I took my station beside an empty stall, one of many that ran the length of the stable, just beyond the main door. My role was the lusty stable lad. Predictably, Jamie was the jockey and the son of the rich stable owner. Cap and whip in hand, he'd moved through the entrance and stood outside and out of shot.

Dave pressed a remote and all the cameras started to roll. "And.... Action!"

I picked up the hose, turned on the water, and began hosing down the red-bricked cobbled area running the length of the stable stalls. A shadow appeared in front of me when the light from the doorway became blocked. Turning toward it, the silhouetted body of apprentice jockey Jamie greeted me.

"Hi, Jamie," I acknowledged. I started to laugh. "Hear you fell off your horse again. Don't worry I'm sure you'll make a good ride one day."

Jamie was furious. "Piss off, stable slave," he barked, skating his riding cap straight at my head.

"Watch it!" I shouted, fending it away with the nozzle of the hose. A jet of water looped in the air and splattered over Jamie's golden silks.

His boyish face reddened in fury. "Idiot! I'll have you washing these silks if you're not careful."

"Better get them a lot wetter then." I began playing the jet against his chest.

Jamie rushed me, his wet silks hugging his compact and powerful chest, defining the shape of both it and his slender waist below. "My dad will sack you for that."

Before he reached me, I turned the tap full on and sent the strong jet splashing against his crotch. "Might as well do your breeches while I'm at it then."

A look of extreme anger spread over his face. Still laughing and acting like it was a game, I began to send the stream from side to side, playing it innocently against the crotch of his riding breeches. The material was so fine the colour of his cock and brown pubic bush began to show through.

Jamie wasn't amused. He slapped his whip threateningly against the side of his boot. "You just wait!"

I decided he needed cooling down further and continued to spray, again directing the powerful jet over his breeches. Jamie's cock began to grow, first in length and then in girth, slowly creeping between thigh and tight white breeches as it travelled ever downward. My lovely jockey didn't flinch or budge.

Suspecting he might be enjoying my seduction, and keen to see how much more cock he had to offer, I continued to work the jet rapidly up and down, concentrating only on the shaft. Jamie's cock continued to grow. The sight was amazing, magical, and ball-breakingly brilliant. He was getting off on my jet of massaging water.

His cock began growing—six, seven… eight-and-a-half and still rising—bloody hell *ten* incredible inches of superb and suckable cock snaking invitingly down the leg of his breeches.

I moved closer, keenly tossing Jamie with the endless torrent of water. His expression suddenly changed to thunder, his face brilliant red from embarrassment. "You're so sacked!" he screamed, sending his whip sailing by my ear and hitting the saddle when he hurled it and rushed me.

I tossed the hose toward the empty stalls. It wriggled like a snake captured by the tail. "Sacked am I? Why don't you admit it? You were loving it."

Jamie's robust little body hit mine with a thud. "Bastard!"

We started to grapple. One by one, the buttons on his silks popped open as we frantically wrestled. He spun around to escape my grasp. On my next tug, I stripped his silks clean from his back. His cock hadn't subsided. If anything, it was trying to escape his wet breeches.

Now wonderfully half-naked, I could feel Jamie's bare chest rise and fall against my own. I wrapped my arms around his waist and pressed into him. "What you need, you spoilt, stroppy little sod, is a damn good spanking."

I felt his hand groping for my cock. "You just try," he hollered. He grabbed my balls and squeezed them hard. "I'll castrate you."

He was a strong little bugger for sure, but weighing in at a mere seven stone three, he lacked the weight to back it up. Before he had time to get a decent grip on my balls, I'd spun him around, threw my arm around his neck, shoved my other hand between his thighs and under his dishy little bum, and with a good grip on that incredible ten inch cock lifted him clean off the ground and carted him away.

"Put me down! Put me down!" he protested, kicking wildly. It was only his mouth complaining, his magnificent cock was still as stiff as it could possibly be.

I carried Jamie to the saddle and slung him over. While holding the back of his neck, as he continued to struggle furiously, I reached down and picked up his whip.

Briefly, I studied his pert little bottom, its pinkness showing through the tight wet breeches. "Castrate me, would you?" With a swift thwack, I sent the whip smacking against his delicate buttock cheek.

"Aaaah!" cried my stunning little jockey. "Aaaah!" he yelped again when the second cheek was struck.

I pressed the whip against his face. "Apologise."

"Up yours!"

I set the whip smacking again, both cheeks this time. A pair of red streaks appeared through Jamie's breeches. He appeared to be struggling less than before after the whip had struck. "What did you say?"

"Just get your balls around here and I'll bite the buggers off."

I placed my hand onto his smooth bare back and held him down. I moved around the saddle and brought my crotch level with his face. "So you wanna have a good look at my dick, do you? Well, I'm here to please the young Master of the house."

Jamie raised his head, his cute face all red and flustered, his fair eyebrows and pale lips standing out against the brightness. "Nothing to look at," he belittled my endowment.

I gave his bottom another smack for his cheekiness, and tugged on the buttons of my shorts. The button on the waistband popped open. With a shake of my hips, the shorts fell to my ankles. Happy to be free my solid cock sprang upward.

The sticky head of my dick pressed into Jamie's face smearing the teenager's mouth with sticky pre-come. "Nothing to see, eh?" I slapped my solid cock from cheek to cheek, spreading the remainder of my pre-come between his parted lips.

"Fuck off!" cursed Jamie, licking his mouth and moving his head from side to side in an unconvincing attempt to dodge my slapping sex.

I raised the whip and continued to sting his arse. "Say you're sorry, Master Jamie."

His head bowed as if defeated. My balls dangled onto the nape of his neck. "I'm sorry."

I stung his backside again. "I bet you've got a right old boner going. Bigger than that stallion you fell off," I tormented. "I reckon you love being spanked. 'Spect you're dying to blow me while I'm doing it. 'Spect you want me to shove my dick deep down your throat."

I spotted Jamie's hand move toward the crotch of his breeches. I was sure he was going for his cock. Gingerly, he began to raise his head. When he glanced up at me, his pupils appeared much larger and more willing than before. "You can try," he dared, his tone seductively soft.

I brought my cock to his lips and flicked the whip against his buttocks. "Suck it!" Jamie's mouth remained shut.

With another harder thwack, Jamie's mouth opened wide. In a flash, all of my cock had vanished down his throat, his palms gripping my buttocks tightly.

Jamie pulled his mouth away and gazed pleadingly up at me, his expression one of expectation. "Spank me again… harder!"

I began to sting his bottom with gentle taps, tormenting and teasing him by keeping my cock far enough away for him not to be able to swallow the whole length. Increasing the frequency of my gentle slaps, I allowed him a few more inches. His long and clever tongue looped around the head of my cock with every provocative strike of the whip. Soon, the head was swimming in a sea of sensitivity as the velvet soft tongue flashed around the sensitive flesh, driving my spunk higher and higher up the stiffened shaft.

"Harder. Spank me harder," came Jamie's urgent request, his palms pulling eagerly at my buttocks, his neck stretching in a frantic attempt to swallow more of my cock.

Keen to please, I reached my left hand over my spankable jockey's naked back and gripped the waistband of his wet breeches. Giving them a decent tug, I pulled them toward myself. The seam vanished into the crack of Jamie's dainty bottom, the material pulling tightly over his reddened cheeks. "Anything to oblige the young Master," I said, but still refusing to feed him all of my cock.

I raised the whip. Jamie gasped with enthusiastic anticipation of it striking his backside. *Thwack* it sang as it struck the right cheek. *Thwack* it repeated on the left. "Mmmm," moaned my little man, his buttocks quivering in pleasure, his neck still stretching and his mouth hungry to eat more of my cock.

I fed a few more inches into Jamie's covetous mouth. *Thwack* sang the whip again. "Mmmm," moaned my increasingly excited jockey.

This time I cracked the whip across both of Jamie's cheeks. When his mouth opened wide in an excited gasp, I flexed my buttocks and thrust my cock deep inside his throat. "Suck the spunk out of me. Suck my balls dry," I encouraged.

Jamie's hand went for his dick and began rubbing the shaft fiercely through his breeches. Gripping tightly on the waistband—as if holding the reins of a horse—I started to build my rhythm. *Thwack* sang the whip.

Deep went my cock. *Thwack* it sang the again. Deeper went my cock.

I was in the home straight and my jockey was alive with passion. The whip continued to sing as it stung. My cock moved deeper and faster inside Jamie's slippery throat. Redder and redder became his cute little buttocks on every delicious strike. Crazily his palm pummelled and pleased his own cock, the other tugging brutally at my balls.

I could see the finishing post ahead. I felt my spunk spiralling up the shaft of my cock as it prepared to propel a plethora of palatable juices into Jamie's joyous palate. Urgency filled my whipping hand. My other gripped the back of Jamie's neck.

Thwack sang the whip. Thrust went my cock.

Thwack. Thrust.

Thwack. Thwack. Thwack. Thrust. Thrust. Thrust.

Jamie's delirious moaning increased. His hand began working ever harder as I fed him more and more of my own delicious dick. His other hand released my balls then shot a finger deep inside my hole. My head began spinning with ecstatic pleasure as I rammed my cock harder and faster into his working mouth.

Thwack sang the whip. Down to the pubics sank my tasty thick cock. *Thwack Thwack* sang the whip again. Passed throat, tongue and soft lips sped my cock as it rapidly withdrew. *Thwack Thwack Thwack* it sang again as I began thrusting my cock swiftly into Jamie's face— tip to base, tip to base, tip to base.

Spittle dribbled over my jockey's chin. His palm began tugging excitedly on my rising balls, the other thrusting several fingers deep into my hole He was desperate for me to send my spunk cascading down his massaging throat.

Repeatedly, I withdrew then buried my cock pubic deep into his gaping mouth. Simultaneously the whip spanked and stung his strong young buttocks. More and more Jamie whimpered as his wonderful mouth worked.

I barely had time for one final lash of Jamie's cute backside and another deliciously deep thrust of my cock, before I was ready to shot my stuff. "Yes!" I cried when the spunk came surging up the shaft.

"Mmmm," Jamie gurgled, keen to receive the lot.

On cue, and per script, I withdrew my cock from Jamie's sucking mouth, desperate though we both were for me to fill it to the brim. His head fell forward.

My first salvo of sweet and scrumptious spunk shot from the eye and splashed over Jamie's satin smooth back. Scooping the juices from his sensuous skin, I pushed my fingers deep into his mouth and let him suck them clean. With my cock still pumping spunk, I raised his head and brought the bud close to his mouth. His expression was electric as he parted his lips.

The next two salvos of scrumptious spunk sprayed over his joyous face. Jamie's hot soft throat took the final three rounds, his mouth slipping over the shaft of my cock and pressing greedily into my pubic bush as he sucked me dry.

"Cut!" sang Dave.

Jamie's mouth continued to massage every droplet of spunk into his magnificent throat. "More!" he demanded after he'd brought himself upright. "I want more."

We'd finished the first scene. I for one hadn't even noticed Dave's intrusive close-up takes. Jamie neither from what I recall. I think we were beyond worrying about such trivial matters, well and truly into one another. The punters would be in no doubt our sex was for real. I sure wasn't. Dave praised our superb ad-libs and the brilliant sex, telling us there was a break available should we wish to take it.

Jamie didn't seem keen. While he was giving me that incredible blowjob, he hadn't been able to free his giant cock from his tight breeches and give it the gratifying wank it so richly deserved. Already he'd turned around and was now resting his rosy bottom upon the leather saddle. Urgently he'd begun to work his cock from his open fly, pulling the thick shaft upward and outward, keen to spring the bulbous head free and get me sucking upon it.

"Action," he prompted, keen to get me gorging upon his massive sex after he'd sprung it free. I didn't need to be asked by Dave if I was ready. Even before he'd called action, and the cameras had started to roll, I had knelt in the soft hay covering the stone flooring.

Jamie had my head gripped in both palms. "Okay, stable slave, let's see what you're really made of." He slapped the enormous bud of his cock across my parted lips. I now knew where Jamie's 7lb allowance had gone. Against his small body, what I'd estimated to be a decent ten inches could easily be upgraded to twelve.

I took the long and heavy sex in my palm and gently peeled the foreskin over the fruit-like bud. Keenly, I began playing my tongue around the smooth surface. My lips soon joined in the action and began to suck down as far as the ridge of the hefty helmet. Meanwhile, my tongue worked wildly inside my mouth—twisting and turning brilliantly, torturing and tormenting the smooth surface of the tremendous head.

Jamie confirmed he was enjoying my sucking by feeding his fingers into my hair and rubbing my head. Although he was relishing my ravishing, he was keen to get more depth. "Love my big fat dick, don't you? Want me to give you the whole damn lot," he said, sticking to script, gripping the back of my head and steadily pushing.

I gradually allowed most of the monster to massage the back of my throat. Soon I was feasting on its glorious length, lassoing the girth with my tongue as Jamie lay into my face with fierce and ferocious thrusts.

I began caressing Jamie's silken chest and strong abdomen, enjoying the texture of his small frame, while sucking deep and hard on the gigantic sex. His stomach felt as tough as corrugated iron against my roaming fingers, the muscles rippling excitedly with my every downward thrust.

For a while my tongue ventured into Jamie's navel, playfully lapping around the boyish knot. Keen to keep my sucking going he swiftly forced his cock back down my throat, again sending his sex sensationally deep.

Jamie raised me by my armpits and brought our mouths together. It was our first meaningful kiss. Passionately we swapped tongues while caressing each other's bodies and cocks. His excitement continued to mount, his sex standing proud and perfect, the head reaching far above his navel and oozing pre-come as I keenly rubbed my own against it.

Giving my buttocks a rough squeeze, Jamie jabbed a finger between the willing cheeks, deep into the hole.

He nodded to the bed-like bales of hay. "I wanna ride you," he said, his expression wild.

As they say in racing circles, my stallion was ready to cover me.

I threw in an ad-lib, giving him a tickle under the chin. "As long as you don't fall off."

Jamie gripped his massive cock and slapped it against his tummy. "No chance of that once I've got this baby up your backside."

"Perhaps you should try shoving it up your horses, then," I tossed in another ad-lib.

Jamie pretended to nibble my earlobe so as not to be overheard by audio. "Can't wait to ram the lot right up you. Fuck you senseless, my young sailor stud."

I couldn't wait for him to do it either. Problem was I hadn't been fucked for a very long time. I certainly hadn't taken a cock of such proportion since my last wonderful film debut. "Too right you will. I'm the best bloody ride you're going to have this season."

We had a playful struggle on our journey to the makeshift bed, Jamie ripping the T-shirt from my chest while I pretended to fight him off.

My bottom hit the soft hay when we reached the bales; my stallion jockey spinning me around and pushing me backwards, keen to get the fucking underway. Before I'd even had time to make myself relaxed and ready to be fucked by him, Jamie had rubbered up his cock, his fingers ladling oodles of slippery lube into my tight and tender hole.

Still in his riding breeches and boots, Jamie speedily parted my legs, placing one on either side of his shoulders. With the expertise of a professional stud, he slipped the head of his enormous cock slickly between the cheeks. A look of absolute joy flooded his boyish face when the bud pressed into the tight flesh and began to enter my hole.

I'd barely managed to suck in a deep and relaxing breath before Jamie's incredible cock began to spread my buttocks wide. A gasp of pain saw my breath rush back out again when the thickness almost split me in two. Before I breathed again, the first five inches of his fantastic cock had completely vanished and was already hammering home.

Calming breaths rushed into my lungs when my insides began to burn with a mixture of pleasure and pain. In a matter of minutes, Jamie's rhythmic thrusting began to do wonderful things to my hole and every other part of my body as his impressive cock massaged the soft and sensitive skin embracing it.

Jamie pushed my legs closer to my chest, raising my bottom higher. To fuck me more robustly he knelt on the bales, adding more leverage to his flexing thighs and thrusting buttocks. A crafty grin illuminated his face. "So you think I can't ride, stable slave?"

I opened my mouth to deliver my next line of camp dialogue. Before I'd uttered a single word a powerful thrust saw the remaining five inches of Jamie's cock vanish out of sight.

My palms rushed to his chest when my hole contracted painfully around the massive sex. My face was grimacing; eyes squeezed tightly shut, my insides exploding as if a tank-buster missile had just slammed into them. "Jesus… fuck!" I cried in gasps, replacing yet another line of dialogue.

Another crafty grin parted Jamie's lips. Bending forward, while still driving his cock hard and deep, he began to ease my pain with a passionate kiss. A nibbled ear followed when he bent and whispered. "Forget your line, Sandy?"

Not to be beaten by a five-foot jockey, I grasped his powerful buttocks and pulled his cock hard into my hole. "That the best you can do?"

My knees met the bales when they were unceremoniously pressed either side of my head and pushed into the hay. I knew I'd opened Pandora's box with my jest. I also knew that once fired up and fucking I'd have little chance of stopping my five foot jockey. Petite he might have been, but each of those thigh and bicep muscles had the formidable power of a fighting machine. Let's face it he was used to having several of tons of horse trapped between his tough and trembling thighs. My average build would hardly present him with a problem ride. There could be no doubt in my mind I was about to get the fucking of my life!

Jamie's face was all smiles when he stood on the bed of bales; my buttocks impaled on that massive cock. Whip in hand, his body arched over mine. I trembled when he raised it high above his head, my thoughts flashing back to Whipcrackaway. It came sailing down shortly afterwards.

A stinging thwack caused my body to jar when the leather thong struck my buttock cheek. They flexed on impact and tightened around his solid shaft. I felt the thickness of the head driving deep as it cleared a path for the rigid shaft. The second thwack saw his cock withdrawn until it was clear of my hole. On his third strike, more forceful than the previous two, he sank the whole ten inches up to the hilt, spearing me like some vulnerable prey. The fourth strike never materialised, though the expression on my grimacing face indicated otherwise.

Jamie had sensed I wasn't keen on being whipped. I think he feared it would ruin our sex. He hesitated before he switched the whip to his left hand ready to beat me again. "You're enjoying that too much," he said, tossing the whip away and changing the script. I was relieved when Dave didn't interfere.

A more loving and passionate Jamie was now gently fucking me, but still with deliberate intent. Purposefully and slowly, he thrust and withdrew his cock, every movement highlighted with pants of pleasure from the pair of us. The prominent ridge of the head sent unbelievable spasms of ecstasy throughout my body on each slow withdrawal, stimulating the fleshy wall like never before. It was clear the pleasure was just the same for Jamie, his buttocks trembling in my palms as I prodded and poked his hole.

"Fuck me harder, faster," I panted, pulling his mouth onto mine and meaning every word now I was more comfortable with the size.

A change of position was called for before Jamie willingly obliged. His cock temporarily withdrawing, he took up a semi-sitting stance. I rolled slightly onto my side ready to accommodate his cock again; my left leg resting on his arm, my right leg stretched wide and pointing away from his body.

When Jamie keenly re-entered me, I raised myself onto my elbows in order to watch his every delicious thrust. Gasps of joy issued from my panting mouth when his magnificent cock began its skilful manoeuvres. In no time I was writhing in ecstasy on each of his prolonged withdrawals and powerful thrusts; my face flushed from a fucking the likes of which I'd never known before.

With a determined gentleness, Jamie fucked me, every minuscule reaction on his beautiful face amplifying his obvious pleasure. My whole being quivered with excitement at the magical sight of his ten-inch cock slipping between my submissive buttocks, his muscled abdomen rippling with every deliberate motion as he aimed to please. For one brief moment I thought I was falling in love with this most beautiful jockey who had the body and looks of a schoolboy but the endowment of a man.

"Like that?" asked my boy jockey stud, his words as soft as his riding silks as he lovingly seduced me.

"Oh, yes," I gushed, delicately stroking a finger over his lips, urging him to press them onto mine, truly make love.

"Me too," he sighed, kissing me passionately and adding more pace to his penetrations.

I brought my palm onto his wonderful cock, allowing its silken surface to slip against my fingers; my gaze fixed on each delicious millimetre as he expeditiously rode me the final furlong. "Faster," I urged, spreading my legs wider. "Fuck me faster."

Jamie began pumping his cock into my buttocks with the speed of an engine's piston. Delightful pants began to spill from his mouth, each punctuated with a compelling urgency as he drew closer and closer to climax. "Oh, yes," he sighed with each excited breath.

The glorious cock had become an ecstatic blur as I watched it furiously fucking my hole. Jamie's face too appeared to be nothing more than an abstract image when he bent and kissed, and fucked, and kissed. It was as if a million explosions were erupting throughout my entire being, bringing me almost to the point of delirium.

"God, yes!" I yelped when Jamie's hand unexpectedly wrapped around my cock and began to crucify it with satanic strokes.

"I'm coming!" he suddenly exploded, his thighs trembling from the indescribable sensitivity rushing along the shaft of his cock when he rammed it home.

Although I was sure he would have dearly loved to come inside of me, he was required to follow Dave's instructions. Releasing my cock, while still fucking me for all he was worth, he prepared for the come shot. My hand quickly replaced his, pumping myself with just as much enthusiasm.

On his next deep and desperate thrust, I sent my foreskin flashing over my cock a final time. There was no need really; his electric expression was more than enough to make me come. Reward came almost immediately, my spunk sailing clear over my tummy and onto my chest and face.

Jamie reached for the back of my head, pulling my face toward his chest. On the precise moment he was about to fill me with a fountain of teenage fluid, he skilfully withdrew his cock, whipped off the rubber and began to thrash himself with the enthusiasm of riding a fifty-to-one winner.

A thick and sticky salvo of spunk splattered over my lips. I waited a few seconds before I keenly lapped it away. His second salvo produced an equal amount of spunk. I'd raised my chin allowing the white juice to ladle onto my neck. His next offerings shot onto my chest, tummy, and cock.

Jamie gasped and panted; his joyous face a thrill to behold. Hand still pumping, he reached for my head a second time. The incredible fourth salvo contained more spunk than the first three. It appeared to fly at me in slow motion. I swallowed the whack mid-air; my mouth engulfing the gigantic head of his cock at the precise moment the juicy cream met the back of my throat. Continuing my forward motion, I sank my mouth down to the base of his cock. His buttocks shuddered in uncontrollable spasms when I sucked the shaft from tip to base and emptied his balls.

I lay back onto the bed of bales and sighed, a gratified sigh. Exhausted, Jamie collapsed on top of me, his naked chest and reddened face glistening with sweat. After kissing me passionately, he began to lick his spunk from my face and neck. His final task brought his tongue lapping down my chest, over my tummy and finally onto my cock, sucking the sticky bud clean.

"Cut!" sang Dave when my cock began to spring back to life.

Dave applauded the pair of us. The expression on his face told us he was more than happy with our efforts. Immediately, he began to review his shots, smiling all the while as he studied the camera's screen.

"We taking a break now?" asked Jamie, keen to wash his mouthful of spunk down with some champagne.

Dave checked his watch. "Fifteen minutes okay? One final shoot and then we're done." The pair of us nodded in agreement, Jamie already filling three glasses with refreshing bubbly.

I took a glass over to Dave then left him to his own devices and joined Jamie on the bed of bales. "Gotta get these boots off," he said, unzipping the backs and working them loose.

I pulled my shorts back on. "Look at all this wasted spunk of yours," I said, pointing to the white globules still decorating my chest and tummy.

"Here," said Jamie, pulling a couple of baby-wipes from a container and handing me one while he used the other to begin cleaning me up.

"You've done it now." I pointed to my rising cock when he worked around my pubics.

"You sailor boys," he joked, pulling up his fly when he realised it was still open. "Talk about a walking hard-on."

I offered Jamie a cigarette. He declined the smoke, telling me it would stunt his growth. I just loved his quick wit. He'd have made a brilliant sailor.

My baby-wipe flew over to the bin. "So what's it like being a jockey? Get many rides?"

Jamie winked. "Not as many as you do, I bet."

"That so? I've heard you jockeys are getting saddled up on most nights of the week; getting a regular ride, with or without a horse."

Jamie squeezed my cock. "And I bet this little beauty's gone off inside more hammocks than Nelson fired his cannons."

"Less of referring to my beauty as little," I scolded. "Anyway, we can't all have donkey dicks."

"Donkey dick? You wanna see it when I'm *really* randy. Even the fillies I ride are champing at the bit for a length."

I made a grab for his cock. "Sure is a bugger to swallow. It's made me a little hoarse."

"I prefer a nice little ass myself," Jamie quickly tossed back.

Dave chuckled at our banter as he went about his task of rearranging the set. "That's good, boys. Keep it nice and dirty." He checked his watch. "Five minutes and counting."

We sank another glass of bubbly apiece. Jamie asked me if I was up for the final shoot. I think he was really asking if I had any spunk left, or maybe he was hinting he wasn't up to it himself. I told him my balls were a "fountain of eternal youth" forever overflowing. He told me he'd better get me in the mood just in case.

For the next five minutes our mouths remained locked together, tongues buried deep, hands fondling cocks. I was really looking forward to the final romp. I hoped Jamie was too. In a short while, I was about to find out.

JAMIE'S BIG RIDE

Dave's voice brought us from our heavy petting, a pat on Jamie's powerful little bottom bringing our lips apart. "Hands off cocks, on frocks," he sang, sending beams of light streaming onto the stable stalls and saddle.

"Didn't see that in the script," said Jamie, looking a little concerned.

"Joke," said Dave, picking up his hand held camera.

I slung my arm around Jamie's waist. "Better be, Dave. We were brought up proper, us two. Not dragged up."

"Ready, boys?" said Dave, ignoring the quip.

The pair of us looked lovingly at each other and nodded.

"And.... action!"

Jamie and me remained lying on the dimly lit bales. We started with some heavy petting and a bit of mutual wanking. A suck on each other's cocks came next, followed by some delicious and more serious sixty-nines. I was reluctant to move on down the script, sixty-nine being one of my favourites, especially when I had such a beauty to bounce my head upon.

A loving stroll, interrupted by some silly frolics and light petting, eventually brought us to the piece-de-re-sistance, the racing saddle where Jamie rested his bottom, his glorious cock already free and standing proud.

I knelt before him and commenced my sucking, working the whole length deliberately slow. As I sucked and savoured, I began to unfasten his breeches, eventually pulling them down to just below his hips. It was the first time I'd seen Jamie's naked tummy below the waistline. Keenly I rubbed my face over its silkiness and then into the soft pubic bush.

I kissed my way up his superb torso, spending time on his tiny navel knot and miniature nipple buds. I also explored under his armpits when he raised them, licking wildly at the tiny tufts nestling in the musty hollows. Our tongues resumed their exploration of mouths while Jamie unfastened my shorts and pushed them over my thighs. My rampant cock sprang free as they fell.

"I want you to fuck me," Jamie lovingly whispered his line of dialogue, turning slowly and revealing the roundness of his smooth buttock cheeks, which were peeping just above the waistband of his breeches. The small crack that separated them begged exploration.

I stepped close again, placing my palms upon Jamie's slender waist. Almost torturing myself with the pleasure, I began to slowly peel the breeches over his buttocks. A whimper of delight escaped my lips when the dainty cheeks were revealed. A more profound sigh of appreciation quickly followed. It was the first time I'd seen them naked.

Jamie's boy-bottom—arse was too crude a word for such a delicacy—was so incredibly divine I could never have done it justice with mere words. Quite simply, it was a holy shrine, a gateway to heaven. Like a devout disciple of delicate and delectable dishes, I fell to my knees and began to worship the heavenly mounds, kissing both cheeks passionately before sending my tongue deep into the hairless crevice.

Jamie gasped and writhed excitedly against my magical tongue, whimpers of joy issuing from his mouth on every probe. Pushing his immense cock down toward the saddle's stirrup, he began to rub himself against the shiny leather, his hips gyrating with my every lap. A silkworm thread of pre-come seeped from the pulsating bud. My tongue was upon it in a flash, savouring the teenage juice before lapping on his dainty balls to encourage more.

The moment had arrived. I began to tremble, my excitement almost uncontainable. Never in my life had I fucked a bottom so divine, a bottom so delicate and small, and a bottom that surely belonged on the body of a boy.

My trembling fingers found the lube and condoms secreted next to the bales of hay. In less than a second, my rampant cock had been suitably covered. A stream of lube soon found its way between those exceptional buttock cheeks after I'd gently parted them. A further nervous trickle completed the preparations when it lubricated my condom-covered cock.

Moving my palm between Jamie's buttocks, I carefully caressed the teenage mounds, smearing some lube around the sensitive surface of his tender hole. Carefully probing, I allowed a finger to slip inside the coveted darkness, stimulating the velvet soft tissue with skilful swirls. Adding a second finger and then a third, I began to push them knuckle deep.

The most minuscule of squeals emitting from Jamie's mouth caused me to stop my exploration. Bending over and pressing my chest against his back, I pretended to kiss his neck. "You okay?" I whispered, not suspecting anything else.

A reddened face turned toward mine and nervously laughed. "I'm a virgin," it confessed.

My eyes lit up with joyous surprise. "What?"

Jamie blew me a kiss and smiled. "But I'm glad you're the first."

My body had shivered excitedly on hearing those magical words. I couldn't believe what a wonderful day I was having. My delightful little jockey, my long awaited fantasy fuck, was a virgin. My excitement was immeasurable.

There's something very special about having sex with a teenage virgin, about being a youth's first, something that is simply mind-blowing, electrifying, and wonderfully intimate. Elated, would not even begin to describe how I was feeling.

Acting as though nothing had changed, I continued the action as normally as I could, kissing my way down Jamie's spine until I reached his tender bottom. Truth was, my heart was dancing inside my ribcage and my head was truly buzzing.

With extra special care, I resumed my preparation for Jamie to lose his secret virginity; an act of lovemaking I hoped he would remember always, for the rest of his life perhaps. Passage nicely lubricated it was time for him to enter the realms of *really* naughty boys.

I pressed my rigid cock into Jamie's hole. I felt his buttocks flex and tighten. When he glanced back, I indicated with a smile that I would be as gentle as I could, but there was no getting away from the fact the first time often hurt. Like hell, from what I recall.

Jamie started to suck in an extremely deep breath, like a submariner taking his last gulp of air before he opened the hatch to escape. As he did so, I pushed a little harder but still taking things slow. Truth was, I couldn't wait to be inside of him, to feel the tightness of that soft teenage tunnel slipping over my shaft.

The air rushed out of Jamie's mouth when his tight little hole began to accept my cock. Without even looking, I could visualise the grimace of pain blemishing his otherwise perfect young face. A second breath speedily inhaled into his lungs in preparation for a deeper penetration. With another forceful push, the head of my cock had completely vanished.

I suppose I should have expected it. Jamie gasped and pulled his bottom smartly forward causing himself even greater pain when the head of my cock popped back out. He turned and glimpsed me. His face was bright red and his eyes watery. "Ouch!" he mouthed, his discomfort obvious.

"Try and relax," I mouthed back, not wanting Dave to know the problem but wondering if he already did.

Burrowing his fingers into the hay, Jamie prepared himself for a second attempt. I massaged his bottom with comforting caresses until I felt his tension begin to ebb. I began to penetrate again. This time the head of my cock slipped inside his hole without complaint.

Jamie gave a smile approval after the pain had subsided. He took another calming breath and nodded for

me to continue. Adding a little more pressure this time,
I kept my penetration at a slow and steady pace until my
cock had safely docked and the shaft was sitting pubic
deep.

I held my cock still for a while longer. Jamie remained silent apart from his heavy breathing. I guessed
he was okay. When I bent over, a smiling face confirmed
he was. I smiled back. My boy jockey was no longer a
virgin.

While I waited for Jamie to become accustomed to
my cock and for him to feel more comfortable, I briefly
studied his superb young torso. His short and slender
neck, sitting neatly upon those powerful young shoulders, was the perfect type to be kissing while you were
lovingly fucking his hole. It led you invitingly to a strong
and muscular back, one that had the strength to restrain
a thoroughbred galloping at full throttle, one that could
easily hold the weight of a beautiful bucking stud. An
impressive pure white, upper torso kindly guided me
down to an enviable eighteen-inch waist. Hidden from
my gaze, the taught and trim abdomen he'd brilliantly
used to power that enormous truncheon-of-a-cock into
my willing body flexed in anticipation. Finally, the most
sought after prize of all, the exquisite sensuality of his
petite and perfect boy-bottom. Now impaled so satisfyingly on my cock, that dainty dish was about to be
thrilled like it had never been thrilled before.

I brought my palms to Jamie's waist, clutching him
tightly. Oh-so-carefully, I began withdrawing my cock.
The feeling was nothing less than sensational when I
felt the walls of his virgin passage constricting tightly
around the sensitive head. Gasps of pleasure pushed my

lips apart with every recovered centimetre. From Jamie there was no response.

Ensuring I didn't withdraw completely, I began a slow re-entry. This time Jamie did respond, his buttocks trembling excitedly as I spread his passage wide, his mouth panting wildly until I'd completed my penetration.

I waited a few seconds until Jamie's buttocks had relaxed. I was more than aware that although a lad might desperately want to be fucked, sometimes they discovered it just wasn't their thing once they'd got a nice big cock buried deep inside of them. Whether sitting on nice big dicks was Jamie's cup of tea, had yet to be determined.

I started to massage Jamie's back and buttocks, drawing my palms over his silken flesh in circular sweeps. As I did so, I began a steady rhythm, slipping a few inches of my cock slowly back and forth. His buttocks remained submissive and receptive, his breathing calm. I responded by working my cock harder and faster into the fleshy darkness. Pleasingly, I soon had the whole of the shaft sailing sweetly back and forth.

My adorable jockey raised his hands and gripped the stable stall, arching his back toward my chest. I briefly slowed my pace fearing I was running on too free a rein. When a gap appeared between his tummy and the saddle, I sent my palm to explore. It was with joy and relief my fingers were greeted, not by a soft and lifeless sex of a disinterested youth, but by the stately flesh of that magnificent and mature ten inch beauty. A beauty now happily oozing prolific amounts of delicious pre-come as it begged for more attention begged for my cock to work wonders from behind.

Gripping the jubilant cock, I speedily worked the pre-come into the foreskin, around the throbbing head and down the shaft. I felt it gaining in girth as his excitement mounted. The desire to fuck him full throttle was now irresistible so I set his cock afire, furiously thrashing the foreskin over the sensitive head. Going for broke, I increased the speed of my cock, thrusting it ruthlessly into his tender hole.

Jamie's response was the desired one, the mind-blowing sensation of being fucked while being tossed simply devastating. "Oh, my god!" he gushed, his bottom all a quiver.

My pace increased both with penetration and pulverising palm. Jamie's knuckles whitened as he gripped the partition tightly. No words of complaint or gratitude escaped his mouth, only the ecstatic O-shape of his lips when he turned toward me and presented the satisfied expression of a youth who was delighting in the joys of loosing his virginity.

My cock was alive from tip to base; the velvet texture of Jamie's tight and smooth tunnel sending my balls dancing in excited spasms as it slipped over my shaft. I returned to the script. "Like that, do you? Like me fucking you good and hard?"

"*Do I?*" squealed Jamie, he too using the prearranged dialogue but meaning every word.

I wrapped my arms around his slender waist, pressing both my palms into his tummy as he came upright. Jamie took control of his own cock. "Hold onto your horses," I warned.

I began to fuck Jamie like I might never get another fuck in my life. "Jesus Christ!" yelped my boy jockey stud when I rammed my cock home. "Hell, no. Oh, yes!"

he screeched again when I pulled my dick clear of his hole then sent it swiftly back in, right down to my pubic bush.

Jamie's legs began to tremble as if he was standing on earthquake soil. With every upward thrust of my rigid cock, I was lifting him clean from the cobbled ground, keeping him hanging in space while joyously impaled. All the while, his palm continued to pummel his cock.

We weren't supposed to come in this scene. "You gotta stop, or I'm gonna shoot," whispered Jamie, his hand falling from his cock to prevent his spunk from spurting all over the leather saddle.

"Me too," I gasped, my mouth pressed into his neck and biting; my cock withdrawing to prevent a similar premature ejaculation.

"What a ride," Jamie sighed, his mouth seeking out mine. "Never thought it would be like this. Hell, I love it!"

I gave him a kiss. "Your best ride ever then?"

Jamie sneaked the loving kiss he'd been searching for. "You bet. You can fuck me any…"

"Eh, you lovebirds. We're supposed to be making a movie," Dave's voice interrupted our unscripted lover's chat.

"Sorry, Dave," we said in unison, our faces flushed and smiling.

Jamie laughed. "Sorry. Got a bit close. Nearly shot me whack."

I took some of the blame. "Me too."

Dave laughed. "Call yourself professionals? I don't know, give a sailor a big cock to play with and he falls in love. We'll move on to the final shot. Okay?"

The pair of us nodded. Jamie gave me a big kiss. I returned with a nifty suck of his cock while he told Dave we were rampant, randy, and ready to roll.

"Thank you," said Dave, a hint of director's impatience surfacing.

Jamie slipped his silks back on, leaving the front open. His riding cap went on his head but his breeches remained off. There was another brief pause while I slipped on a fresh rubber and Jamie ladled loads more lube into his hole. Another minute was also used up while we got ourselves back into the mood with some serious snogging and sucking of cocks.

"And... action!" sang Dave, although the cameras had never stopped rolling.

"Am I a damn good ride, or what?" I set the ball rolling.

"Not as good a ride as when I won the Gold Cup," Jamie boasted.

"You actually won a race?" I quipped. "How?"

Jamie gripped my cock and got it painfully hard with some brilliant wanking. "Up on the saddle," he ordered.

I'd never sat on a saddle before so I knew this part of the scene might well go terribly wrong. With some help from Jamie, my legs were soon astride the monster, my unstable body balancing precariously on the top. Jamie chuckled helplessly as he desperately tried to stay in character.

"The Gold Cup," he continued, picking up that dreaded whip while placing a foot in the stirrup. "I jumps on Action Stations and gets myself comfortable." Jamie slung his leg over both of mine, bringing the cheeks of his scintillating bottom centimetres above my dick. "She's really up for it and ready to go."

"Ride her, Jamie," I urged, my eyes fixed on those delicious buttocks poised only millimetres above my cock.

Jamie centred his cheeks over my solid cock and began to press down, his own cock pointing high and proud, the head resting nicely above his navel. "Boy!" he gasped, sending his hole swiftly and sweetly over my shaft in a single squat. "What a ride that stallion was."

A surge of unimaginable pleasure shot through my cock and spun my balls in sensational spasms. My arms reached out behind me as I fell backwards from the shock. I pressed my hands onto the bale to steady myself. "What a ride!" I gasped in agreement.

Jamie stretched out his left hand as if holding a rein. His right hand had the whip held high. He began to rock slowly back and forth over my cock. His balance was perfect, his featherweight body bouncing elegantly as he continued to enlighten me in the art of riding a nice big... winner.

Jamie clenched his buttocks tightly as they swallowed my cock. "We're in the final furlong, a bunch of horses ahead, another group behind," he continued his tale, his rhythm and balance still perfect as his bottom slowly bounces. "I gives Action Stations a kick and asks him to fly. 'Go on, boy. You can do it!' I yells."

My heart's racing faster than Jamie's imaginary ride. Already my spunk was rising up the shaft of my cock. He continued to steadily bounce. "Ride him, Jamie," I urged him on. "Ride him good and fast."

"The line's coming up," Jamie said excitedly, his movement over my cock increasing, his hole slipping swiftly and smoothly over the entire slippery length.

"Yes!" I gasp.

"The horse in front suddenly veers to the left," Jamie swayed on my cock in sympathy, his whip held high. "It's my only chance," he panted as he bounced. "I goes for the gap."

The whip swished beside my thigh as he bent lower and thrust his bottom hard onto my cock.

I join his enthusiasm. "Go for it, Jamie. Go!"

Jamie's hands were still gripping the imaginary reins, his back arched over as he rode my cock more urgently. "I lets him have it!" shouted Jamie, raising the whip again and sending it smacking down only inches from my thigh.

"Ride him, Jamie. Ride him good," I encouraged again, my concentration on the pleasure surging through my cock.

Jamie was puffing and panting from the exertion and thrill of riding my cock so robustly. "We hit the front," he announced joyfully, his face glowing red and glistening sweat. "You can do it," he yelled to his imaginary horse, his whip flashing beside my leg; his bottom bouncing so fast over my cock I begin to lose my balance.

My palms moved to Jamie's hips to steady myself. I didn't grip but allowed the sensuous skin of his slender waist to slip sensuously through my fingers. Thoughts of riding him bare back and shooting my whack deep inside his soft virgin hole suddenly swamped my mind. "Come on, Jamie," I yelled as an abundance of spunk surged to the head of my cock and prepared to fill his hole. "Ride that big stallion. Ride him good!"

Jamie moved his whip into his left hand, his right going straight to his cock and pumping like crazy. "Come on, my lovely boy!" he shouted, his bottom bouncing furiously over my cock. "Give me all you've got."

"Give me all you've got," I repeated his request, my hands gripping his hips as he slammed his hole hard over my cock and vigorously tossed himself.

Jamie's bum became a bouncing blur as he rode me gallantly toward the finishing post. "Come on, boy, gimme another length," he desperately gasped. "Another good length."

I rammed my cock upward when Jamie next pushed down. "Come on, Jamie. Ride that stallion!" I yelped, my cock in imminent danger of sending a pool of spunk sailing into his hole.

"That's it, boy! Yes. Oh, yes!" Jamie ecstatically called when my cock rammed home and the pubic bush met his hole, his rocking bottom and thrashing palm sending him into blissful oblivion. "That's my beautiful stallion, just another big push."

"Come on, Jamie. Ride. Ride like you've never ridden before," I barked as I thrust my cock upward.

"Go on, boy. Keep going! Keep going!" gasped Jamie, furiously fisting his cock while frantically fucking my cock, his buttocks now a blissful blur.

"Yes. God, yes!" I hollered, my tummy tightening and my body arching upward when my cock siphoned torrents of spunk into my jockey's beautiful backside.

"What a ride. What a fantastic bloody ride," gasped Jamie when he crossed the finishing line seconds later, his jet of spunk firing clean over the stable stall and well out of camera.

Jamie fell backward into my body. We were totally spent. "Weren't we supposed to end this differently? You turning around and coming in my mouth while you continued to ride me?" I puffed, my face red and all smiles.

Jamie gave me a kiss. "No way was I going to stop midstream. Hell, that was fantastic."

"Hope Dave's happy. I'm too knackered to do another take."

"Don't think that will be necessary." Jamie nodded toward Dave. "Look at his shorts. I think we did a good enough job." Sure enough, Dave was sporting a massive boner, something I'd never seen before.

The pair of us fell from the saddle. I rolled on top of Jamie. "Did you really win the Gold Cup on Action Stations?"

"'Course I did." Jamie squeezed my softening cock. "But you were the better of the two rides."

We left the stables and headed to the farmhouse. Jamie and me had been invited to stay the night. It looked like I might be in for a few more photo finishes before the day was through. I certainly hoped so.

Dave slung his arm over both our shoulders as we walked. "Well done, boys." He turned to me. "What did you think of your day at the races, young Sandy?"

I patted his back. "Know what they say, Dave?" Dave raised his eyebrows. I made a grab for Jamie's dick. "Nothing like good WOOD."

SOLDIER BLUE

A bloody big oil tanker, ten times our size, almost sliced us in two as we joined the English Channel in thick fog. After another gruelling time at sea, we were heading towards Pompey for a much-deserved weekend ashore. Freckles got a right old bollocking, poor little sod, for not being alert on lookout duty. I was on the flag deck at the time and could barely see the mast only five yards in front of me, so how the hell could he see a ship bearing down on us at twenty knots, a good ten miles away, however big the bloody thing was?

I smacked his bottom and told him he was a very naughty boy and that I'd punish him later. The Officer of the Watch should have got the bollocking. Thankfully, nothing came of it and lovely little Freckles escaped any punishment so was still able to spend the weekend ashore fucking a frisky filly—number ten, on the last count. I might be shagging someone too if we managed to find our way through the pea-souper without running aground or being sliced in half by another foreign ship running on automatic pilot.

It was funny another ship should almost hit us because we'd just spent a couple of weeks at Portland brushing up on the very skills we might have needed had it done so—Damage Control. We'd done a bit of skilful shooting as well—the missiles and guns, that is.

Damage Control exercises were a nightmare but necessary. We'd all done courses in a special tank designed like the inside of a ship. It slowly filled with water from a variety of jagged holes in bulkheads and burst piping as we desperately tried to block them, while other sailors shored up deck heads and bulkheads.

I remember on my DC course one very tearful young sailor had gotten himself into quite a panic—fear of drowning, I guess. He was shouting up to the training officer, saying that he couldn't find a wedge big enough to block the hole he was currently drowning under.

"Then stick your bloody head in it," yelled the Gunnery Officer. "It's as thick as a plank of wood."

Most sailors passed the course first time, which also included fire fighting. You dared not. You most certainly wouldn't have wanted to go through it again. Dressed in a boiler suit, in a darkened room filled with smoke; your body steeped in ice-cold salt water while trying to shove wedges into razor sharp holes teaming salt water that stung your eyes, was not the most pleasant of pastimes for a pretty young sailor I can tell you.

Even though I found boiler suits quite a turn-on when they were slipped over sailors whose slender teenage torsos were totally naked beneath, not once did I manage to sport a hint of a boner. It would seem some things were more important than sex—not drowning for instance.

Being a Communicator, I was luckier than most when it came to those dreadful DC exercises. All I ever had to do was rig emergency aerials on the upper deck. In my case, only help because even that duty belonged to the boys from the wireless office. And only once was I commandeered by the First Lieutenant to work with Mo the medic—we had first aid training as well—and that was far from unpleasant. I can be a dab hand at taking a temperature—from the rear. As for my kiss-of-life, that was the best and had the potential of reaching unknown depths of depravity when dealing with an unconscious, half-naked teenage sailor.

Naturally, in a real emergency or war situation, we'd all be doing whatever we could to stop the ship from sinking, wherever we found ourselves at the time. Who knows where a sailor might be or what he might be up to when that horrific missile came slamming through the bulkhead?

Tommy had been a constant concern to me while we were exercising at Portland. He never seemed to be off duty. His war with Purdy was more than ongoing. I was worried his 'engage the enemy' button would soon be pressed and that quick temper of his would eventually explode. If he did hit Purdy, then the next time we docked he'd be going ashore all right—straight into the slammer.

He did have a little bit of cheer to his otherwise miserable life though. He'd won the ship's Tombola—a very handy fifty quid. If he asked me nicely, I'd do him a decent blowjob for a quid of that. Maybe that would help raise his spirit.

There was still no news of when we'd be doing our stint abroad. The Ministry of Defence seemed to be forever changing its mind. Nothing in the Navy was certain, only the endless routine of life at sea and, of course, the endless search for sex by us randy sailor-boy studs.

Searching for sex was precisely what most of us were gearing ourselves toward right now, a weekend in the seedy haunts of dear old Pompey town. Hours of drinking, fucking, hopefully not fighting, with whoever might wish to spend their time with a randy young sailor who hadn't been ashore or had sex in two whole months, allegedly.

Sometimes you just needed to get away from the relentless banter of sailor-boy buddies or, in my case, their ever-tempting butts and boners. For a change, I decided I'd not be going on the predictable *shag everything that walks* pub-crawl with my usual bunch of sordid mates. Instead, I'd requisitioned camping gear and grub and would be heading to a countryside retreat, to a place not far from where my folks once lived when I joined the Royal Navy, to the charming and beautiful Bluebell Wood.

At first, I'd thought of inviting Tommy. He was off duty for a change. Sadly, the chances of having fun with him anymore seemed to have died a natural death. I'm sure it would have done him good though, me too if I finally managed to get my mouth over his extremely illusive cock. Matt's bottom had also looked incredibly inviting when I'd watched it wriggling up a ladder, unfortunately not to my flag deck. He'd have been my next choice had he not been duty diver this weekend. It would've been the perfect opportunity to give him that baby he so desperately desired. Freckles' was my final choice. His cock had also been looking pretty hot and sticky for the past few weeks. With this in mind, and memories of our sick bay romp, I'd eventually invited him.

"Spend my precious shagging time with a bunch of fat old mares and cows," had been Freckles' unwelcome response.

To which Chad had replied. "You mean like you normally do."

Chad's witty remark was a common one. The lass with whom you were having sex was always a nympho-maniac super model, whereas the one your mate was bonking was always a boot. Terrible thing, envy.

A couple of hours after the ship had docked I was strolling along a tractor trail upon which I'd strolled so many times as a teenage boy. With my rucksack on my back, I had nothing more than the countryside sounds and welcome tranquillity of my peaceful mind to keep me company, not a sordid sailor in sight.

I don't know if anyone has said it before, probably so, but boys and woods were born to be together, born to share each other's unquestionable beauty. Yes, a woods is that special place where a boy's quest to be spiritually free is born, a place of magic and mystery, a wonderful place to fall in love.

It was the wrong time of year for a carpet of blue-bells to greet me when I entered the delightful Bluebell Wood, searching for a spot on which to pitch my tent. It mattered little. When you loved the woods as much as I did it would be impossible not to be in awe of its splendid beauty through all of its enchanting seasonal changes.

I remembered my own special place in Bluebell Wood and took myself off the narrow path and into the depths of the woodland undergrowth. For so many years of my childhood, this special spot had been my refuge, a place of play, a place to laugh and cry, and much, much more. Retracing long gone footprints, through tangled branches and bramble, I soon found myself standing at a clearing beside the winding stream that separated woodland from field, its far bank crowned by an impressive hedgerow of hawthorn, hazel, bramble and elder.

I loved these special clearings in an otherwise thickened woods. There weren't that many. They were little havens filled with heaven-sent shafts of sunlight that plunged through branches onto grassy soil, then exploded into sunbathing savannahs. They were only known to beaters, badgers, gamekeepers, and other true brethren of the woods and, of course, by boys like I once used to be—still was at heart.

Tent pitched I move down to the stream. At this time of year it was running with ankle deep, clear water. As I'd done so many times before, my feet were soon dangling in its refreshing flow. Memories of happy, boyhood days soon flooded my mind...

I'd searched the stream so many times before, mostly in Wellingtons, sometimes bare foot. I'd been Sinbad the Sailor when I'd found pebbles of coloured glass tumbled smooth by time—jewels and precious gems from far off places. On other days, I'd been Robin Hood's devoted son, my sturdy bow, crafted from a holly branch, to hand as I fought the Sheriff's men. On one exhaustive summer's eve, I even found the Golden Fleece—hair from a horse's mane—tangled in an enormous bramble.

It pricked me ruthlessly when I excitedly claimed the prize as my own.

Then there were the not so happy days. The days I spent huddled against my favourite grandfather oak for comfort—the death of my favourite chicken; the bully who had beaten me at school because I was gay; my broken arm when I couldn't climb trees for two whole months; and other days when tears replaced treasures.

Then there were the very special days. Most memorable of all, the day I lay naked in the sizzling sunshine, feet dangling in the stream, hand wrapped tightly around my cock and pumping vigorously; my thoughts filled with the most beautiful boy in the school with who I was inexplicably in love. Yes, that oh so special and most wondrous day, the day I joyously announced an imminent miracle to the creatures of the wood. The day I hollered, as loudly as I possibly could, those magical words "I'm coming!" A tiny spurt of spunk my reward.

What a day that was. No birthday present ever came close to giving me such a satisfying surprise, not even my new bike.

The corn had been reaped in the field situated on the other side of the riverbank hedge, only stubble left. In a few months time the guns would be standing close to the hedgerow on the far side while beaters thrashed their way through the undergrowth and sent the pheasants to flight. I had done the very same thing myself. Beating, that is. Guns and me didn't get along. It was bloody hard graft but paid well and provided Sunday lunch by way of a free bird for the *special* boy beaters such as myself. I hadn't know it then but even posh men, like the Lord of the Manor, could be partial to a nice

portion of tender rump the likes of which couldn't be
served at dinner.

I pulled a pair of Navy-issue binoculars from the
rucksack pocket and began scanning the tops of trees for
a squirrel scampering playfully above my head. I found
it sitting halfway up a tall pine, acorn in paws, spinning
and nibbling its find without a care in the world.

The squirrel was of the grey variety. I'd seldom seen
the much adored red in Bluebell Wood. The greys were
vermin of course and farmers offered five bob for their
tails if you killed them. I never did, but I did capture
one with the hope of taming it. It wasn't impressed with
its captivity. When I opened my hastily built cage to
feed it, it gave me a very nasty nip before it rushed back
home. I needed a tetanus jab after that. Serves me right,
I guess.

My tent and rucksack were safe in the wood, so it
was with ease I took myself off toward the Common,
and Lover's Gate, trekking through the undergrowth
rather than going back to the footpath. I suppose the
Common was a boring place compared to Bluebell
Wood, but as a boy I liked to venture up there and play
with the wild ponies and annoy the dopey cows.

On one occasion I'd lassoed a stallion with a miraculous piece of rope work as I sat on Lover's Gate.
When the noose pulled taught around the stallion's
neck, it plucked me clean from the gate as it galloped
away, dragging me at least fifty yards into the gorse and
bracken. I had painfully grazed knees and arms that
took several weeks to heal after that rodeo caper. Thankfully, I didn't need another tetanus jab. Funny how you
don't let go even though you know it would be the most
sensible thing to do.

I failed to find the tree I'd secretly carved two names upon as I climbed the leafy slope leading to the Common. I guess I'd purposefully chosen an inconspicuous one. A boy's name was enclosed in that loving heart and entwined with mine; both speared by Cupid's arrow. It was a declaration of my secret love that I'd wanted to share with my forest friends. Pip never knew my love for him had a life of its very own; free to grow as we would both surely grow. Even after we eventually made love, I still didn't tell him.

I was sure the tree was close. Didn't matter really. It was common knowledge for us country folk that trees could wander across a wood if the notion took them. I'd lost many a good tree that way. I knew it would find me again when the time was right.

My thoughts were now on Pip as I continued on my journey; Pip, my lovely Pip, the ever-smiling, gentle Pip.

It had truly surprised me when he made his sexual move on that very special day, brought about by witnessing a couple of mating horses, the stallion's unbelievably long and stiff cock exciting us as it thrust deep into the mare.

We began by kissing. A wank apiece followed. Next a blowjob, Pip telling me I hadn't lived until I'd had one. How right he'd been. I'd been surprised to discover he'd already been given a blowjob, his PE teacher the lucky recipient. Smart, I think his name was. I'd been so damn horny when Pip had finished detailing Smart's sexual skills, I'd have given myself a blowjob had I been able to get my mouth over my cock.

Unbeknown to me Pip had come prepared that day bringing with him KY so's he could fuck me senseless;

take away my virginity. I recall asking him if KY was like Primula cheese and if you could spread it on toast and eat it. The tube made me think so. Silly me. Silly, *innocent* me.

I laughed loud when I remembered the condom caper. Pip had been in a right old state because he couldn't get the damn thing on, his excitement to get his cock thrusting up my hole taking priority. It had only been a guess at the time, but I suggested he might be putting it on inside out. Surprisingly, I'd been right. Pip wasn't as sexually skilled as he'd first led me to believe. It turned out I was the very first person he'd fucked.

The day hadn't quite ended in tears when he'd suddenly revealed on our journey home that he was joining the Army, and that I might not see him again for a very long time. Truth was I was hurting like never before. To be married and divorced in a single afternoon takes some stomaching for a boy who was crazily in love. I'd applied to join the Royal Navy very soon after. It was now almost two years on from my day of sexual enlightenment. I hadn't seen Pip since. I doubted I ever would now my folks no longer lived in the area and I rarely visited, this my first since they'd moved.

I brought the binoculars to my eyes when I detected a rustle coming from beneath the darkness of a rhododendron bush. It wasn't a young badger surfacing early as I'd thought, but a blackbird turning leaves in search of snails and worms. I continued on my upward trudge toward The Common, only the countryside sounds accompanying me.

I hadn't come out of the woods where I'd expected and had ended up about a thousand yards from Lover's Gate. It would seem my directional skills had begun to fade. I could have continued into the bracken and gorse but I wanted to sit on Lover's Gate again. Turning left, I headed in its direction, passing dozing cows and the more lively New Forest ponies.

As I drew closer to the gate, I spotted a face peer from behind a bush and look in my direction, before ducking back. The owner appeared to be sitting on my gate. Although tempted, I refrained from bringing the binoculars to my eyes, suspecting they might think I was some pervert on the prowl.

Acting as though I hadn't spotted them, I continued my approach.

Drawing nearer, I stooped to pluck a ripened berry from a bramble. I took the opportunity to have a closer look at the person up ahead while I popped it into my mouth. I've no idea why my heart danced so nervously when I did so. I can only assume it was because the person appeared to be of about my own age, more interestingly, of the same sex.

Although I was a walking hard-on and always on the lookout for sex, I thought it might be somewhat bold to walk briskly up, introduce myself, and plonk my bottom on the gate beside him. Instead, I chose to stroll on by, bidding him good afternoon while sending the briefest of glances directly onto his combats-covered crotch.

"Sandy!" the unexpected call came from behind, causing me to stop in my tracks and swing around. "Didn't you recognise me?" The stranger leapt from the gate.

No, I didn't recognise him, or the terrible scar on his face which travelled from cheekbone to the corner of his mouth and back like the flap of an envelope. "Do I know you?" I questioned, not daring to move closer.

The young man thumped his fists into his broad chest. I was relieved a tribe of gorillas didn't rush from the woods and join him. "It's me... Pip!" he declared. "Fucking hell. You must remember me."

'Course I remembered Pip. I'd been thinking about him for the past half hour. Surely, this couldn't be him? You could fit two Pips inside the body of this muscled beefcake. "Pip?" I answered, stunned and still disbelieving.

Pip rushed me. I stepped back a pace when he slung his arms about my body and almost crushed the air from my lungs. "What the fuck you doing here, you son-of-a-bitch?" His fist thumped into my back and he laughed rather crazily. "Blow me, Sandy. Who'd have thought..."

I was in total shock. The only thing going through my mind—I had blown him, blown him good and proper on that special day. I doubted I wanted to do so again. He wasn't my type any more. It had nothing to do with the appearance of his otherwise handsome face, more to do with his size and military manner. "Pip!" I reciprocated, patting his big back nervously.

Pip lifted a flap on his combats and pulled half a bottle of whisky from the baggy pocket. "We've gotta drink to this." His new voice had become extremely gruff and manly, even unattractive. He thought for a moment. "The Queen!" he suddenly hollered, taking a hefty gulp before handing me the bottle.

It was far too military a toast for my liking. I was relieved he hadn't saluted. He could have been toasting me, I suppose. "Old pals," I said, taking a very small sip.

Pip sent another slug down his neck when I returned the bottle. "I heard you joined the Navy." He was sniggering slightly. Again his arm went about my shoulder and pulled me roughly into his body. "Tell old Pippy boy what you been up to then."

'Old Pippy boy' screeched in my brain. I felt it whine like a jammed drill. "Not much to tell," I told him, a slight unease beginning to filter through me.

Pip removed his khaki T-shirt, revealing a gallery of tattoos penned into a muscular chest—Union Jack; the head of a bulldog; and other military looking designs. He dragged my body down when he slumped onto the grass, where we must have sat for a good two hours talking about this and that, *that* being the Army, *him*, Pip taking regular sips of scotch, me declining.

He'd been in action, *twice*. His facial wound was from a piece of shrapnel. He'd gotten a medical discharge because of it. He'd won a medal, got married, had a kid, and got divorced, all in two years. The only thing I had done was make a couple of porn movies, been bounced around in storm force seas, and fucked every sailor I could get my disgusting little hands upon, also in two years. I didn't tell him any of it.

"The Army was my *lifeblood*," Pip finished detailing his extraordinary life, his solemn expression speaking volumes.

I suppose we weren't getting along too badly after such a long absence, although I wasn't at all comfortable in his presence. A damn stallion, its enormous cock swinging proudly between its legs, changed things. I laughed quite innocently before I said, "Remember that stallion, Pip? Boy, did we have some horny fun after that."

Pip looked me straight in the eye, the disgust on his face bayonet sharp. "Fucking shit! Don't tell me you're a friggin faggot!"

"What?" I snapped, totally stunned and desperately trying to control my anger.

"I asked you if you were a fucking faggot."

I was up on my feet before he could blink. I was fuming. "I'm a faggot all right," I shouted, putting as much venom into the derogatory word as I possibly could. "So fucking what!"

Pip stood. He unscrewed the cap on the whiskey bottle and shot a hefty measure down his neck. He coughed when it bit the back of his throat. "Fucking hell, mate. Didn't think you'd turn into a fucking perv."

My anger burst into my face. I hated anyone calling me *mate*, especially in that tone. I knew he could snap me like a twig, probably kill me with a strategically placed finger, but didn't care. Had I as much booze inside of me as he'd consumed I think I would have smacked him right in the mouth. I gave him rough a poke in the chest. "What's your damn problem, Pip?"

He took another gulp of whisky. "My problem?" he barked. He slipped his T-shirt back on. "You're the one with the fucking problem. The one who's shoving shit uphill."

My fists clenched. I squared up to him. If he said another word, I was sure as hell going to smack him one. "Don't suppose there's any faggots in the good old army… eh, Pippy boy? All macho men, aren't they?"

Pip began to walk away, like he was afraid of catching my queerness. "You're fucking disgusting."

I went for his jugular. "Really? So whose damn dick was pushing shit up whose damn arse when we were last here? Tell me that *I'm so fucking straight* soldier boy."

The rest of the whisky vanished in a single gulp. I got ready to duck when Pip raised the empty bottle. He twisted his body and hurled it away, sending it high over a gorse bush and toward the horny stallion.

"Well?" I pushed.

Pip didn't answer. He marched smartly away, two fingers pointing skyward.

My body sank to the ground. I bowed my head into my hands. I was shaking like never before. Moments later a revving motorbike brought my head upright. Pip's body flashed by, his face looking straight ahead as the bike roared away.

A gasp of relief, and anger, rushed from my lungs. I waited for the sound of the motorbike returning, for Pip to rush back and give me a friendly hug as he apologised. It didn't happen. I knew I'd never see him again.

My heart heavy, I climbed sadly to my feet. When I turned and faced the woods, I felt my anger welling up again. I decided I no longer wished to sit on my gate of wonderful memories and swiftly headed back to the gap from where I'd exited the woods.

My eyes became watery as I moved back into the woods. I just couldn't believe what had happened. I'd never been one to hold a grudge and began to search my mind for excuses to explain Pip's brutal behaviour. I couldn't accept that he'd turned into a homophobic bastard so easily.

It had to be the army that had created this monster. The endless days of training and the brutal regime of bullying in order to create a fighting machine was to blame. Seeing his mates blown to bits and getting wounded himself couldn't have helped. Or putting a few rounds into guys of his own age. Being discharged from an army he obviously loved, most surely hadn't. The drink hadn't been of assistance either, bringing out the macho side of his nature. Then again, perhaps it had done the opposite, reminded him that deep inside he was more than capable of loving a youth rather than killing him.

The tree with our names carved upon it suddenly appeared. I guessed it must have been following me all along. I gave the heart an affectionate stroke when the love I had for Pip was instantly rekindled. It had to be a good omen.

An explanation suddenly flashed into my mind. Pip's problem was guilt. He'd been riddled with guilt knowing he'd rather be making love to guys instead of killing them. Meeting me had reminded him of this, reminded him of the day we'd made love.

"The poor sod," I whispered. "And he's not even a Catholic."

TASTE BUDS

I was up early this glorious sunny morning; a couple of hours after a sensational dawn chorus had sung me back to slumber. The stream was more than cool when I brushed my teeth and gave my face a jolly good soaking, smelly armpits too. A water vole poked its head from beneath a bush of scrub on the muddy bank opposite as I bathed. It made a hasty retreat when I dipped my billycan noisily into the flowing stream to collect water for my cup of early morning tea, and bade it good morning.

Gone were all thoughts of Pip and the traumas of yesterday as I collected kindling for the fire, soon setting it ablaze. There would be no trips down memory lane today. Today I planned to walk to the village for cigarettes and other bits and bobs, and have a more general look around. Maybe have a lunchtime pint in the local if I stayed in the village until opening time. After that, just take the day as it came. The woods were prone to springing unexpected surprises, pleasant or otherwise.

There's something extremely satisfying about cooking and eating a breakfast in the open air. I reckon half the meat-eating creatures of the woods were gathered around, secretly watching, their tongues lapping around drooling lips as they smelt my sizzling bacon and big fat sausages spitting in the pan. Mine certainly were.

Another speciality I loved was toast cooked over an open fire. You just haven't tasted toast until you've tried it cooked that way. Most grub tasted a hundred times better when you cooked it yourself, especially so if you'd eaten some of the slop the sailor chefs could dish up. An egg floating around in two inches of lukewarm grease was not the most appetising of sights, first thing, when the ship was ploughing through a gale or your tummy was on the turn.

I didn't go by way of The Common on my journey to the village. Instead, I chose to cut across fields and detour through copses. It made the walk more interesting. You never knew what delight might pop from beneath a bush or fall from a tree on sunny weekends, when boys were bounding through the woods rather than banging their heads from unsolvable blackboard problems.

I had thought of bringing a camera with me and taking some snaps to show the lads back on board what the countryside really looked like, the majority being townies. To most, a field was that twenty square foot of grass situated somewhere in the estate and decorated with burnt-out cars or abandoned shopping trolleys. And a wood was that avenue of small trees where the richer folk lived. As for a river or a pond, only gutters and drains unable to cope with torrential rain provided any resemblance.

I'd decided otherwise when I suspected Freckles first words would be, "Very pretty, but where are the tits?"

I laughed when I thought I could have taken pictures of the blue tits that frequented the woods. I imagined Freckles' disappointed face when I told him I had some beautiful tits to show him and produced some snaps of birds from which he couldn't pluck the knickers.

Chuckwell's farm took a good quarter of a mile of my journey. It didn't save me any time though. I'd unexpectedly found myself embedded in a herd of Friesian milking cows on their way to pastures new. I wasn't afraid of course. Being domesticated they are friendly, and rather dopey when it came to brainpower allocation. Only sheep outdid them for sheer stupidity with an equivalent intelligence of a lump of play dough.

The only real problem with being in a herd of cows—to put it crudely—was shit. Boy, could those walking sewage tanks squirt a tidy sum of the smelly stuff. I suspect that's why I never ate my greens as a boy. Vegetarians be warned. A handy smack on the rear with a trusty walking staff would normally keep the rear end out of firing range and on the move.

Cowpats weren't to be frowned upon though, and were a wonderful asset to war gaming country boys, ammunition of the highest quality. You needed to find a pat at least a few hours old—crispy on the outside and soft in the centre. Held Frisbee or discus fashion, these could then be skated through the air toward your target. On contact, they would disintegrate, discharging their soft and smelly contents all over an unsuspecting enemy. A war winner if ever there was.

The other wonderful use for cowpats only came around once a year—Bonfire Night. On those very satisfying and hilarious nights we would find the softest of cowpats—moving them to the target area if necessary—and push several bangers tied together deep into their soft centres. Inserted into the blue touch papers would be a short fuse made from an old shoelace. The polish in the lace allowed it to smoulder slowly, thus giving a delayed ignition time.

The routine went like this: First, we'd wait for a group heading down the path and toward the communal bonfire. When they'd reached the telephone box a few hundred yards away we'd ignite the fuse and scramble through the hedgerow, stifling our excited giggles the best we could. It was still touch and go but if the timing were perfect the bangers would explode at the precise moment the group came strolling by. The enormous bang scaring the pants from our victims was more than enough to make us giggle helplessly, but the expressions on their cowpat-covered faces gave us the most satisfaction.

The Chuckwell twins were at the head of the herd when I'd worked my way through, grubby jeans tucked into boots, their chunky torsos tanned and naked, shirts tied around powerful abdomens. They always were a muscular pair even as fourteen-year-old lads. They were even bigger now.

They bade me good morning with great big smiles when I strolled by. I was pleased they hadn't forgotten my name. I sure hadn't forgotten the handsome pair. They'd had me sandwiched between their naked bodies on more occasions than they'd milked cows. I'd been fucked by both one fantastic afternoon. On another haymaking day, I'd had sixty nines with one while the

other shagged me stupid. All in my sexual fantasies, unfortunately.

Why their parents had named them Bill and Ben
was beyond me—and them, I suspect—but I would have
gladly been their friendly Weed any day of the week.

The Devil's Cauldron was a mile beyond the farm.
As always, I cautiously skirted the perimeter. I guess the
massive cavern was fifty, maybe sixty, foot deep and a
good two hundred yards in diameter. It took a good fifteen minutes to do a complete circuit, even at a steady
jog. Time had covered every inch of it in thick green foliage of every imaginable kind. Naturally, it was a haven
for wildlife and many a breathless fox had darted into
its unexplored depths to escape the more wary hounds.

I'd never ventured into its darkened depths myself,
although I was tempted on more than one occasion.
Not even when a grumpy gamekeeper, who had taken
umbrage at my failed attempt to floor one of his precious pheasants with a wicket-hitting full toss, threw
my cricket ball into its cavernous mouth.

Nobody seemed to know how it came about. "It's
where the Devil's head landed and burnt a hole to Hell
when Ned the Turnip chopped it off," had been one old
farmer's explanation. Apparently, Ned the Turnip was a
gypsy boy from way back, who did chores on practically
all the farms, mainly decapitating turnips as they were
harvested by hand.

Rumour had it young boys who'd been very naughty—not eating their greens for instance—were lured
from their beds into its tangled depths on mysterious
foggy nights. Rumour also had it you could hear the
Cauldron gurgle when the boy was boiled alive and
then satisfyingly devoured, bones and all.

In all probability, it was a bomb crater still filled with unexploded bombs—hence the DANGER signs. Possibly, a German bomber was still buried there. Whatever it was, I never knew of any boy who'd ever ventured more than a few feet below its perilous lip, and only then to hide from the enemy of the day. And if you did dare venture deeper on one of those brilliant war game frolics, you could be sure nobody would find you—ever again!

Cricketers were on the village green when I reached it. I rested for a while and listened to the monotonous thwacks of leather on willow, followed by the occasional run. Cricket was a lot more fun to play than observe. Even greater fun when played with a tennis ball without the fear of broken fingers or ball-breaking bouncers that hit boxless boy's bits.

I stopped at the Turnip Chopper Inn and supped a cool cider in the shade of an elegant willow, buying crisps and more cigarettes for later. A couple of youths kept me occupied while I quenched my thirst. Sexy shorts hugged buttocks tightly as they rode their bikes over grassy mounds and jumped drainage ditches with great dexterity; their bottoms pushed invitingly high and off the saddle. Sadly, shorts that reached the knees didn't do enough to hold my attention for long, the soft flesh of a thigh or the chance of a glimpse of a cock a prerequisite for longer perusal. Even so, I took myself between the pair after they'd stretched on the grass to rest, ensuring I had every detail of their naked tummies and bulging teenage packets etched in my mind.

The sun was on its way down by the time I reached The Common on my journey back to the woods. Very little exciting or unexpected had happened on my jour-

ney, not even another youth to admire. I wasn't bothered. I'd brought myself back to Bluebell Wood to relax
for the weekend and not to hunt for sex.

I joined the woods well before I reached Lover's
Gate. I guess I didn't want to find Pip sitting there and
go through another disturbing reunion. The rhododendron path took me down to where the stream forded the
tractor track. On bad winters, the six-inch trickle could
easily become a raging torrent. A marker on a chestnut tree indicated that back in 1953 it had reached an
amazing fifteen feet, flooding deep into the woods and
across many a field—not today though.

My boots were soon off and I began wading back to
where I'd pitched my tent. For the most part, it was safe,
but you needed to keep an eye open for freshly broken
glass thoughtlessly discarded by careless trippers. Tiny
minnows tickled my ankles and toes in several reedy
patches. Sometimes you'd get even bigger fish taking a
nibble or darting between your legs and down stream.

Several times, I stopped and took in the beauty of
my old surroundings, suspecting I may not be returning
to Bluebell Wood in the near future. A multicoloured
kingfisher held my attention for several minutes as it
plunged into the water until it had a beak filled with
minnows. An undamaged bottle also held my attention
when I tried to make out the worn down writing. It
turned out to be a not-so-valuable ginger pop container
from a distillery long gone.

As I drew nearer to my campsite, my eyes opened
wide and my binoculars made a hasty excursion and
covered them. I was no serious bird watcher but this
rare sight in the woods sure made me twitch. If I was
correct, and knew I was, it was a Lesser Spotted Boy-

buttock my eyes had now focussed upon, delighting in every moment as it bobbed and bounced above and below the waterline.

Moving cautiously forward, I reached a low hanging branch. Desperate not to spook my prey, and to get myself even closer, I gently pushed it into the stream. Silently I stepped my left leg over.

The loud crack of the snapping branch was more than enough to alert the youth. My yelp of surprise, when my body sprawled forward and splashed into the water, could hardly have gone undetected. An almost girlish giggle issued from the adorable face when the youth spun about and spotted me lying prone in the water, the branch jammed uncomfortably into my crotch.

"You okay?" he asked upon reaching me, laughing and giggling at my ungraceful entrance as he waded closer.

"Fine," I replied with a smile. "Just swimming back to sea."

The youth's hand reached down, not to my arm to assist me up, but directly into my crotch. He attempted to disentangle me from the ferocious foliage that was threatening to hold me there permanently. As he bent his head between my legs he couldn't fail to notice I was sporting a fair old stiffy, the wet material of my shorts stretched seductively around the shaft.

I thanked the completely naked teenager, whose only attire was string of coral beads decorating his slender neck, when he eventually released me and gripped my arm, and pulled my drowned body intimately into his own. He told me I was welcome, again with a flurry of giggles.

I suppose it was impolite of me not to have been looking into his gorgeous eyes when he told me his name was Tristan, or Trish to his friends. Instead, I was staring at just over two inches of delicious soft cock and a set of hairless balls that hung neatly below the bud. Even when I returned with my own name, my eyes scanned the dusting of pubic curls sitting neatly above the shaft, before moving onto his microdot navel embedded in a taught and trim, nut-brown tummy. In fact, every inch of his torso was a delightful and delectable, scrumptious nut-brown.

The pair of us climbed the gentle slope leading to my tent. A fire, which he'd kindly set ablaze, already had jacket potatoes hissing in its glowing embers. I noticed no other tent occupied any part of the grassy clearing. It mattered not. He could sleep with me in my tent.

"I've started your fire," he said, oh so poshly. "Bunged some spuds in it too. Hope you don't mind?" 'Bunged' and 'spuds' didn't suit his posh accent and I wondered if they were for the benefit of a working class country bumpkin like me.

"Great," I said. "I'll dig out some bangers and beans to go with them." Then, with an unwarranted bit of sarcasm of his poshness, added, "We are staying for supper, aren't we?"

He was on my case in a flash. He placed his hands upon his hips and began to wiggle his bottom. "Why yes, Vicar." He fluttered his lashes sexily. "You know I wouldn't miss sharing a sausage with you."

I acknowledged his excellent parry with a nod and a smile and began to remove my wet clothing and hang them to dry on a branch overhanging the fire. As I removed my boxers I realised Trish was still stark naked and hadn't gone for his shorts. Suspecting it was nothing more than a temporary oversight on his part, I crawled inside my tent.

I reappeared shortly afterwards, freshly kitted out, sausages and beans in hand. To my astonishment, and extreme joy, he was still in the buff; his nifty little fingers happily prodding at the blazing fire and rolling potatoes with a stick.

I tugged my forelock and tossed the sausages into the frying pan. "Your dinner, me Lud."

Not only was Trish a tasty little treat to find in the woods, he was also a mind reader. "You don't mind me being naked do you?" he asked. "My parents are naturists. I've spent most of my life without any clothes on. All of our vacations are spent at nudist camps, so it's normal to me."

Mind? He could stay in the nude forever as far as I was concerned. It was just a pity that small cock of his hadn't shown as much interest in me as mine was still doing in him.

I joined him by the fire. "No problem," I said. I gave him a wink. "Lucky it wasn't a girl who'd pitched her tent here. You would have sure shocked her."

Trish screwed up his face in disgust. "Girls in my wood—yuk!" As if being punished with instant Karma, a shower of hot cinders suddenly sparked from the fire and landed on his fluffy bush and tummy. "Wahoo!" he yelped, jumping to his feet and brushing his cock frantically before ignition took place.

It was an instinctive reaction on my part. I was upon him in seconds, billycan of water in hand. No way could I see that treasure of a cock incinerated before I'd even had a chance to give it the appreciation it so richly deserved.

Two splashes did the trick, his soft cock now dripping water from the bud, which made it appear even more delicious, my disgusting mind turning the beads of innocent water into droplets of delicious spunk.

"That was close," I said, holding back my laughter.

Trish giggled. He examined his precious cock. "Nearly had an extra sausage for supper. Occupational hazard, cooking." I couldn't resist touching his tummy just above his pubics and pointing out several pinprick burns. I managed to resist touching the other red blotch beginning to develop on the shaft of his cock. I also managed to resist telling him that I'd be more than happy to be eating his succulent sausage rather than the ones I'd soon be frying.

"I'll fetch some cream," I said, keen to keep his equipment in full working order.

The sausages were sizzling in the pan by the time I'd rummaged through my rucksack and returned with a first aid kit. I took control of supper while Trish set about his treatment, dabbing ointment on an increasing amount of red blotches, mostly on his tummy.

He released a wince of pain then giggled again. "I think the bugger's got my hole," he said. Without a hint of embarrassment, he lay on his back, raised his knees to his chin and began smearing ointment into the crack of his sweet young bottom.

"Nasty," I said, disguising my pleasure as he worked his fingers into the hairless crevice and up into his hole. Again, my palms covered my cock, which had begun tenting my baggy shorts the second his knees had raised.

Trish sat back up. "So how come you're in Bluebell Wood and in my favourite spot?"

I thought I detected a hint of *trespassing* in Bluebell Wood in his tone. "I used to live over at Fernyhurst Cottage. Grew up here. Spent most of my childhood in the woods." I began defending myself. "You?"

Trish rolled the sausages in the pan. "My uncle owns Bluebell Wood, you know. I sometimes come over when I visit." I'm sure he didn't mean to sound so upper-class.

"You're Lord Lassiter's nephew?" I said, taken totally by surprise by his revelation. At least it explained his poshness and his unfortunate air of superiority.

Trish bowed. It was more like a sitting curtsy really. "The very same."

"Used to beat pheasants for him when I lived here. Nice bloke. Often gave me a brace to take home for dinner." I didn't tell Trish his beloved uncle would have preffered a mouthful of *me* for *his* dinner.

It was my turn to interrogate. "So how come I've never seen you in the woods before?"

"Boarding college keeps me away. It's up in Scotland. Uncle Rupert usually comes up on term breaks or we go on vacation. If not, then I come down here. My parents live abroad now and are always occupied, so I don't see them that often."

"That's a shame," I said. Trish appeared unconcerned.

The fire spat another shower of sparks into the air. "You don't live around here anymore?" Trish asked as he shuffled backward.

I shook my head. I knew he wasn't intending to do so, but I wasn't happy with his formal tone of questioning. "I'm in the Royal Navy. Spend all my life in a tin can floating around the ocean."

A knowing smile beamed across Trish's face. He folded arms across his chest and began to jig from side to side, Hornpipe fashion. "Rum, bum and backy, me boys," he said with another of his seductively cheeky giggles.

His change of manner pleased me. There was no doubt where that quote had come from. Perhaps Lord Lassiter and his delightful nephew… I quickly let my disgusting thought alone.

"Funny you should mention that. I just happen to have the very same with me," I said, jumping to my feet and making for my tent.

Another giggle rushed from Tristan. "Would that be the backy, rum… or *bum*?"

"All three, *actually*," I said, holding Navy rum in one hand and cigarettes in the other when I reappeared from the tent.

"That's only two, Jeeves." Trish laughed, relishing the play but reducing me to butler.

I dropped my shorts, turned and gave him nice big moony. "Your bum, me Lud."

Trish clapped his hands and laughed a delicious, schoolboy laugh. "Brilliant!"

I stooped to pull up my shorts.

"Leave them off," was the unexpected request from this lively lad who appeared to be without inhibition.

I glimpsed his cheeky face. "You reckon?"

Trish jumped to his feet. "Look." He gave me a twirl, sending his soft cock pointing outward. "Feel the breeze on your body and the freedom you have when you're totally naked." With that, he began a rain dance affair around the fire.

I didn't dance with him but I had thought about joining his nakedness several times while we sat together. Problem was, for the most part I'd been sporting a constant semi-boner. Although it was common for a sailor like me to have, and witness them, I was a little wary to produce one in front of a youth that I'd just met, especially one related to the Lord of the Manor.

Again Trish read my thoughts, or perhaps he'd already spotted my constant arousal. "Don't worry if you get a hard-on. Most lads do when they first go naked. You should see some of them when it's their first time at a nudist camp." Trish laughed. He raised his soft cock upward. "Walking boners."

The thought of loads of teenage lads strutting around a nudist camp sporting uncontrollable stiffies did the trick all right. Even as I began to kick my shorts from my ankles, my cock had started to show its true colours. By the time I'd plonked myself beside the fire it was pointing high and proud.

Again Trish didn't appear to show the slightest embarrassment, but I did notice he'd checked out my endowment when he thought I wasn't looking. "How do you feel?" he asked.

If he was referring to the tingling in my excited cock, and whether I wanted to push it up that pert little bottom of his or between those pouting lips, then the answer was I felt as randy as hell! Suspecting that wasn't his question, I told him I felt as free as a bird. The other truth I didn't tell him was that I'd been naked in these woods more times than I could remember, the last time resulting in the loss of my virginity. If history could kindly repeat itself, then I would be more than happy to oblige again, but this time with Trish loosing his virginity, if he hadn't already. I suspected he had.

I poured rum into mugs and added water. I had no idea of Trish's age. He didn't look anywhere near eighteen. That didn't mean a thing tough. I'd just had sex with a jockey who looked like a schoolboy. However, the last thing I wanted was to be sending an underage lad back to his uncle as pissed as the proverbial parrot.

I held the mug toward Trish and gave him an interrogative look. "You are eighteen, aren't you?"

Trish smiled, reaching out a hand. His cheeks flushed. "Of course."

I kept the mug from his grasp. "Honest?"

Trish thought for a while. "Seventeen." He grinned again. It appeared he wasn't too good at lying. "I will be in a month. But Rupert always gives me sherry and wine with my meals. I've never been drunk."

I couldn't truthfully see a problem. Trish was at college and most likely got pissed every other night. I knew I would never take advantage of him if he did get drunk. Anyway, I was the one who was in control of the rum so it would be most unlikely. "Here you go," I said, handing over my navy career if things should go wrong.

We ate our supper, chatted and laughed, and chatted more. I laughed even more at Trish's jokes. He was a jocular kind of youth and seemed to find fun in almost every situation. The navy came up every now and then. It appeared he'd been to far more countries in his young years than I would probably visit in my lifetime.

On quieter moments, I found myself studying the youth before me, his college-boy haircut that suited his facial features perfectly, his cute stubby nose and those petite ears that protruded pixie-fashion. Then there were those fullish lips that I so desperately wished to kiss but knew I wouldn't. Finally, his smooth chest with its tiny nipples studs; his taught and tender tummy; and, of course, the tempting cock nestling tantalisingly between his tender young thighs that had failed to rise even when the subject moved onto sex.

Boy's games, the likes of Eye-spy, eventually replaced discussion, as Trish became even more fun to be around. A game of *Taste Buds* was introduced by him, not that my mouth wasn't salivating enough already.

Producing his designer rucksack, he told me it contained a variety of crisps and that my task was to guess the flavours. He didn't trust me not to peep and made me wear a blindfold; his very own shorts pulled over my eyes.

My first guess was correct though it wasn't part of the game and wasn't mentioned, it being the wonderfully arousing smell of his cock odour sitting centimetres from my nostrils. I guessed the cheese and onion *and* the salt and vinegar correctly. The beef I mixed up with the OXO. The shrimp cocktail I couldn't get at all and they made me want to puke.

The best part of his game was that our naked bodies were knelt beside each other, allowing me the opportunity to suck in the sweet odour of his teenage body. Sadly, I could only take quick glimpses of his cock each time the blindfold was removed and the result announced. However, on my penultimate incorrect guess, I was sure that tiny treasure had gained in thickness and in length.

"No more, Trish," I puffed. "What with supper, I'm bloated."

"There's only one more. You can do it." His palm rubbed my tummy intimately; his first touch of my body since he'd pulled me from the water. Reluctantly I agreed and the shorts pulled over my eyes, the musty fly resting on my nose.

There was a little shuffle beside me as I waited for the next delicacy to push between my lips. I wondered what was going on. "No nasties. Spiders or anything."

"Of course not." Trish laughed. "Right, open your mouth. Wider. Wider!"

My mouth felt as though it had been wide open for more than was necessary. Beneath the blindfold, my eyes had already screwed up tightly in anticipation of a nasty prank. Just as I went to complain of the delay, he filled it.

My eyes sparkled beneath the blindfold. This one was easy. I recognised the slightly salty taste and texture immediately. For a while, I allowed my taste buds to savour. "Uhm," I said. "Very tasty."

I could hear Trish's gentle breathing above my head. "Like that one?"

"My favourite."

Trish pulled the shorts from my head, placed his palm upon my shoulder, and began caressing. "Thought I'd save the best until last."

I sent my lips down the four-inch shaft of Trish's rigid cock. I watched his tiny balls roll and then draw upward into the sac when it tightened. I stroked them gently, adding to his pleasure. His tummy drew in against his ribs when my mouth met his pubic bush. "Ooooh," he whimpered, his hands falling to his sides.

An even slower withdrawal up the shaft brought my lips to the pinkish-purple head. With gentle swirls, I allowed my tongue to circumnavigate the swollen bud. His tiny balls rose even higher in their hairless sac. "Aaaahh," he sighed.

Bringing my palms to the soft hillocks of his buttock mounds, I gently eased them forward. Simultaneously, I sent my mouth back to the base of his cock and into his quivering tummy. "Yes," enthused my posh young college student. "Oh, yes!"

I gazed up at Trish's pleasure-filled face that was looking down upon my working mouth. I brought my lips back to the head of his cock and began to swirl my tongue again. His expression changed to one of eager expectation. The sound of air rushing from his mouth in an ecstatic gasp greeted my next deep thrust.

I continued with my slow movements—bud to pubic bush, pubic bush to bud—each time lingering on the smooth head and lapping lustfully before the next deep thrust.

"Ooooo. Aaaah. Uhmmm," murmured my young sapling on every sensational swallow, his buttocks flexing tightly from the incredible pleasure.

I allowed my palms to wander over Trish's smooth flesh—abdomen, chest, thighs, buttock and balls. All the while, my mouth was still working as they explored. For a while, I kept my head still, allowing him to thrust into me if he wished.

Increasing my movement over the shaft, I brought my hand to my cock and began to caress. I instinctively knew there would be no sucking of my cock by Trish, no fucking of him or me either. I didn't mind. I was more than happy for him to fill my mouth with teenage spunk and listen to his squeals of delight when I brought him to that fantastic finale.

My increase of speed brought a greater sensitivity throughout Trish's body. Already his tummy had begun to tighten in tiny spasms. When next I plunged my mouth deep into his pubic bush a globule of spunk spat from the eye of his cock.

"Eeeee!" Trish yelped, his buttocks clenching tightly to stem the flow.

My own caressing was bringing me closer and closer to climax. I wanted Trish to come first. Using every sexual skill I had, I set about the task.

Faster and deeper my mouth flashed over the four-inch shaft. More and more Trish's tummy tightened as it tingled with pleasure. A quick suck of his balls, then both cock and balls, and then cock again, produced a tremble in his legs.

"Oh! Uhmmm. Aaahhh. Ooooh," he puffed and panted, his legs shaking so badly he could barely stand.

His ecstatic cries of pleasure had brought me past the crucial point. I knew I would come in seconds. Faster and faster, I sucked. More and more he whimpered. Weaker and weaker became his trembling legs. Still he wouldn't come.

It was if he was standing on the edge of a high diving board, fearing to make that mind-blowing leap. More truthfully, he was just hanging in there, milking the wonderful blowjob with every fibre of his being.

Although I'd discounted it earlier, I pushed a finger into my mouth to moisten it. On my next deep swallow of his cock, I pushed the digit deep into his delicious hole. "Jesus!" he cried, his hands gripping my head when a second digit joined the first.

Trish's legs buckled as I worked my mouth feverishly over the final inch of his cock, my fingers probing deeper into his hole. "Aaah!" he gasped, repeatedly, each emission of pleasure punctuated with a plethora of delicious spunk. "Ooooh!" he sighed and laughed when the final helping of spunk shot to the back my throat.

My own spunk leapt from my cock, splashing on the insides of his tender thighs. "Oh boy," I delighted, savouring all the spunk I'd collected, in one delicious gulp.

"Tristan! Tristan!" The unexpected voice came from the field beyond the stream and hedgerow.

"Rupert!" exclaimed an alarmed Trish. He grabbed his shorts, dashed to the remainder of his clothing, dressed in a flash, then scampered bare foot over the stream and through the gap in the hedge.

"Bye, Trish," I called after him, my disappointment obvious.

Trish's ecstatic face peeped back through the hedgerow. "Come back again, *Hornblower*," he requested with a salute, his face smiling contentedly. "Last weekend of the month. I'll be waiting."

"Try and stop me," I called back as he vanished from sight.

TWO DOWN, ONE TO GO

Miracles of miracles, we were sailing abroad. That is, we were heading for yet another exercise, this time with the Dutch Navy and a few other navies tossed in for good measure. The abroad part, we'd been promised an entire day in delicious Amsterdam if we could prove the Royal Navy was far superior to all the rest. Come tomorrow evening the start of exercise TULIP BLOSSOM would be signalled to all ships and we'd begin the task of hunting down the enemy and pretending to destroy the lot.

For my part, the exercise would be a gruelling couple of days up on the flag deck. Communication would be by lamp or flags when radio silence was in effect. With foreign ships interacting with us there was bound to be a cock-up somewhere down the line. It wasn't unheard of for a ship to dash off in the wrong direction, the signalman having interpreted the flags incorrectly. I hoped I wouldn't be the person responsible. I too wanted to go ashore in Amsterdam and be bouncing on some blond youth's bottom after we'd won the war.

I don't think I'd ever seen young Frecky so excited, brought about by him being informed by some old salt that the *ladies of ill repute* paraded their wares from behind brightly lit windows as the sat in exotically decorated boudoirs. All he needed to do was walk the street and take his pick.

"You mean there's a pair of tits and a tender pussy every ten feet?" had been Freckles' thrilled response. Followed by and even more excited, "I'm going to heaven, lads." Filled with an abundance of enthusiasm he had even created a condom necklace for the occasion, a selection of brightly coloured fluorescent sachets creatively arranged. Flavoured blowjob numbers—banana, strawberry, lemon and the like—carefully distributed between the heavy-duty screwing condoms.

When he showed me his necklace, I remembered on one of our joint *leisure activity* lectures the instructor telling bored Freckles that a sailor should always have a talent in his hands, besides his branch skills. What the instructor didn't know, Freckles' talent was never out of his hands, or some lucky lasses. With so many condom sachets slung around his sexy young neck, he sure intended to demonstrate that fact in Amsterdam, at least twenty times in one day according to my last count.

As usual, when our little rust-bucket set off to sea the weather was on the turn. I'd already handed a signal to the Officer of the Watch advising him to batten down the hatches because a storm force ten was imminent in the North Sea. It mattered not to the gin-guzzling brass up in Admiralty. They couldn't give a toss about poor young sailors like us being bounced around from arsehole to breakfast time from one day to the next. Wars,

imaginary or otherwise, were there to be fought and
won whatever the weather.

"Fifty more lashes of the Cat! Aye, Aye, Mr Fletch-
er."

Already the lads below decks who were off watch
were stowing breakables and lashing down anything
that might move. When you're bearing down on a submarine at twenty odd knots and the ship's doing sharp
zigzags to starboard and port every couple of minutes,
you didn't want any unexpected shocks, like someone's
heavy suitcase filled with contraband fags and booze to
come crashing down on your unsuspecting head. In fact,
you didn't want to be doing anything at all apart from
sitting down or wedged safely in some secure corner.

For those of us who worked on the upper deck, the
greatest danger in these treacherous conditions was falling overboard. When a ship rolls forty degrees or more,
you'd be surprised how easy it is to go over the guardrails, or under them, if a hundred tons of water has just
swept you off your feet and is dragging you across the
deck.

How more ships didn't return to port with half the
crew in plaster after weathering a storm was beyond me.
I guess we all had a natural instinct to keep ourselves
out of danger. Of course, the promise of a decent fuck
in a place like Amsterdam was enough to keep any hot-
blooded sailor on his toes and alive. No way would he
miss out on sex. Mind you, I reckon Freckles would still
somehow manage to get his end away even if he had a
couple of broken arms and legs. He was a lucky little
bugger when it came to dipping his wick.

Come the end of the Last Dog you'd have thought
we were sailing over the Rocky Mountains rather than

the North Sea. Fifty footers were smashing into the bows at regular intervals, the ship rolling heavily to port then starboard as it corkscrewed over or through them. Our poor frigate creaked and groaned like an arthritic old lady when metal strained against metal and she ploughed relentlessly on. All this and we hadn't even begun the pointless exercise.

A bunch of us entered the mess deck one after the other, all having finished the watch. Weather-beaten faces puffed, blew, and cursed as legs bounded tired bodies down the ladder and into the welcome warmth and dryness.

A sodden Tommy appeared a good half-hour after we'd settled down to hot chocolate or beers. "Bet Nelson's crew didn't have to put up with the shit I have to," he cursed.

"Eye spy a grumpy little sailor," Spud quipped, holding an empty beer can to his eye.

Freckles was quick to toss his joke in as he headed for the ironing board to get his kit ready for his tulip-dipping contest in Amsterdam. "It's just armless fun, Tommy," he said with a laugh.

"That prat Purdy..." Tommy began his regular moan.

"Not again!" yelled a group of lads already playing Knockout Whist and supping beer, their hands going straight to their ears.

"You do know what he's like. The bastard!" snapped Tommy, leaping onto his bunk and diving under the blanket fully clothed.

"Well push the bastard overboard," suggest Spud, "and give us all a break."

"I might just do that," mumbled Tommy, his face hidden beneath his pillow.

The ship hit a big one and rolled heavily to starboard. Almost everything on the tables went flying, including a couple of lads who were just about to be seated.

"Who's driving this bloody thing?" called a voice from the port side of the mess.

"That'll be that bastard Purdy." Another little dig aimed at Tommy from one of the lads.

"Bollocks. Me last can of booze," cursed Sprout as he watched his beer roll away, discharging its contents over the deck.

"Don't worry, Sprout, just lap it up like you usually do," chirped Spud.

"Knowing where Spud's tongue's been, you wouldn't want to do it with his," came a quip from an occupied bunk.

"You ain't been licking pussy again have you, Spud?" delighted Freckles.

"Will someone throw a bucket of cold water over that Freckles bitch." Another quick-witted reply was tossed across the mess.

"You seen his necklace?" Jacko joined the fray. "Little bandit's got flavoured ones."

"Can't beat a good blowjob," I joined in.

"Yeah, but he's not supposed to be giving them," laughed Jacko.

"That so, Jacko?" said Freckles. "What about you and that hairy marine?" The lads erupted in jeers and laughter. We loved jests of a sordid nature, especially if untrue, even more so if they could be cultivated into a good yarn.

"Come on, Freckles. Tell all," Spud egged him on.

Jacko made a dive for Freckles' necklace. "You little prick. I'm gonna shove those condoms right up your arse with this broomstick."

"He'll love that," chirped Sprout.

Freckles pushed his luck. "So will Jacko."

Jacko didn't reach Freckles. Another violent roll of the ship saw him gripping the ladder to stay upright.

"Pissing hell!" The alarmed squeal was from Freckles when the legs of the ironing board unexpectedly collapsed and sent it skating to starboard. He went sprawling on top of it, the red-hot iron landing between his legs and only inches from his crotch, the plate beginning to melt the vinyl flooring.

The lads erupted in jeers and whoops.

"Anyone order fried pork balls?" asked Jacko as he grabbed the iron and kindly helped Freckles to his feet.

"Would that be 69 on the menu?" Another quick return.

"Better clean that beer up. Don't want anyone slipping and breaking their neck in my mess. Freckles, can't you do that ironing after the exercise?" sang the authoritative voice of the Leading Hand who was going over information pertaining to the exercise. "Come on, lads, let's have a bit of hush now. Some boys are on watch later."

"I'm not. Thank fuck." It was another muffled grumble from Tommy's bunk.

"Not again!" sang the rest of the lads.

We remained reasonably subdued until 'Pipe Down' whispered through the Tannoy, only the occasional shouts from card-playing lads, each of us quick to bunk down when it did.

My sleep was erratic throughout most of the night. You try kipping in a tumble dryer. At one point, my eyes did flicker open when I thought I heard argumentative voices close to my ear. They lids soon dropped, returning to pleasant places, the hard work I'd done and the prospects of even harder work ahead closing them.

It was an early call for all hands to muster at their respective departments that brought the whole mess into a frenzied spurt of activity. It was well before Reveille when the call came. The air was blue from moaning bodies who'd recently come off watch as boys leapt tiredly from bunks. Even those who'd had a reasonable night's kip weren't happy. It was most unusual for the entire ship to be called to arms without prior knowledge, except for Action Stations or Man Overboard. Before a single one of us had any idea of what was up rumours were being cultivated.

"I think we've hit a fucking whale," was one lad's explanation.

"Engines are fucked and we've got to get out and push." Another wisecrack tossed in.

"Skipper fancies a bit of water skiing," an old chestnut was put forward by a young sailor on his first trip at sea.

The First Lieutenant's sombre voice issuing through the Tannoy eventually solved the puzzle. "First Lieutenant speaking," it began. "I'm sorry to inform you that one of your shipmates has gone missing." Each of us began checking the others around the mess to see who was absent. "Sometime during the night it would appear that Acting Petty Officer Purdy didn't return to his station. We believe it was between 0400 and 0500 hours. If anyone saw him between or after those hours, you should report to me immediately. In the meantime, report to your departments where your Heads will detail you, and we will make and inch by inch search of the entire ship. That is all."

"Yes!" delighted Tommy, who was still snuggled beneath his bedding, in a probability still completing his early morning toss. To that, several lads told him what a prick he was.

The ship had already gone about and we were heading back to Portsmouth in a much calmer sea, our part in exercise TULIP BLOSSOM over. Search and Rescue had also been informed but each of us knew if Purdy had gone overboard he would never have survived last night's storm.

We all loved being sailors and the fun to be had both on board and ashore. But with our sometimes childish behaviour came the utmost respect for both the sea and the dangers a warship held. When refuelling at sea or doing ship to ship transfers the person transferred could suddenly find themselves in the ocean, their helpless bodies swept away in the raging torrent of water if the ships came too close. Or a metal spring, stretching as it took the strain of a docking or towed ship, could snap without warning, cutting a sailor in two as it looped across the deck. No, I'd not met a single happy sailor who didn't have respect for his environment, who wasn't watching out for himself and his mates. Yes, we were more than aware that one day we might not make it home. The 'cruel sea' was fact, not fiction.

It was a depressed bunch of sailors who searched every millimetre of the ship looking for any evidence of Purdy—a body, a note, clothing, bits of a body, blood, anything. Nothing was found. Several sailors had gone to the First Lieutenant to give information. Others, like Tommy, were ordered there. It was common knowledge Purdy and him didn't get along; a motive for murder, not in my book. Mind you, I'd seen that temper first hand. In his present state of mind, he was more than capable of lashing out. But murder?

I wondered whether I should see the First Lieutenant myself. Tell him of the row Purdy and the stoker had that night I'd met Matt. I decided otherwise. In all probability, Purdy had more than likely fallen overboard in the storm. Well, he did drink on duty. Then again, he could have just jumped—suicide.

Tommy had been the only sailor I heard rejoicing at Purdy's demise as we searched the ship from mast to keel. Others might have been doing it inwardly. Even if a sailor was disliked—as Purdy obviously was—he was still a sailor, one of the crew. It was a damn bad omen to lose a sailor at sea, similar to killing an Albatross. We sailors can be a superstitious lot.

Come lunchtime the fruitless search had officially been called off and a normal routine established.

A respectfully subdued bunch of lads sat in the mess this evening as the ship steamed back to Pompey, easy-listening music seeping through the duel-purpose Tannoy. Some of the lads were quietly writing letters to loved ones and friends, while others lay on bunks reading. A few were solving crossword puzzles, while others were already sleeping, no doubt, hoping for pleasant dreams to replace morbid reality. Even the weather appeared to be paying more respect, the swell now a reasonable eight feet.

It was thoughts of our own mortality, unkindly kindled by recent events that occupied most minds. The time between life and death passed in the blink of an eye. Any one of us could have gone over the side in a storm like that. Each of us was very aware the chances of being rescued were practically zero.

There was no larking around or jesting either. Apart from Tommy, that is, who was drinking heavily and constantly trying to bait the guys with outrageous antics, his manner very strange indeed.

Close to Pipe Down Tommy began to laugh quite maniacally. "What's wrong with you lot? You miserable sods," he disturbed the silence. "Purdy's dead. So fucking what." He laughed again. "Good riddance to him, that's what I say. He was a fucking bastard."

A few eyes looked up but nobody spoke. Spud did go to speak but Jacko intervened with a 'leave well alone' look. A couple of lads moved from the table and went to their bunks. The Leading Hand acknowledged the developing situation with a raising of his head.

Tommy staggered to the table, picked up the sugar bowl, and emptied the contents onto the tea tray, the white grains scattering over some of the lad's letters. Laughing uncontrollably, he placed the upturned bowl on his head. "Purdy jumped over the side," he said. He stretched out his hands. "Just like that!"

His cruel Tommy Cooper jest sank quicker than the ill-fated Titanic. He was clearly overstepping the mark and getting out of control. Again, the Leading Hand stopped what he was doing but didn't interfere. He liked us to sort things out between ourselves if we could.

Spud's fuse had been ignited. "You're a fucking prick!" he bellowed, shaking sugar from the letter he'd been writing to his wife and kids.

"What you call me?" slurred Tommy, staggering toward him. Spud remained seated, although he was big enough to floor Tommy with a puff of his breath. He wasn't an aggressive kind of bloke at all.

I blocked Tommy's path. He'd been a good mate until things had started to go wrong. "Come on, Tommy. Let's bunk you down."

He shoved me away. "Piss off. Think I'm fucking a kid?" he snapped, his glare still fixed on Spud. "Perhaps you just want to fuck me, you fucking qu...." Tommy stopped before he went too far.

"You've really got to get that bloody big chip off your shoulder, mate," said Sprout, making matters worse.

Before Tommy could respond, the Leading Hand decided enough was enough. "You causing problems again, Tommy? I think you've had enough booze for one night. Come on. Bunk down. And that's an order!"

It was a terrible sight to witness. I think it took us all off guard. Tommy exploded. "The lot of you need shoving over the fucking side," he yelled. "Fucking wankers!" Then, in a screaming fit of rage, his fists began flying in all directions, a mixture of anger and tears flooding his tormented face.

It took three of us to hold him down. Thankfully, nobody got hurt. Mo the medic was on the scene in no time, an injection in Tommy's bum flooring him. With that, we carted his sedated body up to the sick bay.

"A complete mental breakdown" had been Mo's diagnosis. When we reached Pompey Tommy would be heading to the navy mental hospital, poor sod. What with Purdy and now this, surely things couldn't get any worse.

SUNRISE

It was gone noon when we docked the following day. Tommy was stretchered off as the investigation team embarked. Any questions for him would come later.

Sailors appeared in higher spirits as they worked around the ship. It might have been due to the fact they'd be able to get ashore far sooner than expected, albeit not in lovely Amsterdam. Freckles didn't appear to have the same cheerfulness though. His beloved necklace had even vanished. I told him a shag a night was more than enough for any growing lad. He wasn't amused.

The investigation team ran through statements and events, occasionally requesting some sailor to go to the wardroom where they were conducting their enquiries. Toward the end of the day snippets of gossip filtered out by way of the officer's stewards. It appeared murder had been ruled out and the investigators were now focussing on a tragic accident. That news gave the crew more cheer. It also gave fresh worries that come evening they wouldn't be going ashore after all, but would be head-

ing back to TULIP BLOSSOM. Even the possible return to Amsterdam-tits-aplenty didn't give Freckles any
cheer, and his absent necklace didn't go back around his
neck.

I knew differently of course. I'd been in the Captain's company waiting to take a signal when matters
were being discussed. Nothing had been ruled out. And
no, we wouldn't be heading back to Amsterdam. My
mouth was sealed of course. Being a communicator, I
had my crosses to bear.

By way of a signal from the hospital, I also knew
Tommy was now 'stable and comfortable'. He'd been
classed as P7R, which meant he was unfit for sea. In
the worst of circumstances, it could mean he was unfit
for the navy and would be discharged. Whether he was
a murderer or not, I didn't know. If he was, a plea of in-
sanity might be sufficient to save him. Poor sod.

The rest of the afternoon flashed by and before we
knew it the investigation team had disembarked, brief-
cases filled with verdicts or unanswered questions. Not
long after they'd left "Liberty Men Close Up" sounded
through the Tannoy, accompanied by cheers from those
randy sailors champing at the bit to be back ashore.
Freckles was among them.

Most of the crew appeared to be setting off in ones
and twos rather than the normal rowdy herd. It was
closing on 2300 by the time I walked over the gangway,
also alone. I did the familiar club crawl of sailor haunts,
but without much enthusiasm. I didn't even fancy doing a gay club to search out some raunchy sex such was
my low state at losing one of my best mates to mental health problems. I was wondering too much about
Tommy, whether I should have done more to bring him

from the terrible turmoil he must have been going. In all truthfulness, I probably did all I could. You fight your own battles on a ship. Mates are only there for support and pull you out of the doldrums by taking you on cheerful runs ashore. I guess sometimes it's not enough. That's just the way it is.

I guess it was touching 0200 hours when, still low, I espied Freckles sitting alone outside a closed pub. He was swigging from a half-bottle of vodka, most unusual for him. I perked up slightly when I wondered if this might be the night for me to give him a nice little blowjob. Having no lass in tow, and missing out on his Amsterdam shag(s), he might just be up for it.

"You look like you lost fifty quid and a dog just pissed on you," I joked. A nod acknowledging my presence was all I got in return.

A healthy shot of vodka went down Freckles' throat after an age of silence. "Pssissin' Pompey," he suddenly slurred.

"Dearie me," I said. "Has Freckles got the grumps cos he couldn't use up his necklace? Don't worry you're a long time in the navy."

He went to take another gulp of vodka. I'd never seen him this pissed before, or so low. I grabbed the bottle before it met his lips. "My turn," I said, already suspecting I might need to see him safely back on board.

"I done it, Sandy. I fuckin' done it," Freckles' cursed and slurred.

I took a hefty swig of his vodka, trying to finish the lot in a single gulp so's he couldn't get any worse. "Let me guess, Freckles. You went and got that lass pregnant. You silly bugger. And there's you with all those condoms."

Freckles rocked backward and nearly fell from his seat. I gripped his wrist and steadied him. He laughed a depressed kind of laugh. I pulled him forward.

"I ain't that fucking stupid," he slurred.

"What did you done then?" I tried to make light of his obvious plight.

"I killed him."

Perhaps I was as drunk as he was and was hearing things. "You did what? Killed who?"

Freckles took a big gulp of air. "I killed Purdy."

I was on a wind up for sure. He was baiting me. A drunken prank Tommy might play. But this wasn't funny. "Really? And how did you manage that? I could fit the whole of your body inside Purdy's beer gut. Well… could have."

Freckles snatched the bottle and emptied it. He looked me straight in the eyes. "Night of the storm, about four-thirty, Purdy wakes me up. Tells me I'm on watch. I tell him I'm not. He doesn't listen and drags me from my bunk. The stupid sod's pissed as usual. Not much of a problem usually."

Memories of being awoken stir in my mind. I'm riveted by his yarn and ignore them, and continue to listen.

"He takes me up to the quarterdeck. There's nobody up there because of the storm. He's angry for some reason and pulls me over to the starboard side. It's then I realise what's going on." Freckles tipped the bottle upward and cursed its emptiness. "I look down," he continues. "Purdy has got his fucking cock out. A right old boner going."

I wait silently during another pause.

"He rips off my necklace and tosses it overboard. He grabs my head and starts shoving it down. I'm struggling but he's too damn strong. 'Suck it, you little tart,' he tells me." Freckles thought for a moment. "I don't know why I didn't shout for help. Wish I had."

I remained silent. There's more of his yarn to come.

Freckles lit a cigarette and began puffing away. "Purdy forces me onto my knees. He grips the back of my head, pulling my face into his stinking cock. He's too damn strong and I can't pull away." There was a brief silence, his eyes watery. "His cock's between my lips, he's shoving real hard and gripping my nose so's I open my mouth to breathe." Freckles wiped his mouth. "The ship gives a whacking big roll to starboard, the stern coming right out of the water as she goes over. I sees my chance to escape and give him a real hard shove." Freckles shot me a quick glance to check if I was still listening. "That's when it happened."

"What!"

Freckles stared blankly at the table. "The starboard guard rail dipped right level with the sea. Purdy was stumbling backwards from my shove. Without a word, he rolled right over the top. Plop! Gone!" His expression went blank.

"You're having me on," I said, laughing. "You're pulling my plonker."

Freckles stood and began to stagger away. I called after him, desperately concerned of his drunken state more than his outrageous yarn. He laughed drunkenly. I flinched when he heaved the bottle into the ground and it disintegrated.

Freckles pointed a finger toward me. "Beat that with one of your stories," he slurred, falling against a wall.

"That is so not funny," I yelled as he vanished around the corner. Come my return to the ship little Freckles was going to get a spanked bottom for that one. That was, if he managed to find his way safely back on board.

I needed another drink. Boy, did I need another drink. I lit a ciggie and prepared to make a move.

"Well fuck me with a rolling pin. If it ain't my favourite bum boy." Shells' voice scared the life out of me when he appeared from nowhere.

"Shells," I delighted, cheering instantly. Not only hadn't I seen him since we were on our last ship together, but he was bound to have booze. He was also great company and one of the few lads on board our last ship who knew I was gay and hadn't the faintest problem with it. His other claim to fame, he was the ship's number one gunner, something that will remain a mystery to me for the rest of my life, since he seldom worked without a gallon of rum inside his belly.

Shells plonked his bottom down. He wasn't drunk. Being familiar with his routine, I knew he'd already got drunk, drunk himself sober and was now on the return journey to drunkenness again.

"Got something nice for you," said Shells, his hand reaching toward his bell-bottoms. He laughed when I peered at his crotch. "No, it's not my cock."

I took the rum, unscrewed the cap, and downed a triple measure. "Fancy meeting you after all this time," I said, handing the bottle back. "Killed any pilots lately?" It was an ongoing joke. He was always missing the targets being towed but he'd nearly hit the aircraft towing them on more than one spine-chilling occasion.

"No longer top gunner. Got too good for them," he lied. Well, that was a relief.

We sat there until well after 0400 drinking rum and going over old runs ashore, and the fun times we'd had together. He told me he'd had a bit of a liver scare six months back and ended in a navy rehab. They didn't chuck him out, thank goodness. I couldn't imagine him doing anything except being a damn good sailor. He was now forbidden any alcohol on board his current ship; like that would stop him. Apart from that, like the rest of us, he was content riding the big ones—him waves, me cocks.

When the rum had reached the last quarter of an inch, he suggested we move on. Back in a drinking mood, I agreed.

We'd only reached the main drag, searching for a taxi to take us to the late night drinking club Shells frequented, when he suddenly mentioned the drowning.

"Heard about Purdy going overboard. Saw it coming myself. Years back, when we were on Trepid together." He shook his head. "Surprised someone hadn't bumped him off long ago."

"Really? Why?"

"Don't you know about him?" asked Shells. I shook my head. "Purdy used to be a Petty Officer at a training camp for young seaman. He was always coming onto them, in the showers and after light out. You know?"

"That so?" I shivered but didn't know why.

"He always backed off and dismissed his groping hands as a bit of sailor horseplay if the boys got upset," Shells continued. "But late one night, when he was rat-arsed, he finds this trainee in the showers. What does he do?" I shook my head though I had a fair idea of what was coming. "He tries to get the kid to give him a blowjob. Real rough, apparently." Shells downed the last droplet of rum.

"What happened?"

"The lad goes and shops him, doesn't he? Should have just kicked the sod in the nuts and be done with it. That's how he got demoted to Acting PO."

I didn't wait for Shells to enlighten me further. I was on my unsteady feet in a flash. "Freckles," I murmured. Then, "Taxi!" when an approaching FOR HIRE sign caught my eye.

"Not leaving me, Sandy? Bugger."

"Sorry, Shells. Must dash. Emergency," I apologised as I made a hasty exit.

"Got you going, did I?" said Shells when I ducked inside the cab. "I don't know. You gay boys." With that, he bade me farewell with a wave.

The taxi took an age to get through town, more red lights than a Christmas tree. Even more time was added to the journey, and the cost, when I couldn't find my identity card at the dockyard gate. When we eventually turned right at the Sailmaker's block close to where we berthed, my heart immediately sank into my boots.

It would have been impossible not to recognise the Military Police van parked by the gangway, its light flashing. I asked the cab driver to drop me off short of the ship. Secreting myself behind the leg of a huge dockyard crane I waited, and waited, and waited.

A dejected Freckles, dressed in a white boiler suit, head bowed low, his wrist shackled to a Naval Patrolman's descended the gangway. Another patrolman, carrying documents and a night stick, walked behind them. Behind him, a sailor from our ship carried Freckles' kit bag.

I wanted to rush forward and tell him I was sorry for not believing his story, but remained put. My eyes began flooding tears when he climbed into the rear of the van. The van door made me flinch when it slammed shut and echoed around the dockyard like a bullet from a sniper's rifle. Second's later it sped Freckles away, blue light flashing. Thankfully, there was no siren.

I wiped the tears from my eyes, cursing myself for not realising Freckles had been telling me a true story, cursing my failed attempt to get back to the ship on time. If I had made it back in time, what could I have done? Was I going to tell him to keep mum and all would be well? If so, was he, and me come to that, going to be able to live with the knowledge that he'd accidentally killed Purdy? I guess he'd made that decision for himself and turned himself in.

I banged my fist against the crane with the frustration and hopelessness of it all. I just couldn't believe in less than twenty-four hours I'd lost two of my best mates. First thing after breakfast, I'd ask my DO for a discharge and buy myself out. No way did I want to stay on this jinxed ship, stay in the Navy any more.

It felt as though I were climbing Everest as I solemnly ascended the gangway. The cheerful Bosun's Mate bade me good morning when I stepped onto the quarterdeck. He must have been aware of my saddened state.

"Look at this fantastic sunrise," he said, pointing to the horizon, his arm going about my shoulder.

For several minutes, I stood in an appreciative silent awe as we watched the enormous ball of fire lift from a flat calm sea. "Incredible!" I said sighed when the blue sky exploded in a breathtaking array of reds, gold, orange and purple.

"Who'd want any other life but a sailor's life, Sandy?" said this sailor of twenty year service, his hand affectionately slapping my back, well aware I'd lost two of my closest buddies.

I knew he was right of course. I made my way back to the mess but the way I was feeling at present it would take a miracle for me to believe his wise words, for me to change my decision to quit the navy today.

The door of the diver's den rudely blocked my path when it unexpectedly pushed open. A hand immediately reached from the darkness within and grabbed my arm.

"You've got to fuck me, Sandy. I think I'm turning straight," Matt's excited voice pleaded.

"One day, Matt," I solemnly replied.

"Now!" he demanded, grabbing my cock and dragging me into the den.

I took a deep breath, and sighed. "Okay, Matt."

My face began to fill with renewed joy. Another remarkable day in my life as a spunky sailor had dawned.

About Ken Smith

Ken Smith is a well-known British author of gay erotica and has written many short stories and novellas for both the US and UK market, and has published seven novels. He grew up in his beloved countryside and joined the Royal Navy age 15, where he served for nine years. His novels have a strong feel of the joys of growing up in the countryside and his life as a gay sailor. Semi-autobiographical, they give a realistic account of the raunchy and humorous life both below decks and ashore. He was once described as the Barbara Cartland of gay erotica. "Well, if the frock fits…"

Be sure to read these other naughty nautical adventures written by Ken Smith and available through Lethe Press:

Brad: A Young Man's Adventures
The summer after high school, Brad meets a young man in the woods one day and embarks on a life filled with sexual antics and adventures. Join young Brad on a journey of sexual discovery from his early fumblings in the British countryside until his more experienced days as a rent boy sailor.

Riding the Big One
Going Down
Skin
Run Naked, Run Free
Virgin Sailors

Lightning Source UK Ltd.
Milton Keynes UK
UKOW05f0839160114

224663UK00001B/12/P